I0731814

TOM, NICK, & MARY

A MADCAP ADVENTURE

THRILLOGY PRESS

Books by Terry Fritts

BIO-TERROR SERIES

TAKA
KONA SNOW
KAPU 'ĀINA
(Forbidden land)

The Kevin Bridges Spiritual Warfare Series

BROTHERHOOD OF THE DIVINE
SEVEN OF THE CROSS
CONSUMING FIRE

First Edition by THRILLOGY PRESS 2020
ISBN:978-1-950376-05-6

Tom, Nick, and Mary is quite a departure from the type of
books I normally write. For several years I was a teacher in
South Central Los Angeles and in East Los Angeles and heard
more about the local drug trade than I should have. That is
partially why I waited so long to publish this book. As I stated
earlier, similarity between characters in the book and real
characters is coincidental even though I'm sure many of my
past students who read this book will claim it was them I was
describing. The three teachers are all fictitious although all
the vignettes that occurred on Nick's train commute were
real and did occur during my own commutes. I had fun
writing this book and was inspired by my childhood memory
of *It's a Mad Mad Mad Mad World* for the epic chase scene.

Thanks to Joe Doyle for the cover design and inside art.

Thanks to Myrna Castillo, my teaching assistant, for the
Spanish translations.

Thanks to Michelle Pena-Handley for the photo of Pauline
and I cruising the Alafia River.

TOM, NICK, & MARY

A MADCAP ADVENTURE

TOM, NICK, & MARY

PROLOGUE

Tommy parked his car in the lot of BJ's Pizzeria on the north side of Fourth Street between Milliken Avenue and the 15 Freeway. He had seen the cameras, but figured he was far enough away that no one would be able to tie him to what he was about to do. He also knew he would be back before the restaurant closed and his car stuck out like the lemon it was. He had gone through a dry practice run last Friday and had gone over it every day in his mind, convincing himself that his plan was foolproof. Now it was time to see if he was right.

He reached into the envelope and removed the twenty fifty dollar bills he had placed in there earlier. He had looked at each bill more than a hundred times, but still thumbed through each again just to be sure. The latex paint he had used on his fingers to fill in his fingerprints made the bills slippery. He knew it would only get worse when he started to sweat. He carefully placed the stack of bills in the brand-new wallet he had purchased just for this occasion. Probably not the smartest purchase. He would have to pass off two of the phony fifties just to cover the cost of the wallet. He looked around once more before getting out of the car to make sure no one was near.

He headed for the front of the restaurant as if he was entering, but continued instead on to Fourth Street. He turned west and headed for the bus stop on Milliken. There were two other people waiting for the #81 bus when he arrived. The boy looked to be about sixteen and carried a

1

skateboard. He had a short, spiked Mohawk haircut dyed red. He also had several piercings in his ears, but none anywhere else that Tommy could see. Two wires snaked from beneath his hooded sweatshirt and into his ears. His clothes, expensive designer wear, were made to look like something a punk would wear. He wore just the slightest hint of a deep blue eye shadow. The boy also had added a darker skin tone color to his cheeks to make his face look thinner and more drawn. Tommy could tell this kid was just a punk wannabe from the suburbs who probably removed his piercings, brushed out his hair and removed the make-up before he got home. Tommy noticed these things. He was very aware of how people looked and what they were wearing. The girl was Hispanic and in her early twenties. She wore no makeup and the clothes had a cheap Wal-Mart look to them. She was neither thin nor fat, but appeared to have the body of a young mother. Not too unlike many of the students Tommy had taught over the past few years in his drama classes back at Cudahy High School.

"Probably had a couple of babies before she was out of high school and now is a single parent," Tommy thought to himself, "I bet she works as a salesman at one of the stores at Ontario Mills."

When she turned around, he saw her badge identifying her as an employee of Cost Plus. Tommy had been right.

He stood away from the two and avoided eye contact.

"Got any spare change?" the spiky-haired boy asked.

"Sorry," Tommy replied, shaking his head.

"Got any cigarettes?" the kid asked next.

"Don't smoke," Tommy answered, "and neither should you if you want to live," he thought about saying, but didn't.

2

Fortunately, the bus arrived before any more questions could be asked.

There were few people on the bus, but Tommy knew that's how it would be. That was why he had chosen this line at this time over all the others. As he climbed up the steps, he looked at his reflection in the driver's side mirror and smiled. His own mother wouldn't recognize him in that disguise.

"Eat your heart out, Michael Jackson, you'll never look this bad," Tommy said under his breath.

"What'd you say?" the driver asked.

"Nothing," Tommy replied, looking down and dropping his fare into the automated collector.

"Thank you," a metallic voice replied.

Tommy took a seat near the rear exit of the bus. The punk kid walked to the very back of the bus and sat next to a similarly dressed teenager. The Hispanic girl sat near the front in one of the side-facing seats. It took about fifteen minutes for the bus to reach Tommy's exit on Dry Creek Road. His plan was to walk to the far end of Victoria's Gardens and start at the bar and restaurant in the new Bass Pro Shop which recently opened. He had made a map of the fifteen stops he planned on making, working himself westward as the evening progressed. He had visited each of the restaurants on his list at least three times and knew at what times the crowds were the largest. At a couple of the busier restaurants he even planned to pass off two or three of the phony fifty-dollar bills.

He did not enter the Islamorada Fish Company restaurant directly. He went into the Bass Pro Shop, then wandered over towards the restaurant. Tommy spent about ten minutes looking at the items right outside the door before he finally got the nerve to walk in. The bar was in the middle of the room and was backed by a giant built-in aquarium. When he saw the crowd standing around the bar, he took a sharp turn to the right and entered the restroom.

"Pull yourself together Michael, you can do this," he said, looking at the stranger in the mirror. "What I need is a drink."

Tommy turned quickly and went back to the bar. The crowd was packed two-deep and several people were trying to catch the attention of the bartenders. Tommy had to push his way through. It still took another two minutes until one of the bartenders noticed him standing there.

"What'll it be?"

"Just a Bud," Tommy replied.

"Bottle or draft?

"Draft," Tommy replied thinking a draft beer would be cheaper.

When the bartender returned with his glass of beer, Tommy had already pulled out one of the fifties and handed it to the bartender. Just as Tommy expected, the bartender held up the fifty to make sure there was the perpendicular strip of writing across the bill. Tommy watched out of the corner of his eye as the bartender held it up for just a second and then headed to the cash drawer.

"Here's your change," the bartender replied, putting forty-five dollars and fifty cents on the bar in front of Tommy.

"Thanks," Tommy replied, picking up the bills, but leaving the change. He moved away from the bar and quickly downed the rest of his beer. A second bartender was pouring drinks at the other end of the bar, and for a fleeting moment, Tommy thought about trying his scam again, but decided it would be smarter to stick to his plan. Besides, the bar was not that large and both bartenders used the same register.

Filled with the euphoria of success, Tommy headed to the next stop on his list, Lucille's Smokehouse Bar-B-Que. Here, just like at Islamorada Fish Company, Tommy's little scam worked to perfection. This time he was able to pass off two of the phony fifty-dollar bills. He realized when he

4

started on his second beer at Lucille's, that if he drank a beer with every bill he tried to pass, he would be drunk before he was halfway through his list, so he sat the beer down on the bar and headed for the door. At the next five restaurants, all went as planned. He would crowd his way up to the bar, order a beer, pay with the fifty, take a few sips, collect his change, leave a small tip, and scurry out the door. At a couple of the restaurants the bar was so busy that the bartender did not even bother to look at the fifty. Tommy thought he may just return to these two later to try his luck again.

Tommy had been at his little scheme for almost an hour-and-a-half, visited eleven of the bars on his list, and passed off fourteen of the bogus bills. At the California Pizza Kitchen, the bar was crowded, but not as crowded as Tommy had hoped. He ordered a beer from a bartender that Tommy knew had to be gay. It wasn't that the guy was blatant about it, but it was just something Tommy could readily recognize from having worked around so many gays in the theater.

"Here you go, one Bud draft," the bartender said.

Tommy smiled and began to reach for one of the fifties when he noticed the bartender eyeing him.

"You've got remarkable facial features," the bartender continued. "I don't believe I've ever seen a Caucasian with such an interesting and beautiful face."

The bartender looked deep into Tommy's eyes. He knew Tommy was gay and decided to hit on him. Tommy smiled and instead of pulling out another fifty, grabbed a twenty from his pocket.

"No, this one is on me," the bartender said. "Put your money back in your pants. My name's Troy," he said, sticking out his hand.

"Thank you, I'm T…" Tommy almost gave his real name and faked a cough. "My name's Wendall," Tommy replied, trying not to look directly at the bartender, but losing, as his sexual desires began to stir. The bartender was a good-looking guy and someone Tommy would not mind spending a night or two with, but just not tonight.

"What is your nationality, if you don't mind me asking?" said the bartender. "You have several strong African features. Are you from Zimbabwe?"

Just then one of the waitresses came up to the bar station and requested several drinks, forcing the bartender to move down to the end of the bar away from Tommy.

Tommy took a deep breath and chugged down his beer hoping his chubby would not be noticed as he made his escape. As much as he would love to get together with the bartender, he knew it would be a disaster once the bogus bills were discovered. He could not allow that to happen no matter how turned on he was. When the bartender turned around, Tommy was gone.

Tommy moved quickly to the next bar on his list. This was the one that he hoped to pass at least three of the phony bills. When he entered the Yardhouse, it was packed, just as he knew it would be. He was still a little shaky from his encounter at the Pizza Kitchen and decided he needed a drink to calm down.

The Yardhouse has a huge bar able to accommodate its one hundred and fifty plus beers on tap. There were six bartenders working around the bar when Tommy was able to push himself close enough to order.

"A Piraat Ale," Tommy called out.

When the bartender returned, Tommy had one of his fifties ready to go. The bartender didn't even bother to look at the bill before he placed it in the register and counted out Tommy's change. Tommy was on an emotional high from his success and from the fact that the previous bartender had found him so attractive. He quickly chugged the Piraat, moved to the other end of the bar and ordered another. This time the bartender did look at the bill, saw the perpendicular writing woven into the bill, and stuck it in the register. Tommy pocketed the change and moved to the other side of the bar where several people were gathered around watching a basketball game. The sips of beer had added up, as had the beer he chugged at the Pizza Kitchen and the Piraat Ale he had just finished. Tommy was drunk and just beginning to realize it. The Laker game was on, but it was a timeout and the dance team was performing to a Michael Jackson song. The dancers all tried to moonwalk, some more successful than the others. The people watching all laughed and two tried their own version of moonwalking, failing miserably.

"Wash this," Tommy said, slurring his words. He was an expert at moonwalking and glided backwards across the floor with ease, crashing into a pillar holding several televisions.

The crowd cheered and Tommy held up his arms in victory. Instantly, his arms shot back down to his sides and he headed for the door. When he had crashed into the pillar, he had wiped the white skin-tone makeup off his right elbow and forearm. His natural black skin was glowing through. Several of the bar patrons stared curiously at his multi-colored arm.

"Time to go," Tommy thought to himself.

"I'm an idiot," Tommy said as he hurried down the sidewalk, "a drunken idiot!"

Fortunately, the sun had set over an hour ago and the sidewalk was not brightly lit. Tommy walked along keeping his right-side, close to the stores, to hide his two-tone skin color as he made his way back to the bus stop on Milliken Avenue. Tommy stood in the shadows waiting for the bus and when it arrived, he sat on the right to conceal his discolored arm. At this time on a Friday evening the bus was almost empty. Fifteen minutes later, Tommy was back in his car, headed west on the 10 Freeway.

PART ONE

"Plans are of little importance,
But planning is essential."
Winston Churchill

CHAPTER ONE

Traffic had come to a stop on the 710 South and the two men sitting in the front seat knew they would be late for work. Up ahead a big rig had sideswiped an SUV.

"I hate all the trucks on this freeway," Tommy said.

"Worst freeway in L.A.," Nick replied.

Tommy tuned the radio to one of the news stations to listen to the traffic report. The reporter never mentioned the 710 Freeway.

"Better call school to let them know we'll be late," Tommy said to Nick.

Nick pulled out his cell phone and started to scan his saved numbers when traffic began to move.

"Hold up," Tommy said, "We're starting to move." Nick put his cell phone away.

Nick and Tommy drove to work together every morning in Tommy's old Ford Taurus. Actually, Tommy would pick Nick up at the Alameda exit off the 101 Freeway. Every morning Nick would catch the train at 5:42 a.m. and arrive at Union Station in time to sit and have a cup of coffee before he walked over to wait along the side of the road for Tommy. The only problem was the coffee at Union Station was horrible.

Tommy lived in North Hollywood and Nick lived in Covina. Tommy's full name was Thomas Eubanks. He was born and raised in Los Angeles. At a very early age he realized he liked boys a lot more than girls, and because of that, was overly protected by his mother, which probably saved his life. Every morning she would take him early to Jefferson High School and be there waiting to pick him up at the end of the school day. When Tommy, as she called him, became involved in the drama club and choir, she would be there waiting after every rehearsal regardless of how late it may be. Tommy never had to walk the gang infested streets of South-Central Los Angeles.

Nick Stirling came to California from Oklahoma. When the Sooners came to Los Angeles in the early eighties to play the Trojans in football, he came to watch and never went back. Well, at least he never went back to stay. The eighty-degree weather in L.A. seemed to make much more sense to Nick than the two feet of snow back in Norman. He did go back and pack up his belongings at his dormitory room. He rented a small apartment near the beach and worked for a year before enrolling at Cal-State Dominguez Hills where he earned his teaching credential. Along the way he also met the woman who would become his wife. Who for the past two years was now his ex-wife.

Tommy was a thin black man about five feet ten inches tall with a shaved head in his late twenties. He was gay but did not overtly display his gayness. However, it was no secret to his colleagues and most of his students at Cudahy High School. Tommy was the drama teacher at CHS, but wanted more than anything to be a makeup artist for a big Hollywood movie studio. Not the powder your face and put on your lip stick makeup artist, but the real artist who could age a man a hundred years or turn him into a blood-sucking mutant alien.

Nick was in his late thirties, a few pounds overweight but plenty of muscles, almost six feet two inches tall, and wore a brown wig to cover his bald head. Actually, no one but Tommy knew Nick wore the rug and that was because Tommy designed and created it. Nick had been diagnosed with prostate cancer three years ago, underwent the surgery and began chemotherapy. His hair fell out and Tommy offered to design a wig guaranteed to be undetectable. So far it had passed the test. Nick's hair was starting to grow back, but he thought the wig looked so much better than his thinning hair that he decided to continue to wear it. It was the cancer that was the straw that broke the camel's back for his marriage. Nick had seen it coming for quite some time and was by no means surprised. It took all of Nick's savings and most of his tax-sheltered money to pay off their debts from his illness and get out from under a mortgage on an overpriced house he had purchased four years earlier. At least he and his ex-wife had split on amicable terms.

"Damn, the traffic is stopping again," Tommy said.

Nick looked at his watch. "I better call school," he said, pulling out his cell phone.

"Yeah, this is Nick Stirling. Tom Eubanks and I are stuck in traffic, we'll be a little late." Nick listened for a moment, "Okay, thanks."

"What'd they say?" Tommy asked.

"They said not to worry; several teachers are caught in this mess."

"Good," Tommy replied, and they both sat silently.

Tommy was pretty tightly wound and couldn't keep his feet or hands still for over thirty seconds. He began fidgeting and messing with the radio.

11

"Did you hear about that guy who passed all those phony fifty dollar bills a couple of weeks ago out in Rancho Cucamonga?" Tommy asked.

"I kind of remember hearing something about that. Wasn't it at a bunch of restaurants out in the Victoria Gardens shopping center?"

"Yeah, in the bars of the restaurants," Tommy replied.

"That's right, I remember seeing pictures of the guy on the news. Several of the restaurants had a video of him. A skinny white guy. That's right, they called him the white Michael Jackson, 'cause they had a video of him moonwalking in one of the bars."

"The Yardhouse," Tommy replied. "That was me."

"Yeah, right! You ain't no skinny white guy," Nick replied.

"It really was me. I made myself up to look white," Tommy replied.

Nick looked at Tommy for a second. "You're serious, aren't you?"

"Dead serious. I almost blew it. I got drunk and started dancing around and scraped some of the white makeup off my arm. I had to get out of there in a hurry."

Nick remembered Tommy moonwalking at school for a talent show a couple of years back. "Nah, you're putting me on," Nick said, staring at Tommy.

Traffic had begun to move and Tommy looked straight ahead.

"No, it really was me. I needed money. You know I'm at the bottom of the pay scale. I can't even afford to pay my cell phone bill half the time. I made three hundred and sixty-eight dollars."

"No shit!" Nick said. They both sat silently as Tommy weaved around the accident.

12

"At first, I was really scared but, after I passed the first phony fifty, it was a piece of cake," Tommy said.

"Are you gonna do it again?" Nick asked.

"You know, I haven't given it much thought," Tommy replied.

Nick didn't say anything else for the rest of the ride. He was trying to imagine what it must have felt like.

"We're not even that late," Tommy said, as they pulled into the school parking lot. He was starting to worry if telling Nick had been the right thing to do.

"I don't think I could have done it," Nick said, as they were getting out of the car.

"I didn't think I could either," Tommy replied, as they headed into the school.

CHAPTER TWO

"There are worse places to work than Cudahy High School," Nick would say to himself as he left his house every morning at 5:00 a.m. for the twenty-minute walk to the Metrolink Station. When he first started working at CHS, taking the train every day to save wear and tear on his car was the ecologically responsible thing to do. It was the way people commuted back on the East coast and California was finally catching up. It didn't take long for the novelty to wear off.

Nick had been thinking about what Tommy had told him. He still wasn't sure Tommy had been telling him the truth. Tommy seemed to crave attention and Nick was thinking he might have made the story up to get some attention. Nick hadn't told anybody what Tommy had said to him, and didn't plan on it. Even if he wanted to, Nick didn't really have many friends he could tell. After the divorce, he seemed to drift away from the mutual friends he and his wife had. He never really made friends at work. Not that he was stuck-up, or anti-social, it was just that he would rather stay in his classroom than hang out in the lunch room or work room with the other teachers. For the most part, teachers drove him crazy with their constant whining and complaining. At times, he thought they were worse than the students. There were a few that he didn't mind talking to, and even a couple of female teachers he wouldn't mind getting to know a little better, but one was more interested in women than men and the other avoided socializing more than he did. Tommy was one of the only teachers he considered his friend, and that was only because Tommy had been giving Nick a ride to work every day for the past few years. You get to know a lot about a person riding in a car with them every day. Even so, Nick wasn't sure what to think about Tommy confessing a crime to him.

"Late today," one of the other commuters said to Nick as he stood on the train platform.

Nick looked down the track and saw the glare of the train headlights approaching.

"Coming now," he replied, not looking at the other man.

Nick had been riding this train for ten years with many of the same people and hadn't learned one of their names. If someone did introduce himself or herself, Nick would surely forget them over the weekend. He just couldn't remember names.

The doors opened and the dozen or so people waiting at that spot on the platform rushed to be the first in. By the time the train had reached Covina, empty seats were few and far between. If a seat was still empty, there was probably a very good reason.

Nick wasn't in a hurry, so he lay back as the mass of people squeezed through the door. It was a decision he would later regret. When he did finally board the train, every seat in the lower section was filled and two or three people were standing near the door. He headed up the steps, passing the one empty seat next to the fat man who was snoring louder than the clanking of the out-of-round wheels echoing through the car. He went up to the top hoping for better luck. Nick saw one empty seat a few rows down. It was facing away from the direction of the train and on the aisle. At least he wouldn't have to crawl over someone to sit down. When he reached the seat, he understood why it was still open. Next to it sat a lady who had to weigh close to three hundred pounds. Her butt stuck out and covered almost a third of the aisle seat. On her lap was a grocery bag that looked to be full of snacks, which she was feeding to her four-year-old son sitting across from the empty seat. Next to the young boy was a man, dressed in a very nice suit, trying to read what looked to be some legal documents. His body language did not convey a welcoming attitude to Nick. Nick stood there for a moment and looked both ways for any possible alternative, but saw none, so he sat down in the half empty seat. Nick was able to fit his left butt cheek and a little of his right into the seat. He had to sit at an angle with his right leg sticking out into the aisle. Normally, this would not have been a problem, but today, sitting in the aisle seat across to his right, was the most wrinkled old lady Nick had ever seen. She was not a usual commuter and carried a large roller-suitcase with her that she had sat in the aisle next to her. Nick had to stay alert, for every time somebody walked down the aisle, he would have to shift around to allow them to pass. Still, there wasn't much room and, each time he had to shift, someone's butt would wipe across his right side. When someone fat walked through, and there were many fat ones, Nick would have to lean his head far to the left not to have it wiped across someone's backside. More than once this happened.

Sitting next to the wrinkled old woman by the window, was a young Hispanic woman, probably a student, whose eyes could not hide the abject fear she felt that morning. For sitting straight across from the wrinkled one was a man in his late twenties, who could not stop moving and talking. Nick tried to ignore him, but it was impossible.

"Yeah, it's a machete kind of day," the crazed-looking man repeated.

Nick's head whipped up when he heard the man. The wrinkled one continued to smile and nod her head pretending to follow the ramblings of the lunatic across from her. The eyes of the Hispanic woman grew larger, but the girl

16

sitting next to the lunatic, the one with the pierced nose and eyebrow paid him no attention.

"My roommates always put me on the train when I wake up in one of these moods," the lunatic continued.

Suddenly, the wrinkled one's suitcase fell over and slammed into Nick's leg, pinning it against his seat. The weather had yet to turn cold and Nick was still wearing shorts to work every day.

"Oh, I'm so sorry," the wrinkled one said, pulling her suitcase off of Nick's leg. "Are you all right?" She reached down and started rubbing Nick's leg with her wrinkled hand.

"I'm fine," Nick replied, trying to pull his leg away from the wrinkled one who continued to grin at Nick as she rubbed his leg.

"They hide all the knives and my machetes when I get like this, but I know where they put them."

The wrinkled one removed her hand as someone walked down the aisle.

"I feel like I need to hack the evil out of people. That's what God is telling me to do," the lunatic continued.

Nick leaned back and looked down around the lunatic's legs to make sure he hadn't brought one of his machetes on the train.

"What are you looking at, pervert?" the pierced one asked. "Are you trying to look up my skirt?"

Nick opened a book and pretended to read, ignoring the pierced one's taunts.

The fat lady continued to stuff snacks into her fat little boy's mouth.

"Here eat this," she said, passing him yet another processed peanut butter and cracker snack, which he stuffed into his mouth with the other two he was still chewing.

"Achoo," the little boy sneezed, his mouth popped open. Thousands of partially chewed crumbs of crackers and peanut butter erupted from his mouth, showering the man in the suit, Nick, and his mother.

"Oh my God," the suited man said, looking at the hundreds of saliva-soaked morsels stuck to his jacket, pants, and legal documents.

"Sorry," the mother replied, and tried to hand him a used napkin to clean himself off.

Nick had missed the bulk of the eruption, but still had several of the moist crumbs stuck to his shorts and the hair of his exposed legs. The wrinkled one reached into her bag and pulled out a sealed moist towelette, with the KFC logo, and handed it to the grateful suited man. The mother wiped her son's mouth with the used napkin and handed him a processed cheese and cracker snack, which he promptly stuck in his mouth.

"I just go crazy. It's a machete kind of day," the lunatic said, raising his voice as he started jumping around.

Nick looked back down to reaffirm that the lunatic held or was concealing no weapon.

"You perverted creep," the pierced one said, standing up glaring at Nick.

The wrinkled one continued to nod her head and grin.

The Hispanic girl's look of fear had turned to a look of abject terror.

Nick stood up, grabbed his backpack, and headed for the stairs. "I've got to find a new job," he said to himself.

As he was walking away, he heard the fat little boy sneeze.

"Aw---Jesus Christ, lady," the suited man said.

CHAPTER THREE

It ended rather dramatically, just as one would expect, considering Tommy's lover was a drama queen. They had only been together for two months. Not even enough time to move in together, just sleepovers. They had met at a performance of *Evita*, put on by the Weasel and Fox Theater Company in a small dance studio in Silver Lake. They were the local theater group for Silver Lake, but didn't like to be called a community theater. They thought that would be degrading to their talents. Shantae, that was his name, had played the part of Juan Peron. Tommy had gone there because he heard they were looking for someone who could help them with makeup on their upcoming production of *The Wizard of Oz*. A relationship bloomed between Tommy and Shantae, and between Tommy and the theater company. The bloom fell off the stem opening night when Shantae, who was playing the cowardly lion, turned too quickly and the fake jowls went flying into the audience creating quite a roar of its own.

"You bitch!" Shantae screamed at Tommy. "You are the worst makeup artist I've ever known."

Being called a "bitch" Tommy could take, but being told he was a terrible makeup artist was more than he could bear. Shantae was gone and so was several thousand dollars Tommy had spent wooing his ex-lover.

Tommy had been surly since Shantae had dumped him. The attitude of his students in his drama classes didn't help.

"Why do you even bother to come to school, Noe?" he asked one of the known gangsters in the school.

"Sell the 'chronic'," Noe replied, laughing.

Tommy believed him. Why shouldn't he believe him? Noe was one of the few students who drove to school. Drove to school in style, is more like it. Noe drove a Cadillac Escalade. A new Cadillac Escalade with all the bells and whistles one could imagine. The rims alone cost more than Tommy's Ford Taurus cost new. There was no doubt Noe was into something, and that something was no doubt drugs. Tommy knew that it was more than just the 'chronic' Noe was pushing. Noe was just another one of the jerk students Tommy had to deal with every day.

Having finally told Nick about passing the phony fifties made Tommy feel better. He knew Nick was the only person whom he could tell. Bragging about a crime they have just pulled is usually what brings down criminals. Tommy was confident Nick would tell no one. He knew Nick had very few friends. Tommy was surprised Nick had not mentioned it since the day Tommy had told him about the scam. He was starting to think telling Nick may not have been the smartest thing to do after-all.

Tommy's brakes squealed as he pulled over to pick up Nick.

"I hate that freak'n train," Nick said, as soon as he opened the car door.

"I hate my freak'n car," Tommy replied.

They both sat quietly for the next few minutes listening to NPR.

"Did you read the bulletin about the big community carnival, car show and picnic at school the weekend after next?" Nick asked.

"I saw that. Didn't it say something about the police and the local gang coming together to better understand each other." Tommy asked.

20

"Yeah, they're going to play each other in softball," Nick replied.

"Oh, that ought to work," Tommy replied sarcastically.

"From what I've read, the police and the local gang are pretty much one-and-the-same. We work in a very corrupt city my friend," Nick said.

"No shit," Tommy replied. "Have you seen the cars a couple of our students are driving? It's like they were waving a flag and calling out 'Buy your drugs here'."

"Remind me to stay far away from Cudahy that weekend," Nick said.

"Like you would ever come in to work on a Saturday? Give me a break," Tommy said and, they both laughed.

That day at lunch Nick went to visit Tommy's room.

"Hey Nick, what brings you out of your cave?"

"How'd you do it?"

"How did I do what?" Tommy replied cautiously.

"How'd you get the phony fifty-dollar bills?" Nick asked.

"I made them."

"What do you mean you made them? It's impossible to get a hold of the paper they make money out of, and even if you did, how could you weave this line through the bill? It's impossible!" Nick said, holding up a fifty of his own.

"Difficult, but not impossible," Tommy replied smiling.

"Do you have one I can look at?" Nick asked.

"Not here, but I still have a couple at home I'll bring tomorrow."

"I figured you used that new color copier they have in the workroom," Nick said.

"I did, but it took forever to get it just right."

"I can imagine. But how did you get a hold of the paper?"

21

Tommy reached into his pocket and pulled out his wallet. He opened it up and took out a twenty-dollar bill. "I used these."

"You did what?"

"I used twenties. I bleached them out, then used the copy machine to print the front and back of a fifty on each of the washed-out twenties. That way I had the perpendicular line running across the bill. I figured if it looked like a fifty and felt like a real bill, they would only look to see if there was that perpendicular line woven into the bill, and not bother to read it."

"That seems like a lot of work for less than four hundred dollars," Nick said.

"It was, and if I figure in all the bills I screwed up in the process, I only cleared about a hundred bucks."

"Doesn't seem worth the risk," Nick said.

"No, it doesn't, does it?" Tommy responded.

"I guess I'll see you after school," Nick said, and headed back to his own classroom lost in thought.

"Shit," Tommy said out loud, "it wasn't worth it at all." His mood once again turned surly.

CHAPTER FOUR

Cudahy High School suffered from a severe teacher shortage. Teachers for the most part didn't stay more than a year or two at CHS. Whether it was the ineffective administration or the dangerous environs that surrounded the school is hard to say. All Nick knew was that it gave him and many others the opportunity to make some extra money teaching an auxiliary class during their conference period. For Nick, it was also a chance to get out of the remedial history classroom and teach something he enjoyed to the general education population, art.

It wasn't that Nick was a skilled artist. He enjoyed painting and seemed to have a knack for painting portraits. He even tried to make a living at it right after college. He also had a minor in art at Dominguez Hills which qualified him to teach the class. Easy money as far as Nick was concerned. Art was the kind of class where you show the students what to do and then let them spend the next week doing it. You didn't have to lecture, and for the most part you didn't need to discipline the students, just remind them to lower their voices about every three minutes. It also gave Nick a chance to actually talk to some students.

Nick would walk around the room commenting on the student's work and chatting. One of his favorite students in the art class was Alex. Alex Dominguez. Nick had Alex's older brother, Rudy, as a student several years before in his history classroom. After Rudy left school, he often stopped by to visit with Nick, who became somewhat of a confidant and mentor to Rudy. Rudy grew up in a gang family, but never fell into the life-style of the gangbanger or even dressed like a gang soldier as had his brothers. Rudy was the brightest in the family and the gang recognized early on that Rudy would serve a special purpose in the gang. The Wilcox Street Gang had grown into one of the most powerful gangs in all of Los Angeles. They had worked a sweet deal with several of the local police in Cudahy. They also had a few very smart members who knew you could become extremely wealthy if you organized the gang like a business. A very efficient and successful business. Don't get me wrong, there were plenty of Wilcox Street gangbangers, or soldiers as they were now called, that would just as soon kill you as talk to you. They are just another division in the gang's corporate structure.

When Rudy was a senior at CHS, several of the Wilcox OGs, original gangsters, were arrested by the sheriff's department. They would be spending anywhere from a year to ten years in prison and needed someone to oversee the street-level drug trade in Cudahy, and Rudy had been groomed for just such a task. The only problem was Rudy had to drop out the last semester of his senior year to take over. He kept in touch with Nick over the years, occasionally dropping by to show Nick his kids and tell him how he was rising rapidly through the ranks of the gang organization. For some reason, Rudy felt some need to tell Nick about the gang's drug operation. It was more than Nick wanted to know.

"How's Rudy?" Nick asked Alex that afternoon in class.

"Doing fine. He's now one of the supervisors at the factory in Utah."

"Another promotion?"

"Yeah, now he doesn't have to make the deliveries out here anymore," Alex said smiling. "That was a risky job."

Nick knew that making the deliveries didn't mean driving out with a truck of chickens, but a truck loaded with cocaine to be sold to all the local gangs.

"Rudy just sets everything up and makes sure it goes smoothly," Alex continued. "You remember Hector Contreras? I think he may have been in one of your classes."

"Name sounds familiar but that's about it, why?" Nick replied.

"Hector's the new driver. It was a big promotion for him too. You know you have to have the look and be cool to do the driving."

"I can imagine. I'm sure certain people are always keeping an eye out for you." Nick said.

"Yeah, but we got that covered," Alex said.

"That's what they all say right up until the moment they're caught," Nick replied.

"No man, really. We got a great cover. Hector drives this big-ass motorhome. He even stops at a campground in Vegas both coming and going," Alex explains.

"Hope it works out," Nick said, as he started to walk on to look at another student's drawing.

"Rudy's coming into town for that big community carnival and car show in a couple of weeks. He's just paid seventy-five grand for a new lowrider he wants to show off. You should come check it out," Alex said.

"You know I don't come around here on weekends, but we'll see," Nick replied.

"Can you freak'n believe it, seventy-five thousand dollars," Nick said to Tommy as they waited for the rest of the faculty to make their way to the auditorium for the weekly faculty meeting.

"Just doesn't seem fair," Tommy said. "I hate Tuesdays."

"I hate any day when I have to stay past the 2:58 dismissal bell," Nick added. "I can't even afford to buy a

25

decent car and this high school dropout spends seventy-five thou' on a lowrider."

"I hate this job," Tommy said.

"Me too, but we gotta work," Nick said.

"Not forever," Tommy said.

Nick turned to look at Tommy. "Are you thinking about doing it again?"

Tommy looked around to see who was sitting near them. "I think about it all the time."

"Well, if you do, you ought to try some other way. What you did doesn't make much financial sense. Too much risk for the payoff."

Before Tommy could answer, several other teachers walked over and sat down next to the two of them. Tommy just nodded his head in response.

CHAPTER FIVE

Nick had no trouble finding a seat on the train the next morning. Some days it was packed and some days you had room to stretch out and sit your briefcase on the seat next to you. It wasn't quite that empty, but Nick did have room to stretch out his legs. Across from him two men were talking about what they would do if they won the lottery. It was up to almost sixty million dollars. Nick dreamed about winning too. Just about everybody in California dreamed about it. He bought a ticket for almost every draw. A quick pick away from living your dreams.

"I'd move to Costa Rica," one man said.

"They don't speak English there," the other man replied. "I'd move to Hawaii."

"Too expensive there."

"Hell, with sixty million, no place is too expensive," the man replied.

"I guess you're right about that," his friend agreed.

Nick tried to decide where he would move if he won the lottery. One thing for sure, he wouldn't go near Cudahy for the rest of his life. The guy sitting near him was right about one thing, with sixty million dollars you could move anywhere you wanted.

That got Nick thinking just how much money it would take for him to move away.

"I guess I need to figure out where I'm going so I'll know how much money I need," Nick thought to himself as he closed his eyes, hoping to nap the rest of the way to Los Angeles.

"Where would you move if you could afford to quit teaching?" Nick asked Tommy as he climbed in the car that morning.

"What? What are you talking about?" Tommy asked.

"If you had enough money to get away from here, where would you go?" Nick said.

"Paris," Tommy replied without hesitating.

"Paris, France?" Nick asked.

"No, Lake Perris," Tommy replied," of course Paris, France. Don't be ridiculous."

"Why Paris?' Nick asked.

"Why not Paris? It is the City of Lights, the city of romance, one of the fashion capitals of the world, it is beautiful there," Tommy replied.

"Yeah, but the Parisians are assholes," Nick added.

"That's just not true," Tommy insisted. "Some may be a bit rude, especially if you don't speak French, but I wouldn't call them all assholes."

"Do you speak French?" Nick asked.

"No."

"Then they're all assholes," Nick insisted.

"Where would you go?" Tommy asked.

"Probably Paraguay," Nick said. "I read there is a large American contingent living there. It is supposed to be inexpensive to live there."

"Then what's keeping you from moving there?" Tommy asked.

Nick rubbed his thumb and first two fingers together, the universal symbol for money.

"How much money would it take?" Tommy asked.

"I don't know. I only today thought that is where I want to go." Nick replied. "What do you think it would take for you to move to Paris?"

"A whole lot more than it would take for you to move to Paraguay." Tommy replied. "A Sean John suit would cost me a hell of a lot more *dinero* in Paris than a poncho in Paraguay."

"No doubt about that," Nick replied.

"The men sat quietly for the rest of their commute to school as they each tried to put a price on their dreams.

CHAPTER SIX

"Watch out," Nick yelled, jarring Tommy from his dreams of riches.

A Cadillac Escalade cut sharply in front of Tommy's Ford forcing him to slam on his brakes. Nick and Tommy jerked forward only to be whipped back by the tightness of the seatbelts.

"*Pendejo!*" Tommy shouted.

Nick lifted his finger to flip the driver off, but Tommy pulled it back down.

"It's not worth it. The asshole would probably report you to the principal. That's Noe Gomez. He's in one of my classes. I'll just fail his ass this week for pulling that stupid stunt."

"Well, I sure as hell hope you let him know what a shitty driver he is," Nick said.

"Believe me, I will," Tommy assured him.

"Is that the only pair of pants you own?" one of the girls in Nick's class asked. "You wear that same pair every day. I hope you wash them."

"As a matter of fact, I have several pairs that look the same," Nick replied. "I wear a different pair every couple of days."

"Not for the past two weeks," the girl giggled. "Last week we marked your pants with a red marker on the butt. That red mark has been there every day since then."

The rest of the class burst into laughter.

"I guess you got me," Nick said, making a mental note to lower the girl's grade after class.

Nick was mad and gave the class a meaningless time-wasting assignment so he could sit at his desk and brood. He didn't want to admit it, but since his cancer, his life had been on a downhill spiral. He actually did have several pairs of the same pants, but had been too lazy to bother to take them to the cleaners. Besides, the cleaner charged way too much money. Something Nick never seemed to have enough of.

"Eh *ese*, check out my new watch," Carlos said to Jesus.

"*Firme*. Cool watch man." Jesus replied.

Nick looked up. "What's the problem, Jesus?"

"Nut'n mister, just check'n out Carlos' new watch," Jesus replied.

"Let's see it, Carlos," Nick said.

"No way, you'll try to jack me." All the students laughed.

"Just come up here so I can see it," Nick insisted.

Carlos made a big scene as he walked up to Nick's desk. Nick was still fuming about the pants incident and wanted to embarrass Carlos by pointing out that the watch was nothing more than a cheap replica.

Carlos held out his wrist so Nick could look at the watch.

"Nice watch, Jesus," Nick said. The watch was not a cheap replica, but a real Rolex. A real expensive Rolex.

"It should be, it cost me three thousand dollars."

"Three thousand?" Nick said surprised. "Where did you find it for that price? One like that should cost almost three times that much."

"I got it from a homey," Carlos replied.

"More like from someone who couldn't pay his bill," Jesus spoke up.

"*Callate, pendejo!*" Carlos yelled.

31

"That's enough," Nick said, heading off the confrontation. "Are you slinging. Carlos?"

"Something like that," Carlos said, as he headed back to his seat.

Nick looked at the old Seiko he had on his wrist. It had cost him one hundred and fifty dollars at a half-price sale at JC Penny last year. He thought he had scored big. Now the crystal was so scratched up he could barely tell the time and the date hadn't been right since he bought it. At that moment life just didn't seem fair.

"Noe," Tommy called. "Noe! Noe!!"

Noe had three, as he would say, "fine lookin' mamas" all hanging on his every word and did not want to be interrupted by Tommy.

"*¿Qué pedo?*" Noe replied and all the girls giggled.

"You almost caused me to have a wreck today," Tommy said.

"*Que lastima, lo siento mucho!*" Noe replied causing the entire class to laugh.

"Don't act like a jerk," Tommy said.

"Who you call'n a jerk, *pendejo*?" Noe said, standing up.

"I'm not calling anybody a jerk. I just said don't act like one," Tommy said, with a little fear in his voice.

"That's what I thought," Noe replied. "Who cares about you or that piece o' shit car of yours anyway? I could buy and sell you five times over."

"Get out of here," Tommy snapped. The problem was Tommy knew Noe was probably right.

"Right before the lunch bell rang, Nick walked into Tommy's classroom.

"Let's go out for lunch today, my treat," Nick said. "I need to get away from this madhouse for a while."

"I hear that," Tommy replied.

The two of them walked across the street to a Thai food restaurant. Several other teachers were also there for lunch.

"So how much money do you figure it would take for you to move to Paris?" Nick asked.

"More than I will ever have," Tommy said with disgust. "This place sucks."

"We can eat somewhere else if you want," Nick said.

"I don't mean this restaurant, I mean this whole goddamned corrupt city," Tommy replied.

"So why don't you get out of here, find another school?" Nick asked.

"For the same damned reason you don't. I'm trapped. I can't afford to quit working for this district. I'd take too big of a pay cut," Tommy replied. "Besides, finding a drama opening is a lot more difficult than finding a history vacancy."

Nick couldn't argue that point. He had thought about leaving for years, way before he and his wife divorced. There were plenty of openings, just like Tommy said, but they just didn't pay enough. Nick was as trapped as Tommy.

"I started to talk to that kid who cut us off this morning, and he laughed in my face," Tommy said. "So, I kicked him out of class. The Dean sent him back ten minutes later."

"Just fail the jerk," Nick said.

"It wouldn't matter. He only comes to school to show off to the girls. He probably makes more money than you and I put together."

"I have one of those in my class too. Carlos Contreras. He was showing off a watch that was worth close to ten thousand dollars," Nick said.

"Life just doesn't seem fair, does it?" Tommy asked.

"Nobody ever said it was," Nick replied.

"Guerneville," Tommy said.

"What?" Nick replied.

"Guerneville. I think if I had the money I would move to Guerneville, buy a little house, and travel to Paris a couple of times a year just to buy clothes. That wouldn't take nearly so much money. I bet it could be done for less than a million dollars. I could sell my condo in North Hollywood and probably buy a small house. If I needed to, I could substitute teach."

"Where the hell is Guerneville and why there?" Nick asked.

"It's a small-town north of San Francisco between Santa Rosa and the coast. Several years ago, it became a vacation spot for the San Francisco gay community. Now it is pretty much a gay town." Tommy explained.

"Sounds perfect," Nick replied.

"What about you, how much would it take for you to move to Paraguay?" Tommy asked.

"I figure I could do it for around a million as well. Places there aren't cheap. I could pick up a small condo for around a hundred thousand. From what I read you can live like a king for about thirty thousand a year. A million would be more than enough to last me until I turn fifty-five and can start collecting my retirement. Then I can live on that."

"Sounds like you got it all worked out," Tommy said. "Now all you need is a million dollars."

"Yeah, just a minor hang-up."

Lunch arrived and the two friends ate quietly, each lost in his dreams.

"Mr. Stirling," it was Alex Dominguez.

"What's up Alex?" Nick answered.

"I brought you a picture of Rudy's new lowrider. Check it out." Alex handed Nick a picture of one of the finest '64 Impalas Nick had ever scene. It was parked behind a trailer with a similar paint job. The trailer was hooked to a new top of the line motorhome.

"Is this the new company delivery van?" Nick asked, pointing to the motorhome.

"Isn't it great? Who would ever suspect something that looks like that? Hector is driving out next week and bringing Rudy's Impala for the car show at the community carnival. You really should come check it out."

"Is Hector staying for the car show? I'm trying to remember what he looks like," Nick said.

"Nah, he has to get back to the factory. Next week is a big delivery and he has to get all the cash back before that following Monday," Alex explained.

Again, Alex had shared a little more information than Nick really needed to know.

"Rudy told me to give you this." Alex handed Nick a magazine.

Nick turned it over. It was an issue of Lowrider Magazine with Rudy's Impala on the cover.

"Check out the lady on the cover," Alex said.

"That's not Rudy's wife, is it?" Nick asked.

Alex laughed. "Are you kidding me? Linda never looked that hot even before she had four kids. That's just one of the Lowrider girls who are always posing by the cars. Check out the 'chichis' on that babe."

Nick had to admit, the young lady did add a lot to the picture.

CHAPTER SEVEN

That morning the train was late.

"It's getting so you can count on it always coming about ten minutes late," a stranger said to Nick waiting on the platform.

Nick just nodded his head and grunted.

"Here it comes," the stranger said.

Nick leaned out and looked down the tracks, but saw no sign of the train. He glanced over at the stranger who had reported that it was coming.

"I heard it," the stranger said smiling. "I heard it blow its horns."

Nick nodded his head and turned away from the stranger. Either this guy was a little crazy or Nick's hearing was starting to go. Probably a little of both Nick decided.

About seven minutes later, even Nick heard the loud air horns of the train as it warned of its eminent approach.

"See I told you I heard it," the stranger said to the group of commuters that now crowded that section of the platform.

Some of the engineers had to have a bit of a sadistic streak in them. Today one such engineer was driving the train. He waited as late as possible to apply the air brakes. When he did, he braked hard and a mind-numbing screech wailed at eardrum-shattering volume. The more seasoned passengers had prepared by already covering their ears. As the train ground to a halt, the engineer blasted the air horns a half a dozen times, loud and sustained so as to cause your body to literally vibrate on the cement platform. Even covering their ears could not protect the commuters from the damaging barrage of the headache-inducing decibel level.

A collective sigh of relief went up from all present when the train finally stopped and the doors sprung apart. Then the race for the remaining seats began. When the train was so late, that usually meant more passengers, since those arriving early for the next train could board early. Such was the case again today.

Nick was one of the last to enter and all seats were taken on the lower level. As he headed up to the raised-end sections, he saw two empty seats. One was empty because it would have been impossible for anyone to squeeze into the seat opposite the grotesquely obese person sitting across from it. Nick could not imagine how this person had even made it up the two steps and narrow hallway leading to this seating area.

"How can a body support that kind of weight without crushing the ankle and foot bones?" Nick thought to himself. He looked down at the lady's feet, or at least where the feet should have been. There appeared to be nothing but stumps. There was no clear definition as to where the leg ended and the foot began. It was as though she balanced on two gigantic posts.

"Must be like walking on stilts. Really fat telephone pole-like stilts," Nick thought. He thought about waiting to watch the lady get off the train to see how she did walk, but decided he would rather find a seat and try to nap.

The second empty seat, on that level, wasn't really empty. It was piled with luggage. No matter how many times the conductor announced for the riders to keep the seats clear of bags so passengers could sit down, there was always someone who thought they were exempt from the request. This kind of arrogance really pissed Nick off and he would sometimes go out of his way to ask a person to remove their luggage so he could sit down, even when other seats were available. He would not do that today. The person with the luggage was covered in tattoos and looked like he was just getting out of, or should be headed, for prison. Nick would pass on that seat today.

He headed to the upper level of the train car and the choices were about the same. If Nick really wanted to sit down, there would be some consequence he must endure and, today, Nick just didn't feel like he was up to hassling or dealing with anything. He headed back downstairs and stood with a half-a-dozen other hapless passengers either too fearful or too apathetic to fill one of those empty seats.

When the train arrived at Union Station, Nick headed out to Alameda to wait for Tommy. Getting from the train to Alameda was an adventure in itself. There was always the gauntlet of homeless asking for money to buy breakfast. Several times Nick had given these people money for food or coffee, only to watch them pocket it, collect a few dollars more, and head for the liquor store on Cesar Chavez. If they really wanted coffee, why in the hell did they buy it for a buck fifty a cup at the station, when a block away at Phillipes they could get it for a quarter?

Today as he walked through the station there seemed to be more vagrants than usual. Nick watched as two of them, unsuccessful at panhandling any money, pulled two cups out of the trash and went into the bagel shop and refilled the cups with sodas. The store was so busy that no one even noticed.

"I've got to remember that trick," Nick said to himself.

Nick always liked to walk by the fountains when he headed outside to the street. There were several fountains around the station, but the one he liked the best was the one that held the Koi in-between the station and the Metropolitan Water District building. He stopped almost every day and knew what most of the fish in the pond looked like. Today when he went outside there was a homeless person sitting in the middle of the pond washing off. Fortunately, security had arrived and was pulling him from the water. Nick wondered how many fish would die because of the man's desire for cleanliness. Why couldn't the man take his bath in the restroom sink like the rest of the homeless that hung out at the station seemed to do every morning?

Nick was absolutely hating this commute.

Tommy was unusually quiet when he picked Nick up that morning. Nick could read Tommy's moods fairly well and stayed quiet. He knew Tommy had something to say, he just needed to wait for him to say it.

"Shantae came by last night and took the rest of his things," Tommy finally spoke.

"I guess it's really over then, this thing with you and Shantae?"

"Of course it's over! How could I ever be with someone who said I was a lousy makeup artist?" Tommy said.

"I don't think he called you a lousy makeup artist," Nick said. "I believe he said you were the worst makeup artist ever," Nick said, trying not to laugh.

"Oh, *e tu brute*," Tommy replied, quoting Shakespeare. "I can't believe even you have turned on me?"

"You know I'm just joking," Nick apologized.

"It's only a joke if both people think it's funny," Tommy replied.

The two sat silently for about five seconds, then both burst out laughing.

When they arrived at school, the custodial staff was busy trying to paint over at least fifty areas where a local tagging crew had decided to initiate some of their newest members. The school was covered in gang names and the names of the individual taggers. Of course, there were several references to some of the teachers and what they should go do.

"Don't they have cameras all around the school to catch the fools who do this?" Tommy asked.

"There are plenty of cameras, but they all look about like this," Nick said pointing to the bubble on the ceiling of the walkway that concealed one of those cameras.

"Yeah, so what's the problem. Why didn't it work?" Tommy pressed.

"That glass is supposed to be clear. It's been spray painted over. The camera inside is worthless." Nick lamented.

"Well, that's stupid," Tommy replied. "They should clean the paint off."

"I'm sure they do, or at least did. But as soon as they cleaned it, someone came along and sprayed it again. Now they don't even bother to turn on the recorders. There is nothing to record."

"What a waste of money," Tommy wailed.

"Like this district doesn't waste money," Nick replied. "This is the fifth time in three years they've dug up the campus to rewire the internet system. Somebody is getting rich."

"It sure the hell isn't us," Tommy replied. "By the way, I have to leave early today. I have to meet with my banker about taking out a second mortgage on my condo."

"Good luck, I hope you have plenty of equity," Nick said.

"That's the problem, I think the place is worth less now than when I bought it," Tommy said. "I'm really just testing the waters to see if it'll be possible."

"Maybe you'll be surprised," Nick replied.

"I doubt it, but it's worth a try," Tommy replied.

"I'll talk to Paul about a ride home. I'll see you tomorrow," Nick said.

CHAPTER EIGHT

"Have you thought about trying to pass the phony bills anymore?" Nick asked Tommy the next morning.

"I've thought about it," Tommy replied. "But you're right; it's too much work and too much risk for too little a return."

"Frankly, I'm surprised you got away with it the first time," Nick said. "That bill you showed me wouldn't have fooled anybody."

"Yeah, but you looked at it in the daylight and knew what to look for," Tommy replied.

"If you knew there was a way we could each make a million dollars, would you do it?" Nick asked after a few minutes of silence.

"It would depend on how much risk is involved. You got something in mind?" Tommy asked.

"I've been thinking about something. What if we could rip off the drug dealers?"

"No drug dealers in Cudahy have two million dollars lying around, but they do have lots of soldiers with guns protecting them," Tommy said. "That would be suicide."

"I'm not talking about the local slingers. I'm talking about the mother lode. The guy who supplies all of Los Angeles," Nick said.

"You're freak'n nuts," Tommy said.

Tommy was pulling into the parking lot. Noe's Escalade was parked in one of the handicap spaces near the front.

"Maybe I am," Nick replied. "Let's go to Sizzler for lunch today so we can talk in private."

"You buying?" Tommy asked.

"Sure," Nick replied.

"How does that chump get away with parking there?" Tommy asked.

"He gets away with it because the gang runs this city," Nick replied.

"It's just not fair," Tommy replied.

"Nobody said it would be," Nick replied.

"I think I've heard that before." Tommy replied, as the two men walked into school.

At lunch time, Tommy was waiting by the gate when Nick walked out.

"So, what's your great plan?" Tommy asked.

"Be patient, I'll explain it over lunch," Nick replied.

Nick and Tommy walked into the Sizzler and looked around to make sure no other teachers were eating there. They saw no one they recognized, so they filled their plates and moved to a tall booth near the back of the restaurant.

"So, stop teasing me," Tommy said, "what is this grand plan of yours?"

"It's actually remarkably simple. Do you know a student named Alex Dominguez?" Nick asked.

"Nope,"

"How about Carlos Contreras?"

"Nope," Tommy replied again.

"Good," Nick said. "it's better that you don't know them."

"What makes them so important?"

"Alex's brother, Rudy, was one of my students years ago. I've watched as he's worked his way up the hierarchy of the Wilcox Street Gang. He doesn't look like your typical gang guy. He was groomed to be an officer in their corporate structure."

"Whoa, wait a minute," Tommy said. "You make it sound like these guys are Microsoft or something. They're just a bunch of drug-dealing thugs."

"That's only at the street level and, unfortunately, that's the level that we see around here. Believe me, the Wilcox Street Gang is just like a corporate entity. These guys are the major cocaine supplier for almost every gang in Southern California."

"You're full of shit. You can't possibly know that," Tommy said.

"I know I shouldn't, but I do. Just like you had to tell me about passing the phony fifties, Rudy, and now Alex, can't help but tell me all about the drugs coming into Los Angeles."

"What's your plan?" Tommy asked.

"The plan is to steal the money from them after they make the next delivery." Nick said.

"How are you going to do that?" Tommy asked.

"Not how am I going to do it, but how are we going to do it?
" Nick corrected.

"Okay, how are we going to do it?" Tommy said.

"We're going to rob Hector Contreras when he's on his way back to Utah with all the cash," Nick said.

"Are you telling me one guy carries all the money from selling the cocaine?" Tommy said.

"I sure am," Nick replied, "and I know exactly where to find him."

Suddenly, someone stepped out of the booth directly behind where Nick and Tommy had been talking.

"You're the Michael Jackson counterfeiter?" Maria said to Tommy. "You did a fabulous makeup job. I never would have guessed it if I hadn't heard it for myself."

Maria Aguilar was one of the ELL teachers at CHS. ELL stands for English Language Learners. She was taller than

43

your typical Hispanic woman, about 5'8", and about as friendly as a rabid pit bull. This was only her second year at CHS, but she had been teaching for several years. Nick guessed her age to be thirty-something, but it was pretty hard to tell. Tommy thought she was in her late twenties. Maria Aguilar was about as dowdy and plain looking as anyone Tommy or Nick had ever seen. More than once Tommy had commented on her over-sized frumpy sweaters and her tasteless, dated skirts that went down to her ankles, but Nick always scolded him.

"I just can't understand how any woman could go out in public looking like that. She wears no makeup and, oh my god, her hair, it's just dreadful," Tommy had said to Nick on several occasions.

"Your delusional," Nick would reply, "you fail to see the diamond-in-the rough."

But then again, Tommy couldn't understand why men didn't put on makeup before going out either. Especially, some of the men at CHS.

"You're planning on robbing the Wilcox Street Gang. How much money are we talking about?" Maria asked.

Neither Tommy or Nick answered. They were both too shocked that Maria had overheard their conversation and had sat down at the table.

"I asked a question," she said. "Surely, you've researched this little scheme of yours enough to know how much money Hector will have with him, haven't you?"

"I'm guessing about three million dollars," Nick replied hesitantly. Tommy gave Nick a look that said "what the hell are you doing telling her this."

"Relax Tommy, your secrets are safe with me," Maria said.

"Maria, I think..." Maria interrupted.

"Don't ever call me Maria. My name is Mary."

"Sorry Mary," Nick said," But I don't really think..."

"No, you don't really think," she interrupted again.

"Three million dollars would mean a million for each of us. I think that's fair," Mary said.

"You don't really think you're going to help us rob the gang, do you?" Tommy said.

"Of course I do, what other choice do you have? I already know too much. Besides, you need me." Mary said.

"Need you, why do we need you?" Tommy asked.

"I'll tell you why you need me," Mary explained. "Suppose some *pendejo* comes up to you and says: '*Por qué chingado se acercaon así a mi carro estúpidos.*' What are you going to answer? I know neither of you speak Spanish. '*Y ustedes se van a quedar parados con la verga en las manos tratando de entender que carajos les están diciendo.*' And because you don't know how to respond, he's going to pull out his *cuete* and blast both of you. We wouldn't want that to happen, would we? '*No me molestaría mirar que tan grande tenéis la verga. Especialmente, si yo!*'" Mary said, looking towards Nick

Nick and Tommy sat speechless as Mary spoke.

"Look, lunch is just about over, why don't we meet in my room after school and continue this conversation," Mary said.

Before either Nick or Tommy could reply, Mary was up and on her way through the door headed back to CHS.

"I think we just screwed up big time," Tommy said.

"Did she say what I think she said?" Nick asked. "You're Spanish is better than mine."

"She did if you think she said she'd like to get to know you better," Tommy replied.

"Are you sure that's all she said?" Nick asked.

"Close enough," Tommy replied

"Do you think we should tell her that we know Spanish?" Nick asked.

"No, not yet," Tommy replied. "That might be our only advantage for a while. Let's not give it away."

"Do you think we can trust her?" Nick asked.

"At this point, we have no choice."

CHAPTER NINE

Mary Aguilar had begun her teaching career immediately after completing college. She was only twenty-two years old when she received her first assignment at Huntington Park High School. She spent more time those first two years turning down the advances of students and faculty members than she did teaching. Why Hispanic men and boys thought they could say such things to her just because she was a Hispanic female irritated her beyond belief. Of course, it wasn't just the macho Hispanic men that constantly propositioned her, but they were the ones she found most appalling. It was as if they were using their cultural heritage as an excuse to be abusive to women. It was then she decided to have nothing to do with Hispanic men.

In her third year of teaching, Mary left Huntington Park High School and moved to Venice High School. With the move came a change of appearance. It was then she began to wear the frumpy clothing and worked at being nonattractive. She believed it was the only way to stop the constant fawning by sex-crazed males.

It wasn't that she hated men. She was by no means a lesbian and could not fathom why a woman would choose another woman over a man. It was just she had grown weary of men wanting nothing more than to get her into bed. She had fought it since she was in junior high and finally when she went to Venice, she no longer had to deal with it. It had now become such a habit, she didn't even try to seek an intermediate ground. To her it was a matter of black-or-white, and change was hard.

"Tell me about your plan," Mary said, when Nick and Tommy entered her classroom.

Neither spoke but looked around to make sure no one else was around.

"I'm a little more careful than you two. I already made sure no one is next door who might overhear something.

Nick checked anyway.

"The plan is to steal three million dollars from Hector Contreras as he's returning to Utah with the gang's money," Nick said.

"How many people will be with him?" Mary asked

"None," Tommy said. "At least none according to Nick."

"How is that possible? You're telling me that the Wilcox Street Gang is sending three million dollars to Utah with one person?" Mary said.

"That's right, and I know what he's driving, when he's driving, and where he'll be stopping," Nick smiled.

"I don't believe it. How can you possibly know all of that?" Mary said.

"For the same reason I know Tommy passed the phony fifties, he told me, just like the gang members have told me. It's hard to keep a secret like that without it eating you up inside. You have to tell someone. Someone you trust."

"They'll know it's you that stole the money then," Mary said.

"Believe me, I'm not the only one who knows. Besides, I'll be wearing a disguise," Nick said.

"What! Are you going as Michael Jackson too?" Mary laughed.

"Though I have to admit that was one great makeup job you did on yourself, Tommy," Mary said, smiling. "Let me get this straight. You two are going to dress up in some costumes and rob this Hector guy in the middle of the night of all the gang's cocaine profits?"

"We haven't worked out exactly how it's going to go down quite yet," Nick admitted.

"Oh great! You know we'll be killed if they figure out who did this?" Mary said.

"We know that, but it's our one chance in life to get enough money to get out of this dead-end career. I had prostate cancer last year. Who knows how much longer I'll live? I sure as hell would rather die in Paraguay than here," Nick said.

"Paraguay!" Mary said, surprised. She didn't want to tell Tommy that she had dreamed of moving to someplace like Paraguay for years.

"Nick and I had talked about me making us both up to look like gangsters. Hector would think we were Mexicans," Tommy said.

"I know Hector will be stopping at a campground called Las Vegas Bay at Lake Meade, both on his way to deliver the gang's coke, and again when he returns with the money to Utah. From what I've overheard, and been told, the gang owns a stake in the concessions at the camp ground. He has a nice private spot for his RV right on the water, always available."

"Why do they bother to stop there?" Mary asked.

"They make a delivery to the gangs in Las Vegas on the way to Los Angeles. It's a nice quiet out of the way spot where no one pays any attention to an RV parking for the night."

"So just when is all this supposed to happen?" Mary asked.

Nick pulled out the Lowrider magazine. This is Rudy Dominguez's new car. Rudy is one of the big bosses back in Utah. I had him as a student a few years back. Hector will be pulling a trailer carrying Rudy's car to bring it out for the car show next weekend when he brings the coke out. I heard this shipment is a larger than normal supply which should mean larger than normal cash going back with Hector. Hector won't be staying for the show and carnival, he has to be back by Sunday, which means he'll be spending Friday night at the RV campground. That's when we'll do it."

"Seems like there are a lot of issues and holes in your plan that still need to be worked out," Mary said.

"Nothing says you have to participate in this," Tommy said.

"I say I have to participate," Mary snapped. "Besides, I don't particularly want to spend the rest of my life in Cudahy either."

"Good, then next Friday we'll all take off from work and head to Nevada," Nick said.

"Whoa there, Butch Cassidy," Mary said. "I think we have a lot of planning to do before then. I suggest we all get together at Tommy's and work out the details and try on our costumes. I'll have no problem looking like a homie, but you two, I don't know."

"You may be Hispanic, but that doesn't necessarily make you a homie either," Tommy said.

"We'll see this weekend, which one of us fits in," Mary said. "Now then, do either of you own a gun?"

CHAPTER TEN

"We have to finish off the school year. If one of us quits mid-year it'd look too suspicious," Nick told Tommy that Friday on their way to work.

"I don't know," Tommy said. "I don't think I want to be around for the shit that'll hit the fan in Cudahy if we pull this off."

"When we pull this off," Nick corrected. "And yes, we have to stick it out, and no buying a new car or any other expensive things that might give us away."

"Do you think Mary will agree to it?" Tommy asked.

"I bet Mary will insist we stay around for two more years," Nick joked.

"That's not funny," Tommy said.

Nick and Tommy rode quietly for several minutes.

"Do you have one?" Tommy asked.

"Do I have one what?" Nick replied.

"You know what I'm talking about. Do you have a gun?" Tommy whispered, even though they were in his car on the freeway.

Nick pretended to look all around and in the back seat before he whispered his reply. "No, I don't have one, do you?"

"Good heavens no. Why would I want such an awful thing?" Tommy replied.

"Maybe because we're criminals?" Nick said.

"Well, I'm not touching one, no matter what happens," Tommy said.

When Tommy and Nick arrived at school, Noe had parked his Escalade in the teacher's lot taking up the last two available spaces.

"What an asshole," Nick said.

"I'd tell the campus police if I thought it'd do any good," Tommy said.

"I'll tell them for you," Nick said

"No, don't, the last time I reported a student parking in the teacher lot, I had my car keyed, and I was even parked in the teacher's lot. It's supposed to be secure and patrolled. Here in the student lot, no telling what could happen."

"If you say so," Nick replied. "I'll see you at lunch in Maria, I mean Mary's room."

"Are you absolutely positive this Hector will be at the RV campground next Friday night?" Mary asked Nick.

"I talked to Alex again this morning. He's real excited about getting to see his brother's new lowrider. He said it'll be here Wednesday and it'll be around for a couple of weeks for him to drive. I asked him why Rudy wasn't having Hector trailer it back to Utah right after the car show and he said that's what Rudy had wanted, but Hector had to head back to Utah Friday morning. I didn't want to ask him why," Nick said.

"Are you sure Hector will have the money in the RV when he returns to Utah?" Mary asked.

"That's what I've heard in the past," Nick said.

"I overheard two students in my class talking about how big this delivery is supposed to be," Tommy said.

"What students?" Nick asked.

"Noe and Hector's brother, Carlos. Carlos was telling Noe that Hector said he would show him what five million dollars cash looked like this trip," Tommy said.

"That's hard to believe," Mary replied.

"I swear its true," Tommy said.

"Alex did say this was a larger than usual delivery this time," Nick said.

"And you expect me to believe that the Wilcox Street Gang will not send guards with Hector to protect the money?" Mary said.

"Last year when Rudy was driving, he told me it was strictly a one-man operation. He even bragged about how he was trusted to carry so much money," Nick said.

"Okay, even if this Hector is carrying five million dollars, and assuming he is by himself, how do you plan on taking the money from him and what do you plan to do with him?" Mary asked.

"I was thinking we could get the jump on him somehow at the RV campground," Nick replied.

"And just how do you plan to do that?" Mary asked.

"I thought we'd figure that out when we got there," Nick said.

"I have a better idea," Mary said, as she reached into her briefcase and pulled out the biggest pistol both Nick and Tommy had ever seen.

"Where did you get that?" Tommy exclaimed. "I have an uncle who's into guns. I'm housesitting for him while he's in Mexico for two months. I drop by once a week and water the plants and check the mail. This was in a drawer next to his bed," Mary explained.

"What kind of gun is it?" Nick asked.

"How should I know, it's a gun isn't it, and we need a gun, don't we?" Mary answered.

"Well, I guess so," Nick replied, hesitantly.

"Well, good! Now that we have settled that, tomorrow we'll try on our disguises at Tommy's and start working out the details," Mary said.

Tommy and Nick headed back to their classrooms. "What details do you think she's talking about?" Tommy asked.

"Well, I sure as hell hope it doesn't involve using that canon she had," Nick said.

"I'm starting to think we should rethink this whole idea," Tommy said.

"Do you really want to spend the rest of your life here, or another school like this?" Nick said. "I sure don't!"

"It just seems so dangerous now, with guns and everything," Tommy said.

"It'll be simpler and safer than trying to pass those phony fifties," Nick said.

"And a lot more profitable too," Tommy said.

CHAPTER ELEVEN

Nick had never taken the train into Los Angeles on a Saturday morning. It was much less crowded and there didn't seem to be so many 'crazies' lurking about. Nick took a later train than usual and was running late when he finally got off the red line subway in North Hollywood near Tommy's condo. He was hoping Mary would be running late too.

"Anybody home?" Nick said, knocking on the door.

"You're late," Mary said.

"Where's Tommy?" Nick asked.

"He's putting on his costume and makeup. The same thing I should be doing, but somebody had to wait for you," Mary said, sounding put out. "Let me see the costume you brought."

Nick pulled out a pair of khaki colored Dockers and a long sleeve plaid shirt.

"You're kidding, right?" Mary asked.

Nick turned red. "Well, it's all I had that I thought might work."

"You thought wrong. Didn't you talk this over with Tommy?" Mary asked.

"Don't worry," Tommy called from the bedroom, "I picked up a wardrobe for Nick."

"Thank goodness, one of you is thinking," she said. "I'll be in changing." Mary picked up a canvas bag and headed into the other bedroom.

"Are you ready for me yet?" Nick called into Tommy.

"Just about," Tommy replied. "Have a cup of coffee and relax. I'm just about finished."

About five minutes later Tommy walked out of the bedroom. Tommy's black skin had been transformed to a golden brown and, remarkably, he had well-defined muscular arms. He was dressed in a pair of Dickie shorts and a Pro Club shirt. Tommy was dressed just like Noe Gomez from school. He had the look of a well-positioned member of the gang.

"You look great," Nick said.

"Thank you," Tommy replied. "I can't wait to do you."

"Excuse me?" Nick said laughing. "Don't be silly, you know what I mean. Now get your butt in here."

"Strip to your boxers," Tommy said.

Nick stripped down to his underwear.

"Oh, my goodness. You wear 'tidy whities'. That won't do at all," Tommy said.

"I wear what?" Nick replied.

"Tidy whities, nut huggers, whatever you call them. You need boxers." Tommy said. "And I didn't get you any of those."

"What should I do?" Nick asked.

"Well I would like to say, take them off, but that would surely disgust me and interfere with my work, so you can pick up a pair later. Now, take off your wig."

Nicks eyes got big. "Are you serious?"

"No gangster I know has hair like that. Besides, your bald head will be the perfect disguise," Tommy replied. "Now stand there, and don't move."

Nick did as he was told and Tommy circled him several times spraying a coat of paint, turning Nick a darker shade of brown than he had sprayed himself.

"Beautiful," Tommy said. "Now sit down while I paint on your tattoos."

For the next hour Tommy painted several gang tattoos on Nick. Besides his arms, he had a giant gang name across his chest and another on his back. His arms had a variety of

56

girls, skeletons, and dice, along with a spider web on his right elbow. On his neck Tommy wrote the name Maria. He added two little tear drops under Nick's left eye. "What do you want your last name to be?"

"How about Bravo?" Nick said.

"How about Perez?" Tommy suggested.

"Fine with me," Nick replied.

Tommy wrote the name Perez across Nick's stomach.

"This comes off, doesn't it?" Nick said.

"It better or you're going to look mighty silly at work next week," Tommy said. "Here put this on." Tommy handed Nick a pair of oversized Dickie shorts and a wife-beater white t-shirt that allowed the tattoos to show through the thin material. Tommy handed Nick a long belt to hold up his Dickies. He cinched it tight and allowed the excess to hang down his leg.

"What about shoes?" Nick asked.

"Put these on," Tommy replied, handing Nick a pair of long white socks and black corduroy bedroom slippers.

"I hope I won't have to run in these," Nick said.

"Stand up and let me have a look," Tommy said, when Nick had pulled on the slippers. "You look fabulous. I'm a genius."

Nick looked in the mirror and could not believe the gangster staring back at him. It looked nothing like him. Tommy was truly a magician. Nick practiced a few poses that he had seen students in his classes do. His posturing just didn't look the same, but he still had a week to practice.

"Let's go show Mary," Tommy said.

Nick and Tommy opened the door and started to walk into the living room... and froze in their tracks, both of their jaws fell open, and neither could say a word. They were mute with astonishment.

Mary stood there in a pair of spiked heels and the shortest shorts Tommy had ever seen. However, it was from the waist up that had the two men staring in awe. Mary had on a wife-beater t-shirt identical to Nick's, but inside of hers were the biggest set of breasts Tommy had ever seen. Everything was perfectly defined as they pressed against the overly stretched material of the t-shirt. Mary wore a blonde wig that showed fake brown roots, as if the hair had been recently dyed and was in need of touch–up. The hair was pushed high up on her head. She looked identical to the model Nick and Tommy had seen on the cover of the Lowrider magazine Alex had given him.

"Whoa," Tommy said.

"I concur," Nick added.

"H-h-how...wh-wh-ere, did you get..." Tommy was flustered.

"They're really all me," Mary said blushing. "And you, I can't believe that's really you, Nick. You look downright scary. What happened to your hair?"

"I wear a wig Tommy made for me when I underwent chemo. It looked so much better than my real hair, I decided to shave my head and stick with the wig."

"I never would have guessed," Mary said. "You actually look really nice bald. Old, but nice."

"Well, I would never have guessed about those being hidden away either," Tommy said referring to Mary's breasts. "You could poke an eye out with one of those."

They all stood around staring at each other for several minutes, commenting on the wonderful job Tommy had done on Nick and himself, and on the wonderful job genetics had done with Mary.

"This is why I dress the way I do at work," Mary said. "I have to hide these and my legs or every guy in school would be hitting on me."

Nick turned away embarrassed and adjusted his 'tidy whities'.

"That's why you need boxers," Tommy said.

"Actually, it's good to know I still have what it takes to get a guy going," Mary said.

"Believe me," Nick replied, "you have nothing to worry about."

"Okay, let's go," Mary said.

"Go? Go where?" Nick said.

"Go out and get used to our disguises. We have to live the part we intend to play," Mary said.

"Good," Tommy said, "I'm hungry, let's go to lunch."

Nick was a little hesitant.

"Look, Nick, if I'm willing to go out in public like this, what do you have to worry about, except for other guys hitt'n on your home boy's lady," Mary said, grabbing Nicks's arm and heading out the door.

"Just be careful not to go flashing any gang signs," Tommy said. "That could get us shot."

"I'll take care of all the flashing," Mary smiled.

CHAPTER TWELVE

"Who likes Thai? I know the cutest little Thai restaurant in Burbank," Tommy suggested.

"Sounds great," Nick replied.

"I like Thai," Mary said.

Tommy turned left on Ventura Boulevard and pulled up for valet parking. "There is never anywhere to park around here. This is a very trendy and happening restaurant."

"Maybe we shouldn't..." Nick began to say.

"Don't say it. We need to get used to this," Mary insisted. "This will be a good test."

As the three teachers exited the car, both valets and everyone standing on the sidewalk turned to stare. Of course, they all looked at Mary first, spellbound by her sexiness, then when they saw Nick, they quickly diverted their eyes not wanting to anger the gangster who no doubt was there to make sure the couple was left undisturbed.

"Look mean," Mary said to Nick.

"What?"

"Look like you're really pissed off at everybody. Leer at people and snarl under your breath," Mary said to Nick.

Tommy played his part perfectly. He was like the quintessential homeboy to Nick's bad boy. Mary played her part like she was born for it. She fawned all over Nick and giggled at just the wrong moments, leaving little doubt she was a bimbo beyond compare. Nick needed to work on his image.

When the trio walked into the restaurant, the crowd seemed to part, giving them ample room. The hostess had a look of terror on her face when she looked up and saw Nick.

"Three of us," Mary said, with a heavy Mexican accent. Another group of what looked like studio execs walked in, saw Nick, and quickly turned to leave.

"Right this way," the hostess said moving the group to the top of the waiting list.

"I have to use the rest room," Nick said.

"Just be careful," Tommy warned.

Nick walked into the restroom where several other men were waiting to use one of the three stalls or urinal. Nick thought about waiting for a stall, but decided there was no need to wait. He walked up to the lengthy metal urinal, unzipped his pants, and pulled out what looked like a snow-white penis in comparison to the dark brown make-up that covered the rest of his body. He wasn't the only one to notice and both men on either side did a double-take when they saw Nick's pecker.

"Errrr.." Nick snarled and both men quickly pushed their own penises back in their pants to get away from the crazed gangster who had just snarled at them. They both left a trickle of pee across the floor and across the front of their pants as they hurried from the restroom.

When Nick walked out of the restroom and into the restaurant, several of the men were staring at Mary. "Errrr..." Nick snarled again and all eyes were off of Mary. Nick walked up.

"Next time you need to spray me down there," Nick said to Tommy.

"I need to what?" Tommy asked. Mary also looked up.

"Spray me down there. You know, my penis." He whispered. "I went to pee and it looked like I was holding an albino corn snake," Nick said.

"In your dreams," Mary laughed.

"Well you will never know." Nick replied

"As if I would want to know." Mary answered.

61

Nick and Tommy looked at each other and smiled.

"The two men next to me noticed and I had to snarl," Nick said.

"We'll fix that," Tommy said.

The three received their food in no time. It was obvious to all that the restaurant staff wanted them out as soon as possible. They were happy to oblige, for they all wanted to continue to test their disguises.

"Let's head over to Florence and Pacific," Tommy suggested.

"I don't think we're quite ready for that yet," Mary said. "I think it best if we stay away from an area where we could run into somebody we know, especially students."

"What better way to test our disguises," Nick said.

"The disguises are not the problem," Mary said. "It's the way you carry yourself, Nick. I'm sorry, but you walk and move like a white guy."

"I am a white guy," Nick replied.

"Not next Friday. Next Friday you better act and look like the baddest-ass gangster in all of Southern California," Tommy said.

"You need to spend some time observing," Mary suggested. "Why don't we head out to the Santa Monica pier? There's a Mexican restaurant out on the end of the pier. The place is always packed with gangsters and tourists. We can spend the afternoon having a few beers and people watching. See how the homies walk and talk."

"Let's do it," Tommy said.

An hour later the three were sitting at the outside patio of Mariasol Cocina Mexicana, drinking their first beer of the afternoon.

"Are you sure this is a good place to observe?" Nick asked.

"It is until you act more like a Mexican gangster and less like a white middle class teacher," Mary replied.

"Let's have a shot of tequila," Tommy suggested. "I'll buy."

The afternoon passed quickly and one shot turned into several as did the one beer turn into four. By five in the afternoon, all three teachers were too drunk to drive.

"We need to take a long walk," Mary insisted. "There's no way I am getting in a car with somebody as drunk as me."

"I couldn't agree more," Tommy said, as he slowly tried to stand.

"I need to pee first," Nick said.

"Can I watch?" Tommy and Mary said simultaneously.

"Nobody sees the great white snake," Nick slurred and headed away.

Nick returned and pulled out a credit card to pay their bill.

"Could I see some identification, Mr. Stirling?" the waiter asked.

Nick started to pull out his driver's license and suddenly stopped.

"You know, I seem to have forgotten my license. Mary, it might be best if you pay the bill," Nick said.

"We can use my..." Tommy started to say, but Nick kicked him under the table.

"I guess we could pay cash," Nick said, opening his wallet. "I could if I had some."

"I have no cash either," Tommy said.

"I'll take care of the bill," Mary said, finally catching on. She pulled out her credit card and driver's license and handed it to the waiter. He looked back and forth from the license to Mary several times before deciding the person in the picture and the hottie in front of him were one in the same.

"That was close," Nick said.

"What was close?" Tommy replied, still not sure what was going on.

"Here you are, Ms. Aguilar," the waiter said, handing Mary her receipt and staring at her breasts.

"Errrr..." Nick snarled, and the waiter scurried away.

"Stop walking like a white man," Mary said to Nick as they headed down the pier.

"How about this?" Nick said and started doing something he had heard his student's call 'crip walking'.

"Stop that, stop that this instant!" Tommy said. "You look ridiculous."

Mary was laughing too hard to be angry.

Nick stopped and started slinking down the pier.

"That's even worse," Mary said. You look like a puppy dog that was just scolded.

"Try this," Tommy said and started to strut.

"Nick's supposed to be a gangbanger, not a freak'n peacock," Mary said. "You need to swagger. Act like you're the baddest mother in Santa Monica and anybody who looks at you wrong will get his face punched.

It seemed to work. People began to purposely change their direction as Nick approached just to stay out of his way. Every so often, they would come across another group of gangster-looking thugs who would leer at the trio and throw up some signs. Mary, Tommy, and Nick just ignored them, knowing that there were way too many police around for anyone to start trouble.

All went well until the three teachers felt they had sobered up enough to head back to Tommy's. On the way to the car, two gangsters that had seen them earlier approached.

"*Eh ese, quiero dormir con tu mujer*," one of the gangsters said to Nick.

Without a hint of hesitation Nick, punched the *vato* who had spoken. His friend grabbed Nick but, before either could react, Mary had her pistol out of her purse and stuck in the gangster's ear.

"*Dame una razón para halarle el gatillo pendejo*," Mary said.

They let go of Nick.

"Put your hands on the car," Mary yelled. "Spread your legs."

Tommy and Nick were looking around to see if anybody else was coming.

"Are you cops?" one of the gangsters asked.

"Shut up," Mary yelled.

"Search 'em, Perez," Mary said to Nick.

Nick did as he was told. One of the gangsters had a butterfly knife, but the other was carrying a 9mm Glock. Nick also took his keys and both their wallets.

I believe you boys are in big trouble," Mary said, sounding like a cop. "Now both of you, get slowly on your knees and then lay face down on the ground with your arms out straight." Both of the gangsters complied.

"Go get the car," Mary whispered to Tommy.

Tommy pulled up and Mary and Nick jumped into the car. They were out of the garage before the gangsters knew what was going on.

"You sounded just like a cop," Nick said. "Where did you learn how to do that?"

"Watching the car chases on television," Mary replied.

"What are we going to do with this stuff?" Nick asked.

"Hold on to it for now. Who knows, maybe some of it will come in handy," Mary replied.

"Why did you call me Perez?" Nick asked.

"Because it is written across your belly. Those two gangsters saw it too. They both had 'Westside Capone' tattoos. That's supposed to be a pretty tough gang. You can bet they'll be looking for some payback," Mary explained

"Well, let's get back to Tommy's and change out of these clothes," Nick said.

"Not so fast," Mary said. "Today was a good start, but we still have a lot of work to do. I think the two of you should leave the makeup on and we'll get an early start tomorrow."

"That's a good idea," Tommy replied. "You both can spend the night at my house." Neither Nick nor Mary responded.

"Thank you for hitting that *pendejo*," Mary said. "How did you know what he said?"

Nick hesitated before answering. He wasn't sure if this was the right time to tell Mary he spoke and understood Spanish. "I understood enough to get the gist of what he was saying, and it didn't sound nice. Besides, isn't that the way my character is supposed to act?"

"I can't believe you pulled that gun on those men," Tommy said. "I almost peed my pants."

Nick and Mary just smiled.

It was late when they arrived back at Tommy's condo.

"Mary, you can have the second bedroom and Nick you get the couch. There are clean towels in your bathroom if you want to shower. I'm afraid Nick and I will have to wait till after tomorrow to shower, or Nick, you can have the second bedroom and Mary can..." Tommy was quickly interrupted

"No way that's going to happen," Mary said to Tommy.

"No way what's going to happen?" Nick asked completely clueless.

"Never mind." Mary said.

"I'll get you some clean sheets," Tommy said to Nick.

That night as Mary lay in bed alone, she wondered if maybe she had been a little too hasty with her response to Tommy.

CHAPTER THIRTEEN

"Alex," Nick said in class, "do you still have that photograph of Rudy's new Lowrider?"

"Sure," Alex replied.

"Mind if I borrow it at lunch to show a friend?" Nick asked.

"No problemo," Alex replied and handed the photo to Nick. "I'll get it back from you next period."

"Thanks," Nick replied, and set the photo on his desk. "When is the real thing going to be here?"

"It was supposed to be today, but now I hear it'll be on Wednesday," Alex replied.

"Will Hector be towing it back home after the car show?" Nick asked.

"No, he still plans on picking it up in a couple of weeks when he comes down again. Hector can't stay around for the show on Saturday."

"That's too bad." Nick replied.

"You coming to check out the cars, Mr. Stirling?" Alex asked.

"You know, I just might," Nick replied.

"Hope so, it should be really '*bad*'," Alex replied.

"'*Bad*' as in good, you mean?" Nick said.

"*Orale*," Alex replied.

"Can I help you, Ms. Aguilar?" the Dean's secretary asked.

"I was hoping to look up a student from a few years back," Mary replied.

"I can help you with that, what's his name?"

Mary wasn't expecting to have the secretary's help. "You know, that's part of the problem. I can see his face, but I just can't remember his name. If you have a book with pictures, I should be able to find him."

The secretary seemed a little suspicious of the odd request, but then again, she had heard more bizarre requests in the past. "How long ago did you say?"

"I believe four years ago should do," Mary replied.

The secretary went to a shelf and pulled out a binder that held pictures. "If you need a different year, let me know."

"Thank you," Mary replied, and sat down at a table in back to look at the pictures. It didn't take her long to find Hector Contreras' photo. Now she somehow had to sneak it out. The picture was printed on a page with thirty-five other students. The sheet of paper had a vinyl page protector covering it. Mary would have to take the page along with the vinyl protector. Opening the binder would have made too much noise. When the door to the Dean's office opened, Mary was able to rip the first two holes in the vinyl protector.

The door opened again and the Dean came into the office. Mary did not care much for Dean Cardona. Several times he had tried to hit on her. When he saw her sitting at the back of the room, he immediately went to her and began his macho Hispanic posturing that Mary detested.

"Ms. Aguilar, you're looking ravishing this morning," Cardona said.

"I'm looking for a student who used to go here," Mary said, refusing to look at him.

"Maybe I can help," Cardona said, reaching for the book in Mary's hands.

"I don't think that'll be necessary," Mary replied, pulling the book back.

"What's the student's name?" Cardona asked.

"She doesn't know his name," the secretary yelled from across the room.

Just then one of the campus security men brought in two girls who had been fighting outside the locker room and were still yelling at each other.

Instantly, Cardona was up to intervene and everyone's attention was drawn to the screaming girls.

"Bitch, leave my boyfriend alone," the first girl yelled.

"If you gave him what he needed, he wouldn't be want'n it from me," the second girl replied, and fists were swinging again.

Mary took the opportunity to slip the vinyl page into her purse. She placed the binder back on the shelf and quickly left the office. No one even noticed she had left.

At lunch Nick and Tommy met with Mary in her classroom.

"I think I know how we can do it," Tommy said. "Mary will be the bait. What guy could pass up a beauty like Mary? Look how turned on those two Westside Capone guys were. And dozens of guys turned to check her out as we walked around."

"I don't like it," Nick said. "I don't want to put Mary in a risky situation."

"This entire scheme puts us all in a risky situation," Tommy said. "Besides, you saw how she handled herself with that gun and we'll be right behind her all the time. What do you think Mary?"

"I think it's the most logical solution."

"I still don't like it," Nick said.

"You're just jealous," Tommy said. "Oops, did I say too much?" Tommy giggled.

"I think we should get there and figure out what to do when we case out the situation," Nick suggested.

"I like that," Tommy said. "'Case out the situation', you're sounding like a real criminal, Nick."

Nick gave Tommy the finger.

"I'm glad you're so concerned for my well-being, but I think Tommy's idea is good. We need to go there with a plan, but if the situation requires it, we need to be flexible," Mary said.

"Okay, I'll agree to it, just as long as we can stay within shouting distance," Nick said.

"Good," Tommy said. "Did you get the picture of the RV?"

"Right here. I scanned it and made each of us a color copy."

"And here's a picture of Hector Contreras," Mary said, pulling the vinyl sheet from her purse. I'll blow it up and make copies."

"We have to make sure we don't leave any of these pictures sitting around for somebody to find," Tommy said.

"Good idea," Mary said. "We'll destroy them before we leave on Friday."

"Who's driving?" Nick asked.

"I'll drive," Tommy said. "My car blends in really well and it's reliable."

"Has everybody arranged for a sub for Friday?" Nick asked.

"I did," Tommy replied.

"I was going to call in Thursday night," Mary replied.

"I'll call Friday morning and tell them I missed my train and won't be in," Nick said.

"What if they want you to come in late?" Mary asked.

"I'll tell them that when I missed the train I started to drive in and my car broke down. I have to get it fixed."

"Good answer, good answer," Tommy replied, as if he was hosting Family Feud.

71

"I think we should all spend the night at Tommy's Thursday night so we can get an early start on makeup and our drive."

"Good idea," Nick said. "What about a map? Tommy, did you download a map of the place and how to get there?"

"I did, but I'll also take my Magellan. I'd be lost without it. Literally!" Tommy laughed.

"This will be a piece of cake," Nick said, trying to reassure Mary and Tommy, but mostly trying to convince himself.

"All right," Mary said. "Let's practice your walk."

CHAPTER FOURTEEN

Wednesday and Thursday, Alex Dominguez was not in school. Nick had hoped to talk to Alex to confirm that his brother's Lowrider had been delivered, which in turn meant the RV had dropped off its load of cocaine and was headed back to Utah.

After school on Thursday, Nick had Tommy drive by the Dominguez and the Contreras houses to see if the car and trailer may have been parked there, but they find nothing at either house.

"Maybe we should call the whole thing off," Tommy suggested

"Are you serious?" Nick said. "This is our one chance to get the hell out of here and you want to call it off?"

"We can't be sure the RV even made the trip," Tommy said.

"What's the worst that could happen if it didn't? We put on costumes and drive to Las Vegas. Maybe even gamble a little. We have nothing to lose," Nick said.

"We do if we screw up and get caught," Tommy continued.

"We're not going to screw up. Mary would slap you silly if she heard you talking like this."

"It's just that I'm starting to get a little scared. Those gangbangers in Santa Monica were the real thing. They were mean, fearless, and were carrying a gun."

"And we still managed to get the best of them," Nick added.

"Look, we can talk it over tonight at your house. If we decide it's too risky, then we can call it off," Nick said. "Is that fair?"

"Sure, we'll talk it over tonight," Tommy replied.

They both knew there was no way in hell Mary would let them back out now.

"Let's stop at Phillipes on the way to your place. I have a craving for a French dip roast beef, with bleu cheese. I'm buying," Nick said.

"And the last wishes of the condemned are granted for the final meal," Tommy replied dramatically. They both forced a chuckle.

"I don't know," Nick said. "We drove by, but didn't see the RV, a trailer, or Rudy's Lowrider. I'm not sure what it means."

"It doesn't mean anything," Mary said. "Everything goes just as we planned. If he's there, we're rich and can get out of Los Angeles. If he isn't there..., we'll deal with that if it happens."

"Don't worry, Tommy, it'll all work out just like we planned."

"I thought we might be able to use this," Tommy said pulling out a bottle of powdered granules."

"What is it?" Nick asked.

"Ketamine Hydrochloride," Tommy answered. "It's what most people call a date rape drug."

"Why am I suddenly very nervous having known you for so long?" Nick said.

"I picked it up from a friend, honest. I have never, ever, given this to anyone," Tommy said. "I thought we could maybe slip it in Hector's drink, you know, knock him out so he doesn't remember what happened."

"Does this stuff really work?" Nick asked.

"It does," Mary said seriously. "It was used on me once."

"What happened?" Nick asked.

74

It was when I was teaching at Huntington Park. There was this macho asshole assistant principal who couldn't keep his hands off me and several other of the new female teachers."

"One of you should have filed a sexual harassment suit," Tommy said.

"We were new teachers with no tenure. We needed the job. A couple of us did talk to the principal."

"What did the principal say?" Nick asked.

"He asked if I was sure I wanted to file such a serious charge? He said it would reflect on my career and ruin the career of a good man," Mary said.

"That son-of-a-bitch," Nick said.

"He said he would talk to the assistant principal and put a stop to it. I gave it some thought and decided not to file the charges."

"Did the principal talk to the AP?" Tommy asked.

"He must have, because the guy left me alone, that is, up until the day several of us teachers went to a happy hour. The asshole AP showed up being really friendly and polite to everyone. He bought several of us a drink. He must have slipped the drug into that drink. I woke up the next day in a sleazy hotel room not knowing where I was or how I got there."

"That son-of-a-bitch," Nick said again.

"I didn't even know it was him until another teacher told me she saw me getting in his car that night at the restaurant. I couldn't believe it and I couldn't prove anything. I became a recluse, never leaving my room. I transferred out of there at the end of the year."

Tommy put his arm around Mary and held her tightly as she cried.

"Where is this assistant principal now?" Nick asked.

"He's still at HP, doing the same damn thing to other new female teachers. At least according to a teacher I know who still works there," Mary said.

"That's just not right," Nick said. "People like that should be made to pay for their crimes."

"What about people like us?" Tommy said. "We're criminals too. Should we be made to pay?"

"We're not hurting anyone," Mary said. "We're taking money from the criminals who poison people. They don't deserve the money."

"So I guess we're like Robin Hood," Tommy said.

"Not quite," Mary replied. "I intend to keep the money I steal from the rich."

"You know, I think I better not stay here tonight," Mary said.

"But why?" Nick asked, disappointed.

"Talking about that time at HP has made me upset and emotional. I don't want to say or do anything I might regret in the morning," Mary replied.

"Oh," Nick replied, sounding hurt.

"It's not like you think," Mary said. "It's just that I don't want to screw up what could be the best thing that has ever happened to me because I'm an emotional basket case."

"I think I understand," Nick said.

"No, he doesn't," Tommy interjected. "If he did, he'd be happy as a lark right now."

Mary smiled. "I'll see you guys early in the morning. And Nick, if I were you, I would hold on to the Ketamine tonight."

"The thought never occurred to me," Tommy said seriously as he winked at Mary.

Nick missed the joke. Too many thoughts were laying heavy on his mind.

CHAPTER FIFTEEN

No one slept well that night. Nick lay awake most of the night worrying and thinking about Mary. Her sweet odor lingered in the sheets from when she had slept in the bed just days before. The aroma made him both happy and sad. Happy that he had found someone that he was falling deeply in love with, and sad, because of the horrific experience of being raped by the assistant principal and unable to do anything about it.

Nick had never committed a crime before. At least he hadn't before last Sunday when the three of them robbed the gang members in Santa Monica. But that really didn't count because they had no choice; it was more like acting in self-defense. Although a judge might disagree, especially since Mary had used a gun. Yeah, Nick had broken his share of traffic laws and smoked some pot when he was younger, but you couldn't really call those crimes.

What they were about to do was a real crime. No, it was several real crimes. They were going to hijack an RV, rob the driver of several million dollars, and use a gun in the process. That was real crime. And the best part about it, the guy couldn't report it to the police.

As easy as it sounded, Nick still couldn't sleep. There were just too many things that could go wrong. And what if someone got hurt?

Tommy stayed up late that night packing his car with his spare makeup kit and extra clothing and costumes. He wanted to be prepared for any contingency that might arise, at least any costume malfunctions or makeup touchups. He also packed two army surplus duffle bags that they could use to carry the money in. Three million dollars would take up a lot of room. At least he thought it would. The most cash Tommy had ever seen at one time was just over two thousand dollars and that was when he had to pay cash to get a really good deal on his makeup kit. He hated to part with that much cash, but with the kit he could do anything. That was how he had made his arms look like they were really muscular. With that kit he could turn anyone's face into Michael Jackson, just as he had done when he passed the phony fifties. The kit had definitely been worth the money.

When Tommy did finally go to bed, he quickly fell asleep. The sleeping pills he regularly took helped that. He only took half his normal dosage to be sure he would awaken on time and not be too groggy. The sleeping pills also helped with the anxiety Tommy was starting to feel about this whole scheme. He was scared about what could happen if things went wrong. Actually, he was concerned about being sent to prison and having to endure being constantly raped by the other inmates. At least that's what he heard would happen to a gay man put in prison. He hadn't even considered the possibility that they might be killed. It was probably good he hadn't, for Tommy was already close to an anxiety attack and that would be just enough to push him over the edge.

Mary cried the entire way home. She had never shared the story about her rape with anyone, let alone the man she was falling in love with. She had planned on spending the night at Tommy's and was hoping Nick would share the bed with her. Now that she had aired her deepest and most sensitive secrets, she wasn't sure how Nick would now react to her or, for that fact, how she would react to Nick. She could not risk allowing her now skewed emotions to ruin what in her heart she had hoped for these many years. Nick also needed to focus on the job they had been preparing for, as did she. She knew Tommy would stay focused, but she also knew Tommy, like Nick, didn't fully understand that planning a crime and committing a crime were vastly different. Tommy had approached this as if it was a theater performance for which he was preparing the actor's costumes and makeup. When the time came to pull off the actual robbery, Mary hoped Tommy would take a double dosage of his anxiety medicine. She knew Nick realized this as well and that was why the plans did not require Tommy's direct involvement in the actual crime itself.

If all went as planned, by this time tomorrow, a new life lies ahead for the three of them. A life she hoped would be shared with Nick.

When she arrived home, she called Tommy. She knew Tommy would start on Nick's makeup early and thought of some changes that needed to be made on Nick's tattoos. After her call, she sat at her desk and wrote a long letter. It was more of a confession than a letter. In it she talked about her rape, about her lonely life, about her new-found love of Nick, and about the crime they planned to commit. She tried to justify why she had decided to join Tommy and Nick when she overheard them talking about it and realized this might be her last chance to escape the purgatory her life had become. She then began to write about her new life together with Nick after they succeeded in the crime. As she wrote, the sadness began to leave her and a new hope filled her soul, a hope and happiness she had not felt for years. She finished the letter, placed it in an envelope, and addressed it to herself. She laid it on her desk for someone to find if, for some reason, she never returned. A shiver resonated through her body at the thought of someone else finding the letter. For she knew if they did, things had gone terribly wrong.

Mary went to the kitchen, opened and poured herself a glass of a very expensive pinot noir she had been saving for years for a special occasion. The wine was exquisite, just as she had dreamed it would be those many years ago when she purchased it in Napa.

"Saturday, we will share a glass together, my love," she said softly. She re-corked the bottle, turned off the kitchen light, and went to bed. She fell asleep with a smile and had several pleasant dreams, none of which she would remember when she awoke the next morning.

CHAPTER SIXTEEN

When Mary arrived early the next morning at Tommy's house, Nick's makeup was almost complete. Just as she had requested, Tommy had changed the gang name across Nick's chest from Wilcox Street to Westside Capones, just like the gangsters they had run into last Saturday. On Nick's back he wrote only Capones. She also had requested Tommy add a goatee on Nick's chin.

"Why the goatee?" Nick asked.

"I've always been attracted to men with facial hair," Mary replied.

"Maybe I'll grow a beard," Nick said.

"You do know what all these tattoos mean, don't you?" Mary asked, turning towards Nick.

"Do I need to know?" Nick replied.

"You never know, it might just save your life," Mary said.

"Let's hope it doesn't come to that," Tommy said.

"It won't," replied Nick, "but it would be good to know."

"The ones of the naked girl, the dice, and the lowrider on your arms are pretty much just decoration," Mary said. "I don't remember the girl looking like that."

"Nick had me add it. He wanted it to look more like you," Tommy said.

"Please don't tell me my breasts look that big," Mary said.

Tommy and Nick looked at each other and smiled. "Okay, we won't tell you," Tommy laughed. "The only problem is it weakened my muscle additions a bit, but that shouldn't be a problem."

81

Mary turned her attention back to Nick. "The spider web on your arm means that you spent time in prison," Mary said.

"Any special prison?" Nick asked.

"Not really, just as long as you say it was a state prison."

"I don't even know the name of a state prison," Nick said.

"Sure you do," Tommy said and began to sing.

> *Well, if they freed me from this prison,*
> *If that railroad train was mine,*
> *I bet I'd move out over a little,*
> *Farther down the line,*
> *Far from Folsom Prison,*
> *That's where I want to stay,*
> *And I'd let that lonesome whistle,*
> *Blow my Blues away.*

"Right, Johnny Cash, *Folsom Prison Blues*. I'll tell anybody who asks that I did my time in Folsom," Nick said.

"I didn't know you were such a good singer," Mary said.

Tommy blushed. "That's a secret I've never shared with anybody."

"Let's continue," Mary said. "The name on your neck is of course your woman's name. And those little tears under your left eye are for two homies that were killed."

"Why did I change gangs?" Nick asked

"Hector would know you're not a Wilcox Street soldier," Mary said. "If he does see you..."

"And is able to remember seeing you," Tommy interrupted.

"If he does see and remember you, we want him to think it was the Westside Capones that stole the money," Mary finished.

"Won't that start a gang war?" Nick asked.

"There's a constant gang war taking place on the streets of Los Angeles," Tommy said. "Don't you ever read the news?"

"That might happen," Mary conceded, "but it'll also cut the drugs coming into the city, and that will save a lot of lives."

"Most importantly," Tommy said, "is that we don't want them to have a remote inkling that some high school teachers were behind the theft."

"Amen," Mary added. "Any more questions or are we ready to go?"

"Everything I could possibly need is packed in the car," Tommy said. "I'm good to go."

"I see you've added a few more muscles to your costume," Mary said to Tommy.

"Yeah, I thought it made me look more macho," Tommy replied.

Nick and Mary smiled.

"Whaaaat?" Tommy said. "Are they too much?"

"I think they're just right," Mary said.

"Let's head out," Nick said.

"Oh, I almost forgot." Tommy pulled a container. "Everybody dip your fingers in here."

"What's this for?" Nick asked.

"It fills in the grooves in your fingers so you leave no fingerprints," Tommy explained.

"Great idea," Mary said. "I hadn't thought about that."

"I used it when I passed the counterfeit bills," Tommy admitted.

"Well, I'm hungry," Nick said.

"We can stop when we reach the Cajon Pass," Tommy said.

"I could starve by then," Nick said.

"Looks to me like you could stand to miss a meal or two," Mary said smiling.

"It's the makeup," Nick replied.

"Right," Mary and Tommy said at the same time.

The three friends were in a good mood as they headed down the 210 Freeway. They talked about everything but the crime they were planning to commit that evening.

"So just like that you decided not to return to Oklahoma," Mary said, amazed.

"Just like that." Nick said. "I can't understand why anyone would want to live in Oklahoma."

"Wow, that took some nerve, making a change like that," Mary said.

"Not really. My grades were bad because I was partying too much. I was probably going to flunk out, so instead I decided to drop out and get a job. My parents didn't care where I worked, just as long as I was working and supporting myself."

"Are your parents still alive?" Tommy asked.

"My dad died right after I moved to California. My mom moved in with her sister. She's still alive but now living in a care facility back in Oklahoma."

"Do you ever visit her?" Mary asked

"I haven't for the past couple of years. Not since I had my cancer surgery," Nick replied.

"How come?" Tommy asked.

"She has Alzheimer's. The last three or four times I did go back, she didn't even know who I was. I couldn't take it, so I stopped going and calling."

84

"That's awful," Mary said.

"Awful that I don't go back?" Nick asked.

"Of course not, I mean it's awful that she doesn't remember you. That must be really hard," Mary said.

"Tell me about your first wife," Mary said.

Nick looked at Mary. "Are you sure you want to hear about her?"

"Why, is there something I shouldn't know about?" Mary asked.

"No, it's just that...," Nick hesitated.

"Oh for god's sakes Nick, just tell Mary how she had that affair, and left you for the circus clown," Tommy said.

"Your wife left you for a circus clown?" Mary said in shock.

"I lied about that part," Tommy said, before Nick could respond. "I just thought it made for a better story than saying how Nick's wife left him for a veterinarian."

"The worst part is she must have spent five thousand dollars constantly taking our dog to the vet for useless surgeries and fake ailments," Nick said.

"And she got the dog in the divorce," Tommy laughed.

"I hated that dog," Nick said, and it wasn't a divorce, it was an annulment.

"Don't you have a dog now?" Mary asked Nick.

"Yes, but it's a real dog, not one of those designer dogs created to do nothing but shit on the carpet and sit in your lap all day," Nick replied.

"What's your dream, Nick?' Mary asked.

"To travel and to write," Nick replied

"Write what?" Mary asked.

"I don't know. I know I don't want to write the great American novel. I think I would rather write fun stories that help you escape the stress and humdrum of daily life."

"Mass market commercial crap is what you are trying to say," Tommy responded.

"I guess you could say that. I just want to tell a good story. Have fun writing it, and hopefully make a few people happy who read it."

"Very noble of you," Tommy said. "And I'm sure you wouldn't mind if Hollywood made a movie or two from your books either."

"What about you, Tommy. Tell Mary about your childhood," Nick said.

"What's there to tell? I grew up in South L.A., was overly protected by my mother."

"He was a momma's boy," Nick interrupted.

"I was a momma's boy, I have to admit it," Tommy confessed. "I was gay by the time I reached the third grade. I think that's why momma was so protective of me."

"Gay boys don't do well on the streets of South Central," Nick said.

"Momma probably saved my life," Tommy admitted. "As soon as I graduated from high school I went off to college at UC-Santa Cruz. That was where I blossomed."

"Blossomed and had your rose stemmed is more like it," Nick said.

"Don't be so rude," Mary said

"Thank you, Mary," Tommy said. "As I was saying, it was there that I blossomed and discovered my love for the theater, specifically; for the costuming and makeup aspects of the theater. Teaching was to only be temporary, as I searched for my niche in the movie industry."

"Have you found your niche in Hollywood?" Mary asked.

"No, but now I have other dreams and, if all goes as planned, those dreams will come true," Tommy replied.

"I know they will," Mary said with confidence.

"What about you? How did you end up sitting in a car with two criminals on the way to commit a heinous act?" Tommy asked Mary.

"I was a little too nosey at Sizzlers," Mary replied. "Actually, I saw this as my last chance to stave off being an old maid. Teaching at Cudahy High School is not how I envisioned my life would be. I dreamed of visiting faraway lands, of experiencing exotic foods and drinks, and I know this will sound like a cliché, but I also dream of making a difference in the world."

"I know you travel during the summer," Tommy said.

"I used to, but who wants to travel alone. What's the point in it? The world, the experiences, life itself, they are isolated, meaningless events unless they are shared with another." Mary paused. "Sharing together, that's when life becomes significant and begins to take on meaning. Until you find that special someone, life just doesn't..." Mary paused. "Enough about my philosophy!"

"Did you grow up in L.A.?" Nick asked.

"No, I grew up in Salinas, actually near Salinas in a little town called Spreckels."

"I once had a boy friend named Spreckels," Tommy interrupted.

"Why was he called Spreckels?" Mary asked.

"Let's not go there, shall we?" Nick said and Tommy nodded his agreement.

"It's a little farming community just south of Salinas," Mary continued. "My parents were farm workers."

"Both of them?" Nick asked.

"No, my mom was the typical stay at home Mexican madre who kept a pot of beans on the stove and the dirt floors swept."

You grew up with dirt floors?" Tommy asked in amazement.

"Of course not, that was just a metaphor to symbolize the ingrained culture of my parents," Mary replied. "My mom was a curandera."

"What's a curandera?" Tommy asked.

"I know," Nick said. "My class read a book about a curandera. It's a person who knows how to heal with plants and herbs."

"You believe in that crap?" Tommy said.

"Trust me, it's not crap," Mary said. "I saw *mi madre* do some pretty amazing things when I was growing up. She healed people that the local doctor said were incurable and hopeless."

"Are your parents still alive, do they still live in Spreckels?" Nick asked.

"They did up until the day my papa died. I had already moved away to college in Bakersfield. He came home one evening after picking artichokes. He walked in the house, kissed my mom, sat in his favorite chair and his body decided it had worked hard enough and just quit. At least that's the story my mom told me. My mom moved back to Mexico to live with her sister. She died just a couple of years ago."

"I'm sorry," Nick said.

"Don't be. I visited her often and she was happy to be back with her family on the farm where she was raised. Lots of people to heal and to share her life with there."

"I think I'm ready for a nap," Nick said.

"Are you awake enough to drive or do you need someone to talk to?" Mary asked Tommy.

"After those two double espressos I had where we gassed up, I'm good to go all night," Tommy replied.

"Then I think I might try to catch a nap too," Mary said.

"No need to worry," Tommy said. "Magellan and I will do just fine."

CHAPTER SEVENTEEN

"Man, this makeup gets hot. It won't melt, will it?" Nick asked Tommy.

Tommy lifted his right arm up and shook it around. "If my muscles stay on, you should have no problem with your makeup."

"Yeah, but it's probably thirty degrees hotter outside," Nick argued.

"Relax," Mary said. "The sun will be down soon and it'll really start to cool off."

"Shouldn't we be there by now? It's almost six o'clock. We need to check everything out before it gets dark." Nick had awakened in a semi-panic and the stress of the situation was taking its toll.

"Nick, everything is fine. We thought we'd let you sleep as long as possible. Don't forget, you'll be driving us home after we get the money," Tommy said.

"Oh right," Nick replied, "but..."

"Nick," Mary raised her voice. "Relax, we're there. We have plenty of sunlight left. You're starting to make Tommy and me nervous."

As they drove down the hill towards the campground, it was obvious which one was Hector's motorhome. It was exactly like the picture Alex had unknowingly provided for them.

"Isn't that the trailer for Rudy's Impala?" Tommy asked. "What's it doing there?"

"He must be taking it back to Utah. Maybe Rudy changed his mind about showing it at the carnival."

"Maybe," Mary said. "Park in the lot next to the campground store."

Tommy did what Mary said.

"Let's take a walk up that trail and have a look at the place," Mary suggested.

About one hundred yards up the trail they had a clear view of Hector's motorhome. There were also several large rocks that they could hide behind.

"Look, Tommy said. That must be Hector. What's he doing?"

"Looks like he is packing things up as if he were preparing to leave," Nick said.

"We've got to move fast," Mary said. "Here's what we're going to do."

As they hurried back to the store, Mary explained her plan.

"I don't think I like you going in alone," Nick said.

"Look, we don't have time to debate this. You will have a gun and can watch from back there on the trail. If Hector tries anything, I'll scream and you will come running. Don't forget, I'll also have a gun and I know how to use it."

"Here's the six pack of beer you wanted," Tommy said, hurrying from the store.

"Tommy, I want you to drive down and park by those restrooms just up from his trailer. Give me the Ketamine," Mary ordered.

Nick gave Mary the baggie holding the drug. She popped open one of the beers and poured some of the drug inside.

"Not that much," Tommy said, "you don't want to knock him out completely until we have the money."

"I thought you said you've never used this before?" Nick said.

Tommy just smiled.

"Give me the rest in case I have to pour it into something else," Mary said.

91

"What do you mean 'something else'?" Nick asked.

"Hector may not drink beer," Mary said. "If that's the case, I go to Plan B."

"What's Plan B?" Tommy asked.

"I won't know until Plan A fails," Mary replied.

Mary pushed the top back on the tainted bottle of beer and carefully placed it in her bag to insure it wouldn't spill. She pulled a second beer from the six-pack opened it, and passed it to Nick. She opened a third and handed it to Tommy, and a fourth she opened for herself.

"What's this for?" Tommy said.

"For a toast," Mary replied, "and to help calm all three of us down. Here's to our success." Mary raised her bottle into the air. Nick and Tom did the same and the three school teachers clinked their bottles together.

"To our dreams," Nick replied, as they all took a healthy swig of beer.

"Now take your positions, we're running out of time," Mary said.

"I'll be watching." Nick said. "I'll keep you safe." Nick kissed Mary on the lips. He put the gun taken from the Westside Capones in his waist band and headed up the trail with his beer in hand.

Tommy dropped his full beer bottle in the trash can next to the car. "I detest beer," Tommy said to Mary, "besides one should never drink and drive, it's against the law." Tommy laughed at the irony of what he had just said.

Mary waited till both of her friends were gone. She took another swig of beer, sighed heavily, and headed down the road towards Hector's, singing as she went.

CHAPTER EIGHTEEN

All... my... friends... are lowriders,...
Low...riders... ride... a little higher...

"*¿Que pasa*, home boy?" Mary said, slowing down when she saw Hector standing next to his motorhome.

Hector at first didn't respond, but walked out to the street and looked in both directions to see if anyone was nearby or with the hot mama who now stood in front of his RV downing a bottle of Bud. "Whatchu selling?"

"I ain't selling nothing, I'm giving it away," Mary replied, seeming to ooze sex with her voice.

"You got another *cerveza*?" Hector asked.

"I got a lot more than that," Mary said, pulling the tainted beer from her bag.

Hector took the beer and took a big swig. "Who sent you?"

"What are you talking about? I seen you earlier and wanted to come meet you," Mary replied.

"Don't bullshit me, *puta*, I know someone put you up to this," Hector replied.

"Well, if you don't want any of what I have to offer, I guess I need to find myself a real man who does," Mary said and began to walk away.

"What are you doing?" Nick said, as he watched Mary from the hill.

Hector looked up and down the road again. It was starting to get dark and the families that were near him had all moved into their motorhomes. He chugged the rest of his beer. "Eh good look'n, I was just kidd'n, where ya goin'? Come inside and I'll show you how a real man does it."

It was going better than Mary had expected. She knew the Ketamine worked quickly, and she only hoped she hadn't used too much like Tommy had thought. Mary licked her lips and ran her hand across her crotch, she glanced up to where she knew Nick was hiding along the trail.

"You did that on purpose," Nick said to himself.

Mary followed Hector inside. "Sit down and relax," Hector said, once they were inside. "Your hot little ass will just have to wait for a minute. I have someone dropping by in a couple of minutes. I have a little business to take care of." Hector pulled a pistol from his waist band and sat it on the counter in the kitchen. He seemed to lose his balance and stumbled slightly against the refrigerator.

"Oh shit," Mary thought. "What the hell am I going to do?" She thought about screaming, but knew Hector would grab his gun. "I don't want to be here if you're doing some kinda shit out here," Mary said.

"Shut up, you *puta* bitch, I'll give you what you came for in a few minutes." Hector staggered again.

"*Chingada*," Hector said. Just then Mary heard a car pull in next to the motorhome.

"Who's that?" Mary asked.

"It's those white biker assholes from Vegas," Hector said, starting to slur his words. "They're here to pick up ten kilos of shit and pay their bill. I'm feeling a little high, you may have to help me out. Their shit is laid out in the bedroom and they owe three hundred thousand. No need to count it."

"Amigo, it's me, Scratch," the biker yelled from outside the RV and knocked on the door.

Mary wasn't sure what to do.

"Amigo, are you there?" the biker yelled and knocked again.

Up on the hill, Nick was scared. Mary had only been inside for about four minutes when a van pulled up next to

94

Hector's trailer and four big white men wearing leather jackets climbed out. There was no hiding the fact that they were bikers. Very mean-looking bikers. Nick was about to run down the hill when he saw one of the biker's was holding a rifle.

"I've got to help Mary," Nick said and began to head down the hill when he saw Mary open the motorhome door. He stopped and jumped behind another rock. Fortunately, the bikers standing around the van had not heard him.

"Who the hell are you?" the biker asked, when Mary opened the door.

"I'm a friend of Hector," Mary replied, pretending to fasten her shorts as if interrupted in the middle of sex.

"Tell Hector to quit fuck'n around and take care of business. I got places to be. I don't have time to wait while he gets his jollies."

"Hector's not feeling well, I'll handle the business," Mary said.

Scratch entered the trailer, pushing Mary back as he pulled out his own gun.

"What's happening, Scratch?" Hector slurred as he lay back across the couch.

"This bitch better not be setting me up, or you're both dead," Scratch said.

"I told you Hector wasn't well. I'll take care of business. Your ten kilos are on the bed." Scratch hurried into the bedroom.

"What did I tell you," Mary said. "Now take your shit and leave the three hundred thousand on the bed. That is, if you ever want to do business with us again."

"This better not be no DEA bullshit," Scratch growled. "Tiny, Chilly, bring in the money and grab this shit."

"Oohh mama," one of the bikers said when he saw Mary. "I'll let you sit on my machine any day."

95

"I think you'd look better sitting on my...," the other biker started to say while reaching to grab Mary.

Before he could touch her, Mary had grabbed Hector's gun off the counter and stuck it in the biker's crotch. "What did you say, asshole?"

"Back off, Chilly," Scratch ordered.

"Take your shit and get out of here," Mary said. "You're lucky Hector is too out of it to remember any of this or we might never be doing business again."

"We'll hookup later bitch," Chilly said, as he picked up the kilos. "No damned whore pulls a gun on me."

"Tell Hector this is no fucking way to do business. I don't like dealing with no *cholo's puta*," Scratch said. "Tell him we'll have the money for this load on Monday when he passes back through."

Mary continued to hold the gun. "I'll give him the message, but I guarantee Rudy ain't gonna like the way you treated me. Now get out of here."

Scratch and the two other bikers loaded the cocaine in the van and headed out of the campground. As soon as Mary heard the van pull away, her hands started shaking uncontrollably. Hector's gun fell onto the floor. Mary sat down on the bench by the kitchen table and began crying.

Nick watched as the bikers loaded what he knew had to be bundles of cocaine into the van. He watched as all but one of the bikers entered the van. When the final biker came out of the door of the RV, he could see Mary standing behind him holding a gun. He could not see Hector.

The last biker got in the passenger's side of the van and it pulled away headed out of the campground. Nick waited till he saw it pass the grocery store down at the trailhead and then hurried down the hill to Hector's motorhome.

"Are you okay," he yelled in, not wanting to say Mary's name.

"*Chingada*, I'm feeling *firme*," he heard Hector slur.

"Come on in," Mary called out. Nick could tell that she'd been crying.

"Are you hurt?" Nick asked.

Mary ran and put her arms around Nick. "I've never been so scared in my life," Mary sobbed.

"Well, it's over now, we can get out of here," Nick said.

"I saw the bikers loading some cocaine," Nick said.

"Ten kilos," Mary replied. "They left three hundred thousand on the bed."

"Is everybody all right in there?" Tommy called from outside.

"*Chingada*, we're fuck'n great," Hector responded.

"Come on in," Nick called to Tommy. "Is Hector going to be okay?"

"I think I did put a little too much Ketamine in the beer," Mary said.

"I told you so," Tommy said. "I'm surprised he's not out cold. What happened?"

"Those bikers came to pick up some cocaine and to pay their bill," Nick said. "There's three hundred thousand on the bed."

Tommy rushed into the bedroom to see the money.

"Did Hector say where the rest of the money is?" Nick asked.

"There is no other money," Mary said.

"What do you mean?" Nick replied.

"Yeah, what do you mean?" Tommy repeated.

"When the biker left, he told me to tell Hector that he would have the money for this shipment on Monday when Hector was headed back for Utah," Mary said.

"On Monday? He must have been mistaken," Tommy said. "Didn't Alex say that Hector had to be back in Utah on Saturday?"

"That's what he said, but remember, we never saw Rudy's lowrider parked anywhere in Cudahy," Nick explained. "But I know how we can find out, follow me."

"Is it safe to leave Hector alone?" Tommy asked.

All three of them looked over at Hector. He appeared to be out cold.

"I'm sure he'll be going nowhere," Nick said, "but bring his gun just in case."

Nick picked up a big set of keys he saw laying on the counter. Mary grabbed the pistol off the floor and followed Nick and Tommy out to the trailer behind the RV. Nick fumbled with the keys until he found the one that fit the padlock.

"Wouldn't you know it, it's the one that says padlock on it," Nick said, trying to ease the tension.

Nick removed the padlock from the clasp, turned the handle and gently pulled upward on the roll-up door. As the door rolled up, a light came on inside the trailer.

"Whoa," Tommy said, "that Impala is incredible. Look at that paint job!"

"Shit," Nick said.

"What's wrong?" Tommy asked. Mary already knew.

"What's wrong is that the Impala is inside the trailer," Nick explained. "That means Hector was on his way to Los Angeles, not on his way back."

"Oh shit," Tommy repeated.

Mary had taken the keys and gone around to another door at the front of the oversized hauling trailer. It also had a padlock on it. She used the same key to open it and pulled the door open.

"And this would be all the cocaine he's delivering to Los Angeles," Mary said.

Nick and Tommy hurried over to have a look.

There were at least twenty-five cardboard boxes with the Budweiser logo on them. In each of these cartons were four bundles, similar to the ones Mary had given the bikers, but at least twice as large.

"There must be at least fifty of those packages," Tommy said.

Nick picked one up. "They must each weigh about ten pounds. What is that, about four kilos?"

"Give or take," Mary replied. "All I know is that that's a lot of death and addiction heading for Los Angeles."

Nick opened the trunk of the car.

"What are you looking for?" Mary asked.

"I don't know. I guess I was hoping to find a few million dollars."

"What are we going to do now?" Tommy asked. "Maybe we should each take a hundred thousand and call it quits."

"One hundred thousand isn't going to get you to Guerneville," Nick said, "nor will it buy me my place in Paraguay."

"One hundred thousand isn't even enough to allow us to quit teaching," Mary added.

"Maybe we should take the cocaine and sell it," Tommy suggested.

"There's no way in hell any of us are going to steal that cocaine," Mary said. "That shit is nothing but death. We'll have nothing to do with it."

"Sorry," Tommy said, "I wasn't thinking." Tommy looked at Nick. He knew Nick had been thinking the same thing. Maybe he could talk Mary into it.

"Why don't we go inside and see if we can find some more money," Nick said. "Let's see what Hector has to say."

When they got back inside, Hector was still passed out on the couch. All three of them started going through the cabinets and doors inside the motorhome.

"Look at this," Nick said. "There's an arsenal in here. This guy looks like he's ready for a war." Nick pulled out a fully automatic AK-47 with several clips of ammunition.

Tommy was in the bedroom going through the drawers when he came across another kilo of cocaine. He decided not to tell Nick or Mary about it. He pulled out a clean pillow case. "You want me to put this money in a pillow case?"

"That's a good idea," Mary replied. "We should probably also put it in the car."

"Along with that AK," Nick said.

"Why in the world do you want that thing?" Tommy asked.

"I think that's a good idea, Nick," Mary added. "I don't think we've seen the last of those bikers."

"Why do you say that?" Nick asked.

"Just the way the leader acted when the one he called Chilly tried to grab me," Mary said.

"Tried to grab you?" Nick raised his voice.

"He never got past Hector's gun," Mary said. "He threatened me on the way out the door, as did the leader. I just think it is smart to be prepared."

"We need to know why Hector was getting ready to leave and where he was going," Tommy said.

"It would make sense that he was getting ready to head out to LA. Rudy would be expecting his Impala for the car show at the carnival tomorrow afternoon," Nick said

"Hector won't be telling us anything until he wakes up," Mary said.

"Then wake him up. We can walk him around, maybe take him up to the store and pour some coffee down him," Nick suggested.

"That's a good idea," Mary said. "I'll lock the trailer up and finish packing all that little stuff from outside. Why don't the two of you take the money and that machine gun up to the car and try to sober him up. See if you can find out what his plans were."

"I like that idea," Tommy said. It would also give him the chance to hide the kilo of cocaine he had discovered.

CHAPTER NINETEEN

When the van carrying Scratch and the other bikers reached the main road, they were joined by an escort of three motorcycles. The motorcycles had remained at the entrance just to make sure no unwanted cops or DEA agents decided to drop by during the drug buy.

The van and bikes all sped back towards Las Vegas. A lot of people were waiting for their coke. When the taillights of the van began to fade, a Ford Crown Vic started its engine and pulled onto the road to follow. Two DEA agents sat in the front seat.

"Do you think they made their buy?" one of the agents asked.

"Why else would they have guarded the entrance like that?" his partner said.

"The other car will be here in about a half-hour. Tell them to drive through the campground and write down all the license numbers. Maybe we'll get lucky and get a hit on one of them."

"Why don't we just take these chumps down and squeeze 'em?" the other agent asked. "We got plenty on them to put them away for years."

"These guys don't squeeze," his partner replied. "Besides, these are just local middle men. We want the big dogs that are supplying them."

"Then the boss better damn well give us that helicopter support we requested. Until we get that, we're just whacking off."

"You're preaching to the choir, buddy. Just don't lose that van."

"Ever thought about taking things into our own hands?" the first agent asked.

"What do you mean, going vigilante on these chumps and taking them out?"

"No, not exactly. Forget what I said, I was just thinking out loud."

"Once the cat's out of the bag, it's impossible to put it back in," his partner replied. "I know what you're getting at, and I've thought about it a lot. I hate this damn job. I'm gone all hours of the day and night, never get to see my wife and kids, and I can't even afford to take them on a decent vacation when I do get to see them. Yeah, I think about it a lot!"

"Maybe we should do something about it," the first agent suggested.

"Yeah, maybe we should."

"You looked pretty fuck'n stupid with that bitch's gun stuck in your balls," Scratch said to Chilly. Tiny began to laugh.

"Shut up, asshole," Chilly said, scowling at Tiny.

"Something just wasn't right about that," Scratch said. "I've never seen Hector act like that before. It was like he was drugged or something."

"Maybe the bitch was rippin' him off and had drugged him to steal the shit," Tiny suggested.

"I thought about that at first. But she knew what we were there for and how much money we were supposed to leave," Scratch said.

"If Hector was drugged, he may have told her all of that," Chilly said.

"Yeah," Scratch said, "but she also knew about Rudy. If she was rippin' Hector off, it was an inside job."

"How much cocaine do you think Hector has in that trailer?" Chilly asked.

"A lot more than the ten kilos he sold to us," Scratch said. "I would be willing to bet there's a couple hundred kilos sittin' in there."

"If the bitch is legit, she'll tell them how we messed with her. Those Wilcox Street gangsters might not be so willing to sell to us when they hear what happened," Chilly said.

"Maybe we should rip the bitch off and take all that cocaine for ourselves. Then who gives a shit if Wilcox Street sells to us. We'll have more shit than we can sell in three fuck'n years," Tiny said

"We would also have one major war on our hands," Scratch said.

"Not if they think the bitch ran off with all the shit," Chilly said. "We could steal the shit and make the bitch and the motorhome disappear. They would blame it all on her."

Scratch sat quietly for a minute thinking. "We do know that Hector is headed for L.A. tonight. At least he's supposed to be. Maybe we should pull them over along the way and see what Hector has to say. If he's still all fucked up, we'll know the bitch is up to something. If that's the case, we'll take the shit for ourselves."

"And I can put that bitch where she belongs, on the end of my..."

"I think we're being followed," Tiny said, looking in the mirror.

"Flash your lights at the bikes ahead, they'll know to drop back and slowdown that car behind us," Scratch said.

"Looks like we've been made," one of the DEA agents said. "Turn here, we know where to find Scratch."

"Thank heaven for informants," his partner said, and quickly made a U-turn.

CHAPTER TWENTY

"Let's go, Hector," Nick said, pulling Hector to his feet.

"Go away, let me sleep," Hector said

"No, it's time to wake up, let's go for a walk," Nick said. "Throw the AK in another pillow case. I'll carry it and you get the money. It's going to take both of us to hold this pendejo up."

"*Chingada*," Hector said, "Who are you guys?"

"Sounds like our boy is starting to wake up, we'll be back in about fifteen minutes, be ready to go," Nick said to Mary.

"I will be," Mary assured them.

"It took about five minutes to get the money, AK-47, and Hector up to Tommy's car.

"Put the money in the trunk, but throw the gun in the back seat. Just make sure it stays covered up," Nick said to Tommy.

"So, where are you headed to?" Nick asked Hector.

"What's going on here? Who are you guys?" Hector asked, still not fully awake.

"Westside Capones, holmes. We're going to deliver the cocaine for you," Nick said trying to flash a gang sign.

"You guys are full of shit," Hector replied.

"Let me try," Tommy whispered to Nick. "Eh homie, Rudy sent us down to help you out when he heard you were sick."

"There's no way in hell I'll ever tell you where I am headed," Hector said.

"We know where you're headed, and Rudy is not happy that his Impala is sitting here and not in Cudahy. You know he wants to show it tomorrow at the carnival," Nick said.

"How do you know about the car show?" Hector asked.

"We told you, holmes, Rudy sent us to help you out," Tommy said.

"Why didn't Rudy call me and tell me that?" Hector said, sounding less and less high.

"He said he tried, but you never answered," Nick said.

"No way, Rudy did call, but to tell me where and when to drop off his car," Hector said. "You guys are trying to rip us off. I ain't tell'n you fools shit about nothing."

"Shit about anything," Nick corrected.

"What'd you say?" Hector asked, but Nick didn't answer.

"Sit down by the car and don't move," Nick ordered Hector.

"*No problemo*," Hector replied and laid down still feeling out of it. "But I still ain't telling you shit. Hey, wait a minute, you guys ain't Mexicans."

Tommy and Nick both froze. "Of course we're Mexicans," Tommy replied.

"No way," Hector replied. You guys ain't Mexican, you're Salvadoran."

Nick and Tommy both sighed in relief.

"Get in the car Tommy, we need to talk," Nick said.

"What do you think we should do?" Tommy asked.

"I was thinking we should head to L.A. in the motorhome, deliver the cocaine, collect the money and pretend like nothing happened," Nick replied.

"There is no way Mary will go for that," Tommy said. "Even if she did, we've no idea where or when to deliver the coke and Hector sure as hell isn't going to tell us," Tommy replied.

107

"There must be a way to get him to talk," Nick insisted.

"I don't think so," Tommy said. "Hector is one hard core gangster and he isn't going to roll over. Even if he did, who says the buyers in L.A. will deal with anyone besides Hector? I think we were damn lucky with the bikers. I say we take the three hundred thousand dollars and head for home."

"Maybe you're right, it's just too risky and Hector will never talk," Nick agreed. "Let's go talk to Mary." Nick threw his car door open in anger.

While they had been in the car talking, Hector had gotten to his knees and had begun to crawl towards the back of the car.

"Thump," the door slammed into Hector's face shattering his nose. Blood began to pour down from his nose and into his mouth.

"Don't kill me," Hector screamed, "I'll tell you what you want to know."

Tommy and Nick looked at each other and both smiled.

"Get him something to soak up that blood," Nick said. "So where and when are you making the exchange?"

"I'm meeting Paco and his *vatos* at the Bolsa Chica State Beach RV area at ten tomorrow morning," Hector said, and smiled through his pain. "But knowing that ain't gonna help you if you don't know the code."

"The code?" Tommy asked, "what code?"

"The code that lets Paco know everything is cool. And I'm the only one he'll ask and I'm the only one that knows the answer. And I don't care if you kill me, cause I ain't gonna tell you the code," Hector tried to smile, but both his eyes were beginning to swell. "Paco will only deal with me."

"Now what are we going to do?" Tommy asked.

"I guess nothing if we don't know the code," Nick said. "Put him in the car, let's go back to the RV and see what our friend says." Nick didn't want to say Mary's name just in case Hector was together enough to remember.

I'll ride in back, you drive. I'll put Hector in the front," Nick said.

"Try not to get any blood on the upholstery," Tommy said.

Nick was checking to make sure a towel was in place to protect the seat and didn't notice Hector's hand was still holding the top door jamb of the car. He slammed the door hard and everyone heard the sound of breaking bones.

"Ahhh!" Hector screamed. "You fuck'n crushed my hand. Okay, I'll tell you the code, but Paco still will talk only to me."

Tommy looked at Nick across the roof of the car. "Did you do that on purpose?"

"It was an accident."

Hector was lying on the seat trying to stare at his crushed hand through his swollen and now purple eyes.

"So what's the code?" Nick asked.

"Paco's motorhome will already be parked at the beach. I'm to pull up next to it, get out, and walk around the front of my RV and all the way around the trailer until I get to the side trailer door. He'll ask if I'm having any problems. I'm supposed to answer that I think my trailer is a little out of balance and ask if he could help me move some boxes around. That's when his vato will pile out of his RV and move the cocaine to their RV."

"What about the money?" Nick asked.

"Paco will bring it from his RV to mine. It'll be in four beer cases. Two-and-a-half-million in each case," Hector explained.

Tommy and Nick both looked at each other.

109

"But none of this will go down if I'm not there. He knows to only deal with me and no matter how bad you beat me up, nothing's gonna change that. You guys gotta get me to a doctor."

CHAPTER TWENTY-ONE

Mary was standing next to the motorhome when Tommy, Nick, and Hector pulled up in Tommy's car.

"What did you do to Hector?" Mary exclaimed, when she saw the bloody, bruised, and broken body stagger from the front seat.

"They kicked the shit out of me is what they did," Hector replied. "Somebody needs to take me to the hospital. I can't take the pain."

"Why in the world did you beat him so badly?" Mary asked Nick.

"We didn't. It was an accident," Tommy said.

"An accident? This doesn't look like an accident," Mary exclaimed.

"Believe me, it really was. I accidentally hit him in the face when I opened the car door. And then when we were about to bring him back, I accidentally slammed his hand in the door. I think he broke several bones in his hand," Nick explained.

"His nose is for sure broken," Mary said, looking at Hector's face.

"Did you find anything out?" Mary asked.

"He told us everything," Tommy said. "Where and when the drugs were to be exchanged for the money and even the passwords to let Paco know everything is cool. He's supposed to collect ten million dollars. Ten million!"

Mary was taken aback by the amount. "I thought you said it would be three million."

"That's what Alex had said. He must not have known," Nick replied.

"What's that noise?" Nick said. "I thought I heard some splashing."

"It's probably just the fish jumping," Mary replied.

"That sounds like a hell of a lot of fish jumping," Nick said. "Tommy, turn on your headlights."

Tommy turned on the headlights and the lake in front of the RV lit up,

"Look at all the fish jumping," Tommy said. "They're all over the place. Hundreds of them."

Everyone stared in amazement as hundreds, if not thousands, of fish were flying up out of the water. Several had even jumped out onto the land.

"I've never seen anything like this," Tommy said. "What do you think is happening?"

"I have no idea," Nick replied. "But I have heard about animals behaving like this right before an earthquake."

Nick looked at Mary and saw that her head was down and she was rubbing her forehead. "Are you all right?"

"Sorry," Mary said. "I knew you would come back and try to talk me into delivering the cocaine. I couldn't take the chance of you talking me into it. Now that I know it was for ten million dollars, I kind of wish I hadn't done it."

"Done what?" Tommy asked.

Fish continued to fly out of the water, but now the top of the lake was covered with dead fish.

Nick noticed the empty Budweiser boxes strewn around the ground on the opposite side of the trailer.

"You threw all the cocaine into the water?" Nick exclaimed.

"All of it." Mary answered.

"You threw the coke in the water? We're all dead men. The OGs are going to rip our heads off," Hector said.

Tommy ran down to the water and picked up an empty ripped-open package.

112

"You were right, Tommy, there were fifty of them," Mary said.

"That was almost a ton of coke you destroyed," Hector said in disbelief.

"I know, my arms are really beginning to ache," Mary replied.

Hector was now almost fully awake and becoming agitated. "Why don't you fix Hector another drink to help calm him down. Maybe a little something to help ease his pain," Nick suggested, nodding at Tommy to be sure he understood.

Tommy went inside the RV and pulled a beer out of the refrigerator. He pulled out another baggie of the Ketamine and poured it into the beer.

"This should help with the pain," Tommy said and handed Hector the beer.

Hector instinctively reached out with his right hand then suddenly pulled it back as pain shot through his body.

"Try the left hand," Nick suggested.

Hector grabbed the beer with his left hand and chugged it.

"Have a seat at the picnic table, Hector. I don't want you to fall over and hurt yourself," Nick said

"As if there was much else left for him to hurt," Mary added.

"You and I had better pick up all those ripped-open bundles. Keep an eye on Hector," Nick said to Tommy.

"He should be out in a couple of minutes and then I'll come join you," Tommy replied.

Both Mary and Nick nodded.

"I'm sorry I destroyed all the cocaine," Mary said.

"Don't be. That much coke on the streets of L.A. could kill dozens of people. None of us would want something like that on our conscience. I don't care how much money was involved. It would never have been worth it," Nick replied.

Mary walked over and put her arms around Nick and kissed him. "I can't tell you how wonderful it makes me feel to hear you say that."

"We better get busy cleaning this mess up. We need to get out of here before somebody reports all those dead fish," Nick said.

"Well, I can help," Tommy said. "Hector is down for the count."

It took about ten minutes to collect all fifty of the ripped-open bundles. Most were still in the water by the shore. A couple of them partially on the shore still had some cocaine left in them, but a little dip in the lake took care of that.

"I sure hate to lose all that money," Tommy said. "Too bad it didn't work out like we had planned."

"At least we all will come away with a hundred thousand. That's better than nothing," Nick said, trying to put a positive spin on things.

"Well, it wasn't worth it as far as I'm concerned," Mary said. "I was beginning to think I might just want to move with you to Paraguay and two hundred thousand isn't enough to make that happen."

"There's nothing else we can do," Tommy said.

"Are you sure?" Mary replied. "When the bikers picked up their coke, they didn't bother to check it out at all, nor did our friend Hector tell me to count the money. They dealt with each other often, so neither questioned the honesty of the other."

"I'm not so sure it is a matter of integrity," Nick said. "More likely it is a matter of somebody dies if they try to cheat."

114

"Maybe so, but I would be willing to bet this Paco in L.A. won't question or test the coke either," Mary said.

"Are you willing to bet your life on that?" Tommy asked, "because if you're wrong, we're all dead."

"I don't believe you guys are actually considering trying to rip off these drug dealers," Nick said.

"What the hell are you talking about?" Tommy said. "We knew that was the chance we took from the very beginning. And that was when we thought it was for a million each. Now we are talking over three million each. That would buy a villa in Paraguay and unlimited trips to Paris or anywhere else in Europe."

"You heard what Hector said. This Paco guy will only deal with Hector and Hector is in no shape to deal with anybody, even if he was willing to. And he sure won't be willing after what we did to him," Nick said.

"You're about the same size as Hector, don't you think, Tommy?" Mary asked. "I'd be willing to bet this Paco has only met Hector a few times. I think with your makeup skills you could make yourself look just like Hector and probably convince Paco that you are him. Didn't you bring your makeup kit with you?"

"You do know the code," Nick added. "Nobody but Hector knows the code. At least that's what Paco thinks. Once you give him the code, he'll know it has to be Hector."

"I don't sound anything like Hector," Tommy said.

"You can tell him you have a cold. Hell Tommy, you're a trained actor, a thespian, you could pull it off," Nick said.

"But what are we going to give Paco in place of the cocaine. He knows what the bundles look like and feel like. Where are we going to get something that looks and feels like a ton of cocaine and get it packaged like the real thing by tomorrow morning?" Tommy asked.

Nick picked up one of the original ripped bundles Mary had opened and thrown into the water. "It looks like butcher paper wrapped around saran wrap, held together with packing tape."

"It can't be done," Tommy said

"Oh ye of little faith! You worry about passing yourself off as Hector, I'll take care of the fake cocaine."

"What about Hector? What are we going to do with him?" Mary asked.

"Help me put him in the car, I'll figure it out on the way. Mary, do you think you can drive the motorhome?"

"Sure. I drove the moving truck and towed my car last time I moved."

"Good," Nick replied. "Tommy, grab your makeup kit out of the car and put it in the RV. You have an hour to make yourself look like Hector. Here's his driver's license picture. I'm afraid that's all you have to work with."

"That should be enough," Tommy replied.

"You ride with Mary in the motorhome. You need to be Hector's twin by the time we reach Vegas."

Nick pulled Mary to him and kissed her deeply. "Everything will work out, I promise." Mary nodded her head.

"Drive slowly and stay focused on your tasks." Nick said.

Mary nodded her head. She understood exactly what Nick meant.

"We'll stop by the grocery store on the way out and get rid of all but one of those soggy old wrappers," Nick said. "Let's roll. We have a lot to do before we reach L.A. in the morning."

"Get the number of that one," the DEA agent said to his partner. "It might have come from the campground."

His partner grabbed the camera off the seat and snapped it quickly as the motorhome sped by in the opposite direction.

"Shit, it was pulling a trailer, I missed the number."

"Well, did you get the number off the trailer?"

The agent pulled the picture back up on the digital camera. "I got part of it. The tail lights were a little bright for the night vision lens."

"A few of the numbers should be enough. We'll run it through the system when we get back to the office. First, we got a couple hundred more pictures we have to take."

"And it has to be tonight?"

"That's what the boss says. He thinks we're getting close to finding the main supplier."

"Like I haven't heard that before!"

"Just drive. I'd like to get home before sun up for a change."

"Then you should never have left the FBI and joined the DEA."

"No kidding. Look, there's another camper leaving the campground," the agent said, and snapped a picture.

PART TWO

"When all else fails, complicate matters."

Aaron Allston

CHAPTER TWENTY-TWO

"Thank you for calling Wal-Mart, how can I help you?" a cheerful voice asked.

"I was just making sure you were still open," Nick replied.

"Open 24/7, sir, almost all Wal-marts in Las Vegas are open 24/7."

"Just how many Wal-marts are there in Las Vegas?" Nick asked.

"I believe about thirty, sir. How else can I help you?"

"You've helped me enough already, thank you," Nick said, and closed his cell phone. Nick punched the address of the Wal-Mart into Tommy's Magellan. Estimated time to destination was still seventeen minutes.

"I wish Hector's face wasn't banged up so badly," Tommy said to Mary. "I could have made a mold of it just like Tom Cruise did in Mission Impossible."

"Tom Cruise made a mold of Hector's face?" Mary asked, being silly.

Tommy looked up at her and sighed. He saw her looking back at him through the rearview mirror. "It doesn't make sense to have a mirror there," Tommy said. "The motorhome is too long and there isn't even a window in the back."

"It's so the driver can keep an eye on the kids playing around behind her," Mary explained. "You're a genius, Tommy. If I didn't know it was you, I would swear I was looking at Hector."

Tommy smiled. "See, I even did his gold tooth."

"That's right," Mary said. "I had forgotten about that. Does his ring fit you?"

"The one Nick took off of his left hand does, but Nick couldn't get the one off of his right hand, his finger was already too swollen. I think it was broken."

"I think several of his fingers were broken," Mary replied.

"Do you still see Nick?" Tommy asked.

"He's right in front of us, but I have no idea where he's going," Mary replied.

"Nick is smart, he'll know what to do," Tommy assured her.

"Looks like we're pulling into Wal-Mart," Mary said.

Tommy stopped putting on his makeup and came up to the front to see what was going on. Nick was already out of the car and headed to the motorhome.

"You look great, Tommy. What about the muscles? Are you going to leave those on? Hector wasn't that buff."

"I don't think I have enough makeup to cover my arms to make them the right color if I take off the fake muscle appendages," Tommy replied. "Maybe I could put on a long sleeve shirt to hide them."

"It's too hot for a long-sleeve shirt, even for a cholo," Nick replied. "Let's just hope Paco doesn't notice."

"If he does, tell him you've been working out," Mary suggested. "How's the real Hector doing?"

"Sleeping like a baby," Nick replied.

"And he will for another eighteen hours would be my guess," Tommy said.

119

"What are we doing here?" Mary asked.

"We're going shopping," Nick said.

"All three of us?" Tommy asked.

"What, you don't like shopping at Wal-Mart?" Nick asked.

"Not really, it's kind of a..." Tommy hesitated.

"Like stabbing a knife in the side of American society and ripping out the middleclass?" Mary asked.

"Or destroying the entrepreneurial spirit and future of the small business owner?" Nick asked.

"I was thinking more along the lines of it's kind of trailer-trashy," Tommy replied.

"What is it we have to get?" Mary asked.

"I'll know when I see it," Nick replied," Although I do have a fairly good idea."

"I pulled five thousand dollars out of the biker money for each of us. I'm hoping more than one check-stand is open so not to raise too much suspicion. Let's go, you guys stay behind me. I'll tell you what to get. When your basket is full, pay and take the stuff to the RV, then come back in for more."

"Welcome to Wal-Mart," an older gentleman said as they entered and gave each of them a cart.

"Did you see the way he stared at me?" Mary asked. "What was his problem?"

"Did you forget how we're dressed?" A lot of people are staring at us," Tommy said.

"You know I'd completely forgotten how I looked," Mary replied. "Where to first?"

"I bet I know," Tommy replied. "I heard cocaine dealers sometimes use powdered baby laxative to cut their cocaine before they sell it. Is that what we're going to use?"

"I seriously doubt they're going to have two thousand pounds of baby laxative in the store. Besides, a powder is too

120

hard to work with. First, we're getting the packaging material."

They headed to the office supply aisle. "Grab all those rolls of brown butcher paper and every roll of strapping tape you can find," Nick told Tommy. "Then head over to the grocery area and buy at least ten rolls of the really wide Saran Wrap."

"Does it have to be Saran Wrap? I always thought the plastic cling wrap was easier to use."

"Whatever! Just get it, pay and take it to the RV. Then meet me in the outdoor home center area, over there."

"Now where to?" Mary asked.

"Linens."

"What's in linens?" Mary asked, as they approached that area of the store.

"We need at least one hundred packages of the largest sheet sets they've got. If they're not that big, then we need two hundred packages."

Mary started filling her cart. "I don't know if this will be enough," Mary said.

Tommy picked up one of the sheets sets to feel the weight. "Take it to the RV and come back and buy as many packages of men's underwear and socks that you can fit in a basket. Then wait for Tommy and me."

Mary headed for the checkout, while Nick headed for the outdoor home center.

"That's a lot of sheets," the checker said to Mary.

"I know, I can't believe it either. We opened a campground for inner-city kids out by Lake Meade and we forgot to tell them they had to bring their own sheets. We're going to lose money on this group," Mary replied.

The checker looked at Mary standing there in her short shorts, and her t-shirt with no bra. "They sure didn't

121

have camp counselors like you when I went to camp. Aren't you afraid the mosquitoes will eat you alive?"

"I eat lots of vitamin B," Mary replied.

"I see," the checker nodded, as if now it all made sense and he began to ring up the sheets.

Mary saw Tommy headed back into the store.

"Welcome to Wal-Mart," she heard the old man say for the thousandth time that night.

When Tommy found Nick, Nick was loading bricks into his basket.

"We need two hundred of these. I already have fifty in my basket, but I don't think it can take the weight of too many more. We'll have to each make two trips."

"I got it," Tommy said, and began loading bricks.

"I need to grab a couple of more things, wait for me up front. We'll go out together."

Nick was hurrying through sporting goods towards the house wares section when he saw the two-way radios. The package said they had a twenty-six-mile range. "We could talk back-and-forth with those. No cell phone records that way. Damn, I'm starting to think like a criminal," Nick said to himself and threw the radios into his cart.

When he got to house wares, he couldn't find a kitchen scale that went to ten pounds. He wasn't even sure such a thing existed and wasn't about to ask for assistance. Instead, he grabbed a flat bathroom scale that seemed to be the best one. At least it was the most expensive one.

Tommy was waiting at the front for Nick. The checker rang them up like someone buying a hundred bricks at ten o'clock at night was not unusual. Actually, in Vegas, the time you purchased something really had no relevance what-so-ever. It was a twenty-four-hour city and a lot of people worked at night.

When they arrived at the motorhome, they unloaded the bricks.

"I need you to grab a hundred more of these," Nick said to Tommy.

"Picking them up is scratching the makeup off my hands," Tommy said. "I don't have any more to cover up the scratches.

"I'll help you get the rest of the bricks," Mary said. "Maybe you can find some makeup as well.

"Good idea," Nick said. "I'll get started in here."

Mary had already organized things in the motorhome. She had opened the butcher paper and had even remembered to buy three pairs of scissors as she was heading out with her sheets. The sheets were stacked next to the kitchen table, which had been cleared to serve as the workspace for assembling the bundles. The tape was open and the cling wrap was sitting on the seating bench. A second area had been set up on the kitchen counter. Nick stacked the bricks on the kitchen floor and set the scale on the table. He sat the bathroom scale on the table. It was time to begin. He figured they had until midnight to get the hundred bundles built.

Nick cut his first piece of butcher paper large to make sure it would be big enough and to determine what the ideal size needed to be. Next, he grabbed a package of sheets and laid them on the scale. On top of the sheets he placed two of the bricks. He broke open the bundles of men's socks and laid several pairs around the bricks. On top he added another sheet set. It was still a little less than four kilos, which he knew the bundles of cocaine had weighed.

"Damn," Nick said, as he pulled the stack from the scale to wrap it and the bricks slid out. "That's not going to work." He looked around the motorhome for ideas. "The towel!" Nick grabbed a bath towel that was hanging behind the door and laid it out on the scale. Then he placed the sheets, bricks, socks, and second set of sheets as before, and folded the towel up and pulled it tightly around the stack. The towel was much too large and too heavy. Nick cut off sections from the towel until the needle on the scale was just at the bottom of the number ten.

"This damn scale better be right," Nick said to himself. He lifted the bundle off the scale and sat in on the butcher paper. Before he wrapped the paper around the towel, he wrapped the entire stack with strapping tape to secure it tightly together and take away the cushioned feel of the towel. He next folded the butcher paper around the taped bundle. As hard as he tried, he just couldn't get the butcher paper folded correctly.

"Let me show you," Mary said, coming in with a load of bricks.

"Better yet," Nick said. You wrap the package and I'll bring in the bricks."

"Sounds like a deal," Mary replied. "You forgot the Saran Wrap. All the bundles had plastic wrap underneath the brown paper."

"Damn, I knew something didn't look right."

Mary grabbed the giant roll of plastic wrap and wrapped the taped towel several times. Then she wrapped the bundle neatly in the butcher paper and taped it to be identical to the real cocaine she had destroyed. "Perfect," she said. "What do you guys think?"

Tommy and Nick both stopped bringing in the bricks to look.

"Looks like the real thing," Tommy said, taking the package from Mary. "It feels nice and solid and even throughout. It would fool me."

"Good," Nick said. "I'll get the rest of the bricks. I need you to go back and buy a hundred bath towels. Preferably white."

"Anything to stop lugging these god forsaken bricks," Tommy muttered.

"Let me finish moving the bricks and I'll show you how to put the bundles together," Nick said. "I'm sure we can find a couple more towels to use until Tommy gets back. Sit down and relax, you've had a tough night and it's going to get longer if not tougher.

"You'll get no argument from me," Mary said, and sat down in the driver's seat and closed her eyes.

By the time Tommy returned with the towels, Nick and Mary had put together four more bundles that looked identical to the first.

"I figure we can knock out all fifty bundles in less than two hours if we put together an assembly line system," Nick said. "I'll put together the bundles including wrapping them in Saran Wrap."

"Cling wrap," Tommy corrected. "Saran Wrap doesn't stick as well."

"Mary, you'll do the final butcher paper wrap and Tommy you'll put the bundles into the trailer. Just make sure you put them in a bag so no one starts asking questions. Everybody got it?"

Both Tommy and Mary nodded.

"Then let's do it."

CHAPTER TWENTY-THREE

"Chilly, go bring in some of the boys," Scratch said, as he sat in the back room of a local bar that the bikers now owned, thanks to drug money.

Scratch, Chilly, and Tiny had broken down three of the four kilo bundles and sent out several of their gang members to make the nightly deliveries to the mid-level dealers. Two of the bundles were sent in their entirety to one of the larger hotels where a mafia lieutenant was waiting. He in turn would send it along to his men at the various hotels to meet the needs of the various high rollers and other special guests.

"What's up, Scratch?" one of the biker's asked as he walked into the back room accompanied by four other dangerous looking bikers.

"I need you to get the word out that I'm looking for a big brown and white motorhome pulling a large trailer with a picture of a lowrider Impala on the side of the trailer. I sent Spike back to the campground to keep an eye on it, but it was already gone. I know it's heading for L.A., but so far none of the boys have seen it on the 15 South. I also need men covering the 93, the 95, and the 160 South. Better put somebody on the 95 and 15 North too, just in case. I need that motor home found within the hour. Call me if you see it. Chilly, Tiny, and I will head south on the 15 to Baker and hole up there. I figure it has to eventually head that way. I want one of you to head out in the van to Primm and wait there for further instructions."

"What's so special about this motorhome?" Spike asked.

"The bitch that made Chilly's dick shrivel at the end of a gun barrel is in it," Tiny laughed.

"Shut the hell up," Chilly said. "That bitch is mine when we find them."

"That motorhome is carrying at least a hundred kilos of shit and three hundred thou of our hard-earned money," Scratch said. "I'm tired of being at the mercy of those Wilcox Street bastards. The best part is that they won't even know it is us who did it. So don't tell the world what you're doing."

"Should we stop them if we find them?" Spike asked.

"No, just call in and keep an eye on them, but don't let them know you're following them. There's an ounce of shit in it for whomever spots them first and calls. Now get out of here."

The bikers all hurried away arguing who would get which freeway. Spike of course got the 95 since it was the most likely route the motorhome would have taken from Lake Meade if it didn't take the 15 and, according to Scratch, the 15 was already being covered. Spike knew Scratch didn't want the word out on the streets, but what better way to insure he was the one to pick up that ounce. Spike was a mid-level dealer for the gang and had a number of street-level dealers he supplied. A few quick phone calls later, Spike was assured to be the first to know if the motorhome was still in Vegas.

"Looks like a jail break," one of the DEA agents watching the biker bar from down the street said. Several bikers came out of the bar and headed out in every direction.

"I'd say they're looking for somebody," his partner replied.

"Sure looks that way. Look, there goes Scratch with Chilly and Tiny. That's who we should follow."

The agent started his car and began to pull out. "No, wait. The van is leaving. That's who we need to follow."

"It looks like the van is following Scratch."

127

One of the agent's cell phones began to ring.

"Agent Smith," he answered.

"Agent Smith, it's Zeke." Zeke was one of the street level dealers working for Spike whom the DEA had flipped. Zeke had agreed to keep dealing and report everything he heard about the gang's dealings and suppliers. Zeke was the one who tipped them off about the campground. His information was usually good, but not always helpful because it came so late.

"Whatcha got for me, Zeke, and it better be good or we're going to have to talk to the judge about your cooperation," Agent Smith said.

"It's real good and I just heard it a minute ago. Spike called me."

"What did our friend Spike have to say?"

"He told me there's an eightball in it for anyone who spots a certain motorhome. I bet it's the same one that was out at Lake Meade that I told you about earlier," Zeke said.

"Quit yanking us around," Smith replied. "What's the big deal with this motorhome?"

"Spike didn't say. All he told me was that Scratch needed to find it tonight and whoever found it and called him first was in it for an eightball."

"Did he tell you what this motorhome looked like?" Smith asked.

"Only that it was big, brown, and pulling a trailer with a painting of an Impala on the side."

"An Impala, what kind of Impala?"

"You know, an old car, a lowrider he said, like the beaners drive."

"Call me if you hear anything else."

"I will and you guys will let the judge know how I helped you out, right?" Zeke said, but Agent Smith had already ended the call.

128

"Call Johnson and see if they saw any brown motorhomes pulling a trailer with a lowrider Impala painted on the side when they toured that campground." Zeke says the word is out on the street that Scratch is looking for this motorhome."

"Well, he must be thinking its heading out of town, because that's where he and his boys are heading, south on the 15 towards Los Angeles."

"Zeke did say Las Vegas was just a stopover for the big shipment he heard was headed to L.A. Maybe Scratch has decided he wants a little more of the shipment than he already got tonight."

"Should we mobilize everybody?" Smith's partner asked.

"Mobilize them for what? If we're lucky, maybe these bastards will kill each other off. I was thinking we shouldn't even call about the motorhome."

"If they kill each other off, we'll never find the source."

"If they kill each other off, what's keeping us from taking the money?"

"I like the way you think, Agent Smith."

"Let's stick with Scratch and see where he leads us. Odds are he'll lead us to the motorhome. Maybe we'll get lucky," Smith said.

"You forget this is Vegas. The odds are always in the house's favor not the gambler's."

"Like I said, maybe we'll get lucky."

CHAPTER TWENTY-FOUR

"And that makes fifty," Mary said, handing the last bundle to Tommy.

"Twenty minutes ahead of schedule," Nick said. "Now let's hit the road."

"What about Hector," Tommy asked. "Are we taking Hector with us to L.A.?"

"No," Nick replied, "I think it would be better if we left Hector behind. I was thinking about putting him on a bus heading east, but I'm afraid the driver may ask too many questions when we tried to put him on board. So I think it would be best if we get him a room somewhere nearby, so he can sleep it off. He's been through enough and is going to be hurting big time when he wakes up. It's the least we can do."

"I agree, even though he's a jerk," Mary said.

"I'll find a hotel and check him in," Nick said.

"Whose identification are you going to use?" Tommy asked. "If you use his, I'll need it back."

"Take one of these," Mary said, reaching into her bag and pulling out the license of one of the Westside Capones she had taken the previous Sunday.

"Great idea, thanks," Nick replied. "You two need to fill the RV with gas and then head for Los Angeles, but not on the 15. I trust Mary's intuition that we haven't seen the last of those bikers tonight."

"Which way do you think we should go?" Mary asked.

"I was checking Tommy's Magellan and think it wouldn't take too much longer to head back towards Boulder City on North Boulder Highway until it joins the 93, but turn south on the 95 just before Boulder City. You would stay on the 95 until you reach the 40 then turn west. The 40 meets up with the 15 at Barstow. I think Scratch will have given up by that time."

"That is, if he even bothers to look for us," Tommy replied.

"I'm not willing to take the chance," Nick said. "Here, take this radio so we can talk back and forth without using our cell phones. But remember, anybody could be listening, so use no names."

"What if we do run into Scratch and his friends?" Mary asked.

"You still have that 50-caliber pistol and Hector's 9mm. And there's a whole arsenal under the bench seat in the kitchen, but let's hope it never comes to that. I'll have the AK-47 with me in the car. I'll try to hang back far enough behind so it doesn't look like we're together. That way I can warn you if I see trouble coming and help out if it does without being expected. Any more questions or comments?"

"What are we going to do when we get to L.A.?" Tommy asked.

"I've got about nine hours of driving to figure that out," Nick said. "When you stop for gas, make sure you buy some snacks. I don't want to be stopping at any restaurants along the way."

"Be safe," Mary said, and kissed Nick.

"You as well," Nick replied as they parted ways.

There were several motels along N. Boulder Highway for Nick to choose from. He finally decided on one called the Outpost, just because the parking area seemed a little darker than the rest.

The desk clerk on night duty didn't even bother to look at Nick as he checked him in.

"Cash or credit card?" The desk clerk asked.

"Cash," Nick replied.

131

"You want the room for all night or just a couple of hours?"

"All night," Nick replied. "And can it be on the first floor?"

"Right," the desk clerk replied. "That will be one hundred and twelve dollars, plus a seventy-five-dollar deposit you'll get back at check-out if nothing is missing."

Nick wasn't going to argue. He pulled out two hundred-dollar bills and handed them to the clerk. The clerk held them up to the light and then pulled out a special pen to mark them. "We get a lot of phony bills in here."

"Good thing Tommy didn't run into a guy like this when he was passing his paper," Nick thought to himself.

The clerk wrote out a receipt and handed it to Nick along with a room key.

"Enjoy yourself," the clerk said as Nick headed out the door.

"Nick got in the car and could see the clerk watching him as he drove around to the side where his room was located.

"Shit," Nick said. He had forgotten that the cameras would record the license plate number on his car. "This won't do." He continued driving right out the exit at the back of the parking lot. Nick headed down the highway towards Boulder City. He would try again at the first motel he came to, but this time he wouldn't pull the car into the lot.

The first motel he came to was the Starview Motel. It looked about the same as the rest he had seen, but here he could park on a street near the hotel lot. All went pretty much the same way with the desk clerk, only this time the hotel was only ninety-five dollars and the deposit was only fifty.

"I'd like one on the first floor near the back," Nick asked.

"Sure," was the only reply he received.

Nick walked back to the room to check it out before he went to the car and carried Hector inside. It was still too early for the gamblers and partiers to get home and any families would already be in for the night, so all was quiet. It took less than a minute for Nick to get Hector and lay him peacefully in his room.

As Nick was walking towards his car, a woman approached.

"Looking for a little fun? Need a date for the evening?" the woman asked.

"No thanks," Nick replied curtly.

"Only fifty bucks and you pay for the room," the hooker responded.

Nick continued to walk away, but suddenly stopped.

"Change your mind, honey?" the hooker asked.

"I've got a friend who is passed out over in Room 146. He's had a rough night. He got in a pretty bad bar fight and got his nose broken and his hand busted up."

"So what?" the hooker replied.

"I'll give you a thousand dollars to go over there, climb in bed, and spend the night with him. Then when he wakes up in the morning, you take him places he has only imagined," Nick offered.

"Are you serious? You want me to spend the night in bed with this guy and then toss him in the morning when he wakes up?"

"That's right," Nick said.

"And you'll pay me a grand to do it?"

"Yep," Nick replied. "But if you pocket the money and don't perform as agreed, I'll come looking for you. And do I look like the kind of person you want to have looking for you?"

"Let's see the money," the hooker replied.

"So do we have a deal?" Nick asked.

"If you have a thousand dollars, then we have a deal."

"You promise not to bail on me, 'cause if you do and my friend says you weren't straddling him when he wakes up in the morning, then I'm gonna be pissed."

"Relax," the hooker replied. "For a grand, I'll do you right now, too."

"That won't be necessary. Here's the room key and here's the money." Nick counted out ten hundred-dollar bills. The hooker stuck them in her purse.

"You sure you don't want me to..."

"Just do what I asked," Nick said.

"It's your loss," the hooker said, and headed for the hotel room. Nick watched as she went inside.

When Nick got back to the car, he tried to call Tommy on the two-way radio, but got no answer. That meant either the radios didn't work or the motorhome was already more than twenty-six miles away. Nick wanted reassurance that Hector would indeed sleep through the night, but he wasn't going to get it.

"Time to catch up," Nick said, and stepped on the gas.

"It only took eighty dollars to top off the tank," Mary said to Tommy as she entered the mini-mart and paid the cashier in cash for the gas.

"You want a corndog or something?" Tommy asked.

"A corndog? You've got to be kidding! Mary exclaimed. "Do you know what's in those things or what they fry them in?"

"No I don't, and don't tell me either," Tommy replied.

"You're a hot one," a big white guy in a cowboy hat said from across the store. "I sure would like your number. How much you charge?"

"*Besa mi culo*," Mary said.

134

"I'll kiss anything you want me to kiss, if you dump the chump and strut your sweet stuff over here, honey," the cowboy replied.

"Fuck off," Mary said.

"Ooh-weee, we got ourselves a spicy one," the cowboy said to his friend. "I think maybe we should use our hoses on her to try and cool her down a bit."

"Ignore them, let's get out of here," Tommy said to Mary and they both turned away from the two drunken cowboys and walked out the door.

"This one here's a scrawny little fellow," one of cowboys said as he wrapped a big hand around the back of Tommy's neck as they followed them out the door.

"Let me feel them big titties, baby," the second cowboy said reaching towards Mary.

"Holy shit, this one's arm fell off," the drunken cowboy holding Tommy said. He still held Tommy tightly. The fake muscles Tommy had added to his right arm had come loose and when the cowboy grabbed his neck it fell to the ground.

"Oh my god, I ripped his arm off!" the cowboy screamed in terror.

When the other cowboy turned to see why his partner was shrieking like a woman, Mary kicked him hard in the balls. When he bent over in pain, she shoved the barrel of the 50-caliber pistol into his mouth ripping his lip and breaking away one of his front teeth. She lifted it up and pulled until the sight caught on his other front tooth.

"I think you better let my friend go before your friend's brains splatter all over everybody," Mary said.

The cowboy tried to pull away, but Mary cocked the hammer back.

"Lleee iiim gggo," the cowboy tried to talk but couldn't. Mary had pressed the gun down hard on his tongue and now blood was pouring from his lip.

"I think he said to let him go," Mary said. "Now!" she screamed. The second cowboy let go of Tommy, but stood dumbfounded staring at the fake muscles from Tommy's arm lying on the ground.

Tommy bent over and picked up the fake muscles, but froze when he saw Mary's expression. He saw the hatred in her eyes and her hand begin to shake. "Don't do it, Mary. He isn't worth it. He's not the one you hate."

The cowboy, with the cocked 50-caliber Smith and Wesson stuck in his mouth, lost complete control of his bladder and bowels, soaking his pants in front and back.

Mary seemed to snap out of her trance. "I think your friend may have soiled himself. Why don't you two go screw each other." Mary ripped the gun out of the cowboy's mouth breaking his other front tooth.

"I said get out of here." Mary screamed. They both took off running, one of them in a lot of discomfort and the other continuing to stare at Tommy's arm.

"Thanks," Tommy said.

"You would have done it for me," Mary said. "Now pick up your arm and let's get out of here before someone calls the police."

"Or calls a paramedic. I knew the glue was getting loose," Tommy said. "I think I need to do some body work."

"I think that would be a good idea. I don't want your arm falling off in the middle of your negotiations with Paco. It might cause him a little consternation," Mary replied, and they both smiled.

CHAPTER TWENTY-FIVE

Nick was doing about fifteen miles over the speed limit. He had tried the portable walkie-talkie again, but there was still no answer. He was in a hurry to catch up and watch their back. He wanted to make sure no trouble headed their way. His mind was on Mary and he didn't notice the red light of the police car approaching behind him until the spotlight illuminated the inside of Tommy's car.

"Oh shit," Nick said out loud.

Nick was sitting in a car that wasn't his, dressed like a hardcore gangbanger. In the backseat were two pillow cases. One contained close to two hundred and ninety thousand dollars and the other held a fully automatic AK-47 with several extra clips and a four-kilo bundle of cocaine. Nick didn't know a whole lot about guns, but he knew a loaded machine gun was not legal to have in your possession at home, let alone in a car. Things were looking mighty grim.

As Nick signaled to pull over, the thought of running entered his mind, but he had seen too many chases on television and knew the runner rarely got away in the city. Out here in the desert chances were even slimmer.

Next was the problem as to whom he should tell the cops who he was. He did have the Westside Capone gangster's driver's license and wallet. He also had the Capone tattoo across his chest. For a fleeting second, he considered trying to pass himself off as the gangster, but chances are they would then surely search the car. He decided his best chance was telling the police who he really was and explain how he was on his way to a costume party. Whatever way Nick decided to play it, he knew he was screwed.

"Well, let's get it over with," he said, as he pulled to a stop.

Just as the two police officers prepared to exit their car, a pickup truck carrying the two drunken cowboys that Mary had run into sped by in the opposite direction running into every car it tried to pass. You could hear the crunching of metal grow closer and closer until they passed and hit another two cars spinning them into oncoming traffic. Both the policeman jumped back into the car, did a quick U-turn, and sped after the out-of-control pickup truck.

Nick had started to hyperventilate, knowing his world was about to collapse around him. Suddenly his attention, like the police officers' attention, was focused on the approaching truck. He started to laugh hysterically when the police jumped back in their car and began chasing the truck. God had intervened and he wasn't about to wait around for more police to show up. He quickly started his car and headed down the road, this time at the speed limit.

"Try him again," Mary said.

"I just did. There's still no answer. He must still be too far away and out of range," Tommy replied.

"Who knows if those damn things even work," Mary said.

"That damn cricket is driving me crazy," Nick said out loud. "It sounds like it's on the seat right next to me." He turned over both wallets and the walkie-talkie but saw nothing. "Tommy needs to fumigate this damn car."

Nick picked up the walkie-talkie and pushed the button, "Can you guys hear me yet?"

"I don't think I could have done what you did back there," Tommy said to Mary.

138

"Of course you could have," Mary replied. "Adrenaline kicks in when you see a friend in trouble. All fear leaves you and you just react."

"Maybe for you, I'm too big a chicken."

"Don't be absurd. You passed all those phony bills, didn't you? A chicken couldn't have done that. That took a lot of *juevos*," Mary said.

"Yeah, but I haven't even touched a gun before and I don't think ever I could," Tommy replied.

"Sure you can. Here, take this one." Mary held out her pistol. Tommy hesitantly took it in his hand. "That is a Model 500 50-caliber Smith and Wesson Magnum Revolver, the most powerful handgun in the world."

"I thought Clint Eastwood said in one of those Dirty Harry movies that his 44-caliber was the most powerful handgun in the world," Tommy replied.

"That was a double-action Smith & Wesson Model 29 .44-cal. Magnum revolver, and it was the most powerful at that time. Now it's the one in your hand that Dirty Harry would probably carry," Mary explained.

"How come you know so much about guns?" Tommy asked.

"I lied when I told you I borrowed it from my uncle. It really is mine. I bought it thinking I would kill that assistant principal who raped me. I came to my senses shortly thereafter."

"So you really do know how to use it," Tommy said.

"Of course! I took several gun safety classes and went to the range and practiced shooting it. I also discovered that it's way too big of a gun for me. I actually have three others at home. Just not so powerful. This one is mainly to intimidate. If you shot someone with that, you could blow their leg off."

"Ooh," Tommy moaned, and started to set the gun on the counter.

"No, you need to get used to it," Mary insisted. "Stick it in your waist band like the gangsters do. It'll help with the look."

Tommy didn't like the idea, but he did as Mary told him to. "There's that cricket again. It sounds like it's inside the walkie-talkie."

"What am I thinking," Mary said. "That chirping tells you somebody is trying to call. These are made for hunters out in the wilderness. They chirp so they won't scare away the animals. Pass me that thing."

"This is 'sitting pretty', is that you 'lone dog'?" Mary asked, pushing the talk button.

"Well, it's about time I got a hold of you, 'sitting pretty'. I was beginning to worry."

"No need to worry. We just didn't know how this damn thing worked. We've been looking for a cricket for the past half-hour. We didn't realize it was the walkie-talkie signaling us."

Nick had thought the same thing about a cricket being loose in Tommy's car, but wasn't about to admit it. "I'm just glad you're safe."

"We have tried to call you several times. Did everything go okay with our friend?" Mary asked.

"It was a little more difficult than I thought it would be, but all is in order. I even bought him a little surprise for the morning when he wakes up." Nick didn't think now was the time to tell Mary and Tommy about his near disastrous run in with the police.

"I got a feeling I don't want to know what you bought him," Mary replied.

"Did you guys have any trouble gassing up and picking up food?" Mary and Tommy looked at each other. Tommy was shaking his head "no".

"Everything went fine," she replied. There was no point in troubling Nick with more worries, she thought. "Where are you now?"

"Magellan says I passed a road a couple of minutes ago called Eldorado Valley Road. Where are you guys?"

"We just passed a sign that said Cal Nev Ari, four miles," Mary answered.

"Let me see what Magellan says." Nick worked with the GPS unit. "It says that I'm about forty-five miles behind you."

"Then how in the hell are these walkie-talkies working? Their range is supposed to only be twenty-six miles." Mary said.

"I guess there's not much interference out here. We're in the middle of nowhere, remember?"

"I got to go, I'm speeding a little and a motorcycle is coming up behind me really fast. I'll call you back in a few minutes."

Nick watched as the light grew brighter and closer. Suddenly, it shifted to the other lane and shot past Nick like he was standing still.

"That was no cop," Nick said to himself. I'd better call Mary back."

Nick tried the walkie-talkie several times, but got no response." Probably some hills in the way," Nick said out loud. "I'll try again in a few minutes."

Spike paid no attention to the cars he flew past as he barreled down Highway 95. If a cop tried to stop him, then heaven help the cop. Spike was on a mission. It wasn't so much that he wanted the ounce of cocaine Scratch promised to whoever found the motorhome, but the prestige it would give him. Spike was ready to move up in the gang and what better way to prove his worth.

When Spike passed Nick, he had no idea that in just one hour he would catch the motorhome pulling the trailer, but Nick knew. And at Nick's rate of speed of seventy miles per hour, he wouldn't catch up to the motorhome until it reached Barstow. Nick decided he better speed up a bit, but just a bit, for he knew the next time he was pulled over, things wouldn't turn out too well.

CHAPTER TWENTY-SIX

"What the hell are they doing?" DEA agent Smith asked his partner who was staring through the binoculars.

"Looks like they're having a beer," Smith's partner replied, "and waiting."

"Waiting for what, I wonder?"

"Probably waiting to hear from one of their scouts as to where the motorhome is would be my guess."

"I wouldn't call them scouts. It makes them sound a little too honorable. We might as well relax too. Go get us a couple of burgers and coffee. I got a feeling it's going to be a long night."

"When is this fine new ride of yours going to get here?" Noe asked.

"Hector will bring it by the carnival, *ese*. I want it to be a grand entrance. He's got business to take care of in the morning, but I expect he'll get the car here sometime around noon."

"Isn't that the time the home boys and cops start their softball game?"

"*No se*, I don't give a shit about no softball game," Rudy replied. "All I care about is showing all you *pendejos* what a fine lowrider looks like."

"Shit *ese*, it ain't nothing compared to my new Escalade. You got hydraulics on your Impala?" Noe asked.

"Shit yeah, but I ain't gonna bounce it around like some dumb ass *cholo*. She's too fine for that. They fuck'n shouldn't even allow new cars in the competition as far as I'm concerned. You got balls to even call that Escalade of yours a lowrider anyway."

143

"You'll change your mind when I drop that bitch down to the ground during the judging tomorrow," Noe bragged.

"Whatever homie, we'll see who's got the most badass car tomorrow."

Rudy pulled out his cell and gave Hector a call. Again, the phone rang and rang until it kicked over to voice mail. "Why ain't you answering your damn phone, *pendejo*? Don't be late for your meeting in the morning. Just handle the business with Paco and get the hell out of there. I'll make sure there are some soldiers in the neighborhood to escort you here. I know we ain't never had any trouble, but this is a lot more dough than usual, so don't mess it up. And don't fuck'n be late dropping off my car at the carnival."

Rudy checked his watch. Hector should have left the campground by now. Rudy decided he was going to have to talk to the OGs about supplying shit to those Vegas bikers. He had never trusted Scratch from the very beginning and Hector had even said Chilly and Tiny had smarted off to him on the last trip. That was no way to run an operation. Scratch was getting sloppy and sloppiness led to arrests. Maybe it was time to move a few of the Wilcox Street homies up to Vegas. Let them handle the dealings with the mafia and casinos. It wouldn't take long to set up a network of local dealers. Some of the OGs in prison could work it out with some of the other gang leaders doing their time. A lot of the gang business was handled in the state prisons. Should be a simple matter. Rudy didn't want a war with the bikers, but they needed to be put in their place.

"Ten million dollars! You ever seen that much money at one time before?" Paco asked Chuy.

"I ain't seen that much money my whole life," Chuy replied. "Why we payin' those Wilcox gangsters so much this time?"

"We just paying them for the coke they been frontin' us the past six months."

"Why'd they front us so much?" Chuy asked.

"OG Victor saved the ass of one of the Wilcox OGs in a riot up at Atascadero. Victor took the shiv meant for the Wilcox OG."

"I remember hearin' about that. How is Victor?"

"He lost a kidney, but gained us a lot of territory. The OG told Wilcox to front us the shit so we could get control of the Southside. Now that we supply all the local gangs, we gots money to pay 'em back and deal in cash from now on."

"You sure these Wilcox busters won't start cuttin' the shit or shortin' us now they gettin' their money?" Chuy asked.

"Why would they? It would be bad for business and this is a business. Someone starts getting' greedy and people start dying. Nobody wants that to happen."

"If you say so, but I got a hard time trustin' any dem Eastside sons-a-bitches. They killed too many of my homies over the years," Chuy said.

"We gots to forget the past and look to the future, homie. Forget all that gangbanging shit. That's for the little soldiers to learn how to be men. Now let's head over to my house and kick-it. We gots a big day tomorrow and we need to be in place tonight."

CHAPTER TWENTY-SEVEN

"Doesn't it make you nervous when Hector's phone rings like that? That's the third time and they're all from the same number. I hope he wasn't supposed to check in or something. Maybe we…"

"Tommy!" Mary snapped. "Relax, everything is okay."

"Yeah but it's been over an hour since we last heard from Nick and he isn't answering when I try to radio him. Maybe I should call him," Tommy continued to ramble.

"We cannot take the chance using our cell phones to call him. Somewhere down the line someone may check into that sort of thing. Besides, Nick turned his cell phone off just like you and I did. There are GPS units in them that allow them to be traced if they're turned on," Mary patiently explained.

"I could use Hector's to call him," Tommy suggested.

"Stop and think what I just said. Nick's phone is turned off and, even if it wasn't, if you called him on Hector's phone Nick's number would not only be on Hector's cell phone, but on the bill statement when it arrived wherever the hell it arrives to." Tommy could tell Mary was losing her patience.

"What the hell was I thinking?" Tommy said. "I'm just getting really tired."

"Why don't you try to sleep for a while? I'm still wide awake. You sleep and in a couple of hours I'll wake you and you can drive while I get some rest."

"Are you sure?" Tommy asked.

"Positive, now go lay down," Mary told him.

Tommy did as he was told and in less than two minutes, he was fast asleep. Mary was also wondering why they hadn't heard from Nick, but didn't want to say so to

Tommy. He was already too stressed out. If he knew Mary was concerned, it would only have made matters worse. As if things could even get much worse.

Mary didn't see the motorcycle coming up behind her. She only saw it as it raced past at what she estimated to be more than a hundred miles an hour. A chill ran down her spine at the sight of the biker. She knew it probably was not one of Scratch's gang members, but just the thought scared her. She eased off the gas slightly, hoping Nick would soon catch up.

"I wonder if Nick saw him coming? If he did, why didn't he warn us?" Mary said to herself. Now she was really beginning to worry why Nick had not radioed them. The motorcycle never seemed to slow down and Mary watched as it disappeared into the night ahead.

"Out of sight, out of mind," Mary said, trying to raise her spirits and diminish her fear. It didn't work.

Nick was driving faster and faster. Each time he saw headlights approaching from ahead or behind he would slow back down to seventy. He figured seventy was a safe speed. No state trooper would pull him over for doing seventy, or so he hoped.

Nick had been concerned when the motorcycle passed him as he approached Needles, but having seen no others, his fear had somewhat receded. Twice the walkie-talkie had made its cricket chirp, but each time he tried to answer he received no response.

Spike smiled as he roared past the brown motorhome pulling the trailer. It was the break he had hoped for. He raced ahead until he was out of sight of the motorhome and then pulled down a side road to make his call. Scratch answered on the first ring.

147

"This better be good news," Scratch growled into the phone.

"I found the motorhome," Spike replied. Scratch immediately tensed up.

"Where are they?"

"Headed west on Highway 40, about fifty miles west of Needles."

"Who was driving?" Scratch asked.

"Some chick, I didn't see anybody else," Spike replied.

"How fast was she going?"

"About fifty-five. It'll take her at least an hour and a half to reach Barstow," Spike estimated.

"We're on our way. Stay behind her, but far enough back that she doesn't see you," Scratch ordered. "We should meet up with you before she reaches Barstow. Call us if anything changes."

"We got the bitch," Scratch said to Tiny and Chilly, but we got to move fast."

Chilly pulled out two twenties and threw them on the bar. "This oughta cover it," he said to the bartender. Tiny and Scratch were already headed out the door.

"Call Pecos in the van and tell him to head to Barstow as fast as he can," Scratch ordered Chilly as he walked outside.

"Tell him yourself, he's pulling in now." Chilly replied.

"Scratch walked over to the van window and began explaining something to Pecos. Immediately the van pulled out of the parking lot and headed for the freeway on ramp.

"Let's ride, boys," Scratch said, "time to get rich."

"Wake up Smith, they're moving," agent Jenkins said to his partner.

"Look, the van finally caught up to them."

148

"Just in time to move on, it looks like," Jenkins said, as he watched the van squeal out of the parking lot and head for the 15-west onramp. Seconds later the thunderous roar of the three big bikes rattled the windows of the diner and the bikes sped off after the van.

"I'd say they're in a pretty big hurry," Smith said.

"Then I guess we are too," Jenkins said, as he fishtailed through the gravel lot as he made his U-turn to follow the gang. "Should we try to keep up with the bikes?"

"If we can, but I don't want to be too obvious or have to explain to some CHP officer what we're up to, so keep up if you can, but if not, we can follow the van."

"As you wish."

"Looks like we'll soon be able to quit this stinking job," Smith said.

"We need to talk about that. I've known too many cops who messed up by quitting too soon or spending money on things they shouldn't have been able to afford. Internal Affairs looks for shit like that," Jenkins explained. "Especially when you're dealing with the kinds of people and money we deal with."

"Who's to say I didn't have a rich uncle that died?"

"I didn't say it was impossible, just that we have to be smart about it," Jenkins replied.

"What would you do with that kind of money?" Smith asked.

"It depends on what kind of money we're talking about," Jenkins replied.

"Well, how many kilos do you think are in that motorhome? Two or three hundred?"

"I would say at least that much. If you're going to take this kind of a risk, I'd make it worthwhile," Jenkins replied.

"Who are we going to sell the coke to once we steal it?" Smith asked.

149

"Probably the same people who are buying it now," Jenkins replied.

"What about selling it back to who we stole it from?" Smith offered.

Jenkins thought for a moment. "Not a bad idea, buddy. I'll have to give that some thought. But first things first, we got to steal the shit before we can sell it."

"That's the easy part," Smith replied. "Just follow that van."

Neither Smith nor Jenkins saw the CHP car's lights until he sounded a short blast of his siren to get their attention.

"Now what?" Jenkins said. "Just be cool, show him your badge and give him one of your cards. Tell him we're pursuing a suspected drug dealer and can't wait around."

"Morning, officer," Jenkins said. "Here's my badge and card, we're following a suspected drug dealer and can't stick around."

The officer looked at the card. "I hope you realize when you fishtailed out of that lot back there you threw up quite a bit of gravel. One of the pieces hit my windshield and cracked it. The DEA will be getting the bill."

"All units please respond to an accident 30 miles east of Barstow on the 15," the CHP officer's radio blared.

"I guarantee we will be in touch. You're free to go."

"Great," Smith said. "Now we have to worry about explaining that one to the boss. Go, go, we can't afford to lose them.

As the Crown Vic of the DEA agents merged onto Interstate 15, the Crown Vic of the CHP officer rocketed past.

"I sure hope he doesn't scare off Scratch and his buddies," Jenkins said.

"The way Scratch tore out of here on the cycles, I doubt if he'll even catch them," Smith replied. "Just get behind the van and stick with it. The night is only getting longer."

CHAPTER TWENTY-EIGHT

Mary kept looking in her rearview mirror. She was sure she had seen the single headlight of a motorcycle laying back behind other cars that would catch and pass her, but the single headlight never moved closer. She was just about to wake Tommy to share her concern when she heard the cricket chirp of the walkie-talkie.

"God, I hope that's you," Mary said.

"Is everything alright?" Nick's voice said over the radio.

"No, but now that I hear your voice, things are a lot better."

"I've been trying to reach you for miles, but I guess I was still too far away," Nick explained. "I heard it chirp a couple of times, but when I answered no one was there."

"Tommy tried several times to reach you. Where are you now?" Mary asked.

"I figure I'm about seventy miles past Needles. Where are you guys?" Nick asked in return.

"I'm not real sure. I haven't been watching the signs too closely. I think I'm being followed by a motorcycle."

"A guy on a bike passed me a couple of hours ago. He must have been doing over a hundred," Nick said.

"The same guy must have passed me. He shot by me like I was sitting still, but I know there's another cycle behind me. Did a second one pass you?"

"No, only the one."

"And I haven't passed anybody. I'm not sure where this guy came from," Mary sounded worried.

Nick didn't like what he was hearing and pressed down on the accelerator. He was willing to chance getting stopped if it meant keeping Mary safe.

"Slow down a little to see if he passes you," Nick advised.

"I already did that, but he's still back there.:

"How fast are you going?" Nick asked.

"I slowed down to fifty," Mary replied.

"I should be catching up pretty soon," Nick said. "Where's Tommy?"

"He's asleep in the back. He was starting to get really antsy and stressed. I told him he needed to rest because he'd be driving soon."

"How are you doing? I mean, besides being scared to death."

"Are you asking about my personal life or my life in relation to what is going on at this very moment?" Mary replied.

"Both, neither, hell I don't know. I'm only trying to distract you and make you feel better," Nick said.

"I know, and I really appreciate the effort," Mary smiled. "So why did you decide you wanted to move to Paraguay?"

"I don't really know why for sure. One day AOL listed the top places in the world to retire to. I think they got it from *Money* magazine. Paraguay was near the top of the list. There were all these great pictures of these beautiful villas you could buy for next to nothing. At least next to nothing compared to prices in the LA area. The cost of living was really low and I figured with the money I have saved, even if I retired at fifty-five, I could still afford to live there. Maybe not live in luxury like the people in the pictures, but live well. Of course, this was when I was feeling sorry for myself. My wife had just divorced me and I was still taking chemo for my prostate cancer."

"How is your prostate?" Mary asked

"Are you asking for personal reasons or just out of sympathy?" Nick laughed. "I am totally cancer free, or so the doctor says. And everything is working like it should."

Now Mary laughed. "Are you really set on Paraguay?"

"At least as my home base. I really want to travel again, see more of the world, and maybe I will get ideas for stories," Nick replied.

"That's right, you want to be an author," Mary said. "What kind of stories do you want to write? Mysteries, thrillers, biographies, what?"

"A little of everything I guess. I've always wanted to write a historical thriller about religion."

"Then I guess you need to spend some time researching in Italy. I've always wanted to see Florence."

"The city that brought the world the Renaissance," Nick said. "Did you know the Medici family is almost solely responsible for commissioning most of the Renaissance art in the world today?"

"That's right, you teach an art elective at school too. Are you an artist as well as an author?"

"Quit turning this conversation back to me. Let's talk about you. Why do you want to see Florence?"

"It's the city that brought us the Renaissance," Mary laughed, repeating exactly what Nick had just said.

"No really, why do you want to go there?"

"I don't necessarily just want to go there. I want to see all of Europe. And all of Asia, Africa, and even South America. I want to experience the whole world. It's always been my dream. I saw this scheme of yours as my last chance to actually reach my dream. I would rather die than spend the rest of my life teaching in Los Angeles."

"Nobody is going to die," Nick promised

"I almost had to kill a man at the gas station. I didn't want to tell you. I was afraid you'd worry too much," Mary said.

"What happened?" Nick asked.

"A couple of drunken cowboys grabbed Tommy and tried to grab me. All I could think about was that assistant principal who used to try to grab me in the same way."

"What did you do?" Nick asked.

"I kicked him hard in his privates and stuck my 50 caliber in his mouth. I broke his tooth and cut his lip pretty bad in the process. I cocked back the hammer and came really close to pulling the trigger. I was enraged."

"So why didn't you? Why didn't you pull the trigger?"

"The smell!"

"The what?" Nick asked.

"The smell! The guy was so scared he lost control of his bowels and bladder."

"Are you saying he shit his pants?" Nick asked.

"Yes, but not quite in such vulgar terms. When I smelled it, I realized that he was as scared of me as I was of the assistant principal and I felt sorry for him."

"What happened next?" Nick asked.

"Tommy calmly talked me into letting them go. I pulled the gun out of his mouth and he and his buddy stumbled back to their pickup truck and sped away bouncing off of parked cars and running oncoming cars off the road."

Nick thought about the pickup truck hitting the cars when the police were pulling him over. Could it have been the same two guys? Nick decided not to tell Mary about what had happened to him.

"I just passed a sign that said Barstow twenty-eight miles," Mary said.

"I should catch you before you reach town," Nick said. "How are you doing on gas?"

"This thing must have had extra tanks installed. I should be fine until we reach San Bernardino."

"I may need to gas up in Victorville," Nick said. "I think we should gas the motorhome there too."

"Have you thought about what we're going to do in the morning when we get to Bolsa Chica?" Mary asked.

"I'm still working on it, but I do have a few ideas" Nick lied.

"I can't believe this gang is so organized that they're able to reserve side by side spaces in an RV campground as popular as Bolsa Chica. Have you ever tried to reserve a space at a state campground? You have to call ahead like six months to the day when you want the space and chances are slim at best that you'll even get through to reservations," Mary complained.

"Somebody must know what they're doing," Nick replied. "Do you have the reservation in front of you?"

"Yeah, Hector has reserved Space B009 for Saturday and Sunday nights. On the map somebody has highlighted Space B011 right next to Hector's spot. That must be where this Paco will be parked."

"How close to the exit are the spaces?" Nick asked.

"Only about three spaces from the access road, but then it's about a quarter mile to the exit onto PCH," Mary replied.

"Is the road to the spaces a one-way road or a dead end?" Nick asked.

"No, the road circles around, but I can't tell from the map if it's a dead end or not," Mary explained. "The entrance is about a mile-and-a-half south of Warner Avenue."

"Is there an entrance to the 405 on Warner Avenue?"

"I think so, but I really can't say for certain. It's a main thoroughfare so there should be if there's not"

"Well, that's reassuring." Nick replied.

"Best I can do on such short notice," Mary laughed. "You're starting to break up."

"I'm going through some hills. It should be okay in a minute or two. Did I tell you I'm falling in…"? The transmission was lost.

"Damn," Mary said. "I've been waiting for someone to say to me what I think you are about to say for years." Mary said to a now silent walkie talkie.

"…and that is why I would like you to …" Mary heard other snippets of Nick's message. …ever love somebody like…"

Mary's attention was suddenly drawn to three approaching headlights, about two miles ahead.

"…so would you marry me?" Nick asked finishing his lengthy proposal and confession of love. He waited for an answer but the walkie talkie was silent. Deafeningly silent! "Or maybe not," Nick continued. "I might be rushing things. I know you are your own woman and would never…"

"Shut up, Nick," Mary said finally hearing his voice. "There are three motorcycles coming towards me."

Nick pushed the gas pedal to the floor. He knew Mary and Tommy were in trouble.

"I'm on my way, just keep going, and wake up Tommy. I'm sorry if I spoke too soon a minute ago."

"Nick, the radio just now started working again. If you were talking, I didn't hear anything." Mary told him.

"Great." Nick thought to himself. "I bare my soul and no one hears the greatest speech of my life."

"Tommy, Tommy," Mary yelled, trying to wake him, but he continued to sleep.

157

The three bikes had come to a stop. Mary looked in her mirror and saw that the single headlight she believed was following her was now right behind her. She reached into her purse for her 50-caliber pistol, but it wasn't there.

"Shit, I gave it to Tommy," she said. "Tommy!" she screamed his name again. Still he didn't move.

"Nick, it looks like the three bikers from the campground. They're right behind me. "And you were right about Tommy, I can't wake him."

"Vroom, "Spike roared by and gunned his engine, vibrating the entire motorhome.

"Jesus Christ, one of them just shot past me. His light wasn't on so I didn't see him coming.

"Is he trying to stop you?" Nick asked.

"No, he just took off like he was in a big hurry," Mary replied. "Wait, the other three are starting to pass me, they're flashing their lights. I'm going to try to run them off the road."

"Be careful and keep going, I'm on my way," Nick implored.

Scratch, Chilly, and Tiny didn't wait for the van as they roared towards Barstow. About fourteen miles before Interstate 15 met up with Interstate 40, the three of them turned off on Harvard Road and headed south. At Riverside Road they turned left, then right on Fort Cathy Road. Scratch knew they'd save a good half-hour taking the shortcut to connect with the 40 and Fort Cathy Road had an onramp. Besides, the checkpoint was up ahead and that could really slow them down if traffic was heavy. In less than ten minutes they had reached Interstate 40 and headed east. They slowed down to the speed limit and watched closely as each oncoming vehicle whizzed by. Several motorhomes were on the road that night and passed them, but not the one they waited for. They had traveled east about ten miles when Mary drove past.

Scratch signaled for the other two bikers to pull over. By the time they came to a stop, Spike had pulled up on his cycle.

"That same bitch that pulled the gun on you was driving," Tiny said to Chilly.

"I saw," Tiny replied. "I'm gonna make her pay for that!"

"You ain't gonna do shit till we get our hands on the rest of that cocaine," Scratch warned them.

"I told ya I'd find the motorhome," Spike said. "I told ya."

"And you will get the ounce I promised," Scratch said.

"I don't need no ounce," Spike replied. "I did it for the gang."

Scratch knew Spike had wanted to move up in the gang hierarchy, but he also knew Spike liked to do as much cocaine as he sold. He also knew Spike wasn't the smartest soldier that rode with Scratch's gang. Spike just couldn't be trusted. Not that he would purposely rat you out, but Scratch was afraid Spike would slip up and say too much and get them busted. He didn't need guys like that in the inner circle.

"What's the plan?" Spike asked.

"I need you to head back to the 15 and meet up with Frank. He's driving the van. He doesn't know about the shortcut. I need you to show him," Scratch explained.

Spike didn't like the idea of missing whatever was going down with the motorhome. He had seen the hot-looking babe driving it and he had heard that the gang scored its coke from a motorhome as it headed to L.A. to make deliveries. This had to be that motorhome. And he sure wouldn't mind seeing that babe up close.

"Is the chick driving the one that almost shot off your balls?" Spike asked Chilly.

In a flash Chilly was on Spike with his bowie knife out.

"Back off, Chilly," Scratch said. "You better get out of here and do like I told you," he said to Spike.

"I was just joking on you," Spike said to Chilly.

"Making fun of Chilly is liable to get your throat slit," Scratch said.

Chilly put away his knife, but kicked Spike's bike hard, knocking it over and breaking the headlight.

"Now how in the hell am I supposed to drive without a headlight?" Spike asked.

"There's plenty of moonlight," Tiny said. "Just get outta here like Scratch says before Chilly kicks you in the head."

Spike picked his bike off the ground and tore out towards the west and Fort Cathy Road, where he would cut up to the 15 and wait for the van. Scratch, Chilly, and Tiny were right behind him.

CHAPTER TWENTY-NINE

Nick kept watching in his rearview mirror for any headlights catching up to him. He also carefully checked out every car that passed in the opposite direction to make sure they weren't the highway patrol. Mary had stopped using the walkie-talkie. He knew she'd would need both hands to drive now.

"If I only knew how much further ahead she is," Nick said, hoping to see red taillights.

Nick reached into the backseat and grabbed the pillow case containing the AK-47 and spare clips and poured the contents onto the seat. Along with the weapon and clips was the bundle of cocaine he had taken from the motorhome.

"I don't know why the hell he brought that," Nick said aloud. "None of us uses the shit and Mary would kill him if she knew Tommy had taken it." He stuck the bundle under the passenger's seat. He put the AK back in the pillow case and laid it on the seat, but stuck the clips in his pockets. He only prayed he wouldn't have to use it.

Tiny and Chilly started to pull around the motorhome, signaling for Mary to pull over. Chilly flipped Mary off.

"Not even in your dreams, asshole," Mary said, and swung the motorhome sharply to the left.

Chilly and Tiny had expected her to try that and easily were able to avoid being hit. They both dropped back behind the trailer that the motorhome was pulling.

Mary slammed on the brakes causing them to lock and the trailer to begin to fishtail.

Chilly had just looked over to Scratch to see what to do next and did not react quick enough to avoid slamming into the trailer. He was able to lay his bike down and avoid a major impact.

As quickly as she had hit the brakes, she hit the gas and the trailer straightened out and fell into line behind the motorhome once again.

Tiny and Scratch both stopped to help Chilly.

"I'm gonna kill her," Chilly said. "Look what she did to my ride."

"Look what she did to your jacket," Scratch said.

Chilly pulled off what was left of his leather jacket. The two sleeves were held together by a small five-inch strip of leather around the collar. The right front and side were still intact, but the left side along with the back had been shredded when Chilly slid down the highway.

Tiny had pulled Chilly's bike off the ground and put the kickstand down. "Looks like you just scraped off some paint and dented up the fuel tank."

"My seat is all ripped up and look at my handle bars, they're all bent to shit," Chilly whined.

"We got to ride," Scratch said. "We can't let her get away."

"She ain't gittin' away," Chilly swore. "She's gonna pay for this." He slowly climbed on his bike and tried to start it. It took a couple of tries, but soon the engine thundered to life. Moments later the threesome was once again behind the motorhome.

"What the hell," Tommy said, as he was suddenly awakened as he rolled off the bed and onto the floor and heard the skidding tires. As he started to stand, the momentum of the motorhome shifted again and he toppled back onto the bed.

"Did you fall asleep at the wheel or something?" Tommy yelled to Mary.

162

"Tommy, thank God you're awake," Mary yelled." The bikers are back and trying to stop us."

Tommy rushed to the passenger seat and looked into the mirror. He could barely see them standing far back on the road. "What's going on? What are they doing?"

"I hope they're scraping a dead body off the highway," Mary replied.

"You ran over one of them?" Tommy gasped. "No, but I did suddenly stop and I think at least one of them ran into the back of the trailer."

"Have you heard from Nick yet?" Tommy asked.

"I have, but you need to call him back and tell him what's happening."

"Where's the walkie-talkie?" Tommy asked.

"It was right here. It must have flown somewhere like all this other stuff when I slammed on the brakes."

"I'll look for it," Tommy said.

"Looks like they're coming back," Mary said, staring into the side mirror.

"All three of them?"

"So it appears," Mary replied.

"Maybe they just want to talk or buy more cocaine," Tommy suggested.

"I don't think so," Mary replied. "They didn't seem like the socializing type. More like the rape, burn, and pillage type."

"Are you saying our only choice is to have to kill them?" Tommy asked.

Mary sat stunned by what Tommy asked. Was that the only choice? Was she ready to kill three people that she didn't even know? Could she actually kill someone? She had come close to killing the drunken cowboy back at the gas station, but could she really have done that? Was her life so threatened that she could justify such an action? Mary

163

realized she couldn't. She couldn't even kill the assistant principal who raped her. That was why she had bought the gun, but even with ample opportunity and justification, she couldn't do it, nor could she do it now.

"I'm pulling over to talk to them," Mary announced.

"Are you nuts?" Tommy yelled. "They'll kill me, then rape and kill you. Is that what you want?"

"I just can't kill them without due cause," Mary insisted. "You stay hidden and come out with the 50-caliber if they try to hurt me."

"There's no way I could ever shoot them," Tommy said.

"Even to protect me?" Mary asked.

"I just don't know," Tommy replied. "

Mary looked at Tommy and knew he'd never shoot a person, no matter what the circumstances. She doubted if she would be able to either.

"Just threaten to shoot them, but shoot their motorcycles instead," Mary suggested.

"I could do that," Tommy said. "I hate those god-awful loud things anyway.

"Then here's what we'll do."

CHAPTER THIRTY

"Shit!" agent Jenkins swore, as he swerved the car back into the slow lane. "I didn't see that bike coming at all. The son-of-a-bitch didn't even have his headlight on."

"Do you think it was one of Scratch's guys trying to make us?" Smith asked.

"No, he was going too fast and didn't even look this way."

"Look, he slowed down next to the van. Maybe he is one of Scratch's men." The van is pulling off at that next exit. Pull over to the shoulder and turn off the lights. The van is stopping."

"Pass me the night scope," Smith said, and he began to watch.

"What are they doing?" Jenkins asked.

"Looks like they're loading the bike into the van," Smith replied. "They both got in and the van is taking off."

"Is it coming back onto the freeway?"

"No, it looks like they're heading south on that road ahead. Let me see if I can find the name."

"It's called Harvard Road," Jenkins said.

"How in the hell do you know that?" Smith asked.

"Look out the window next to us, Sherlock." The agents had pulled over right next to the Harvard Road next-exit sign.

"Let's get going, I don't want to lose them."

"I found the radio," Tommy yelled.

"Call Nick and let him know what we're going to do," Mary ordered.

"Are you sure you want to do this?" Tommy asked.

"No, but I'm even surer that I don't want to kill a man unless I absolutely have to," Mary replied.

"Now call Nick, but stay out of sight. We want them to think that you're either still passed out or gone," Mary ordered.

Before Tommy could push the send button, the walkie-talkie began to chirp.

"I hope that's you," Tommy replied.

"You're finally awake, what's the situation?" Nick asked.

"Not good! Mary caused one of the bikers to crash into the trailer, but he looks to be okay. All three are behind us trying to get us to pull over," Tommy explained.

"You need to keep going, they'll kill you if you stop."

"That's what I tried to tell Mary, but she thinks differently. She thinks we should stop."

"Why in the world would she think that?" Nick asked.

"She says they probably have guns and could blow out our tires whenever they want. She seems to believe they just want to talk to see if Hector is okay and to buy some more coke."

"There is no coke," Nick said. "I told her that, but she insists that we stop."

Mary had been following the conversation.

"Tell Nick it's the smartest thing to do. Tell him I'm not willing to run these guys over and kill them, not knowing for sure what they want. If it comes down to them or me, then I'll shoot. You tell Nick that," Mary said.

"I heard you, Mary, and I think you're wrong, but you're the one who knows these guys. Just leave this thing on so I can hear what's going on," Nick ordered.

"Tommy, what are you going to do?" Nick asked.

"I'm going to stay hidden and only come out if Mary is in danger. I hope we can talk our way out of this," Tommy said.

"So do I," Nick replied.

"I'm pulling over," Mary said. "Wish me luck."

"You'll need more than luck," Nick said to himself, and he began to pray.

Scratch was surprised when the right turn signal began to flash on the motorhome. He signaled for Chilly and Tiny to follow him as he roared around the motorhome, but didn't pull over until it had come to a complete stop at the side of the road. He had seen what she had done to Chilly's bike and wasn't going to risk his own hog to such damage. By the time they had parked their cycles, Mary was standing in front of the motorhome.

"Just why the hell are you guys trying to scare me to death?" Mary demanded. "I guess you never want to do business with Wilcox Street again."

Chilly started to rush towards her, but Scratch called him back.

"You better keep that mad dog on a leash, before he really gets hurt." Mary said. "What happened to your jacket, have a little accident?" Mary smiled.

"You're just a little too smart for your own good," Scratch said. "Where's Hector, why did Wilcox send you on this trip with Hector?"

"Hector's been sick and we didn't think he could make the drive and deliveries on his own. We wouldn't have sent him at all, but we knew you or Southside Big Dog wouldn't deal with anyone but Hector. So as sick as he's been, he had to make the trip. That's why we couldn't come sooner like we originally planned."

167

Mary had hoped Nick was right when he had told them that the deal was supposed to have already gone down. She could see that Scratch was unsure of what to say or do. Tiny and Chilly also noticed Scratch's reticence.

"Let's just take the shit from them," Chilly said. "We don't need them anymore."

"Shut up," Scratch barked. "You're too dumb to see the whole picture."

"We should at least get our money back. If Hector is okay on the return trip, we can give it all to him then. I don't trust this bitch. I think she's the one trying to rip off the Wilcox *vatos*." Chilly insisted.

"You're making a life ending mistake, my friend. There are hundreds in Vegas that are loyal to Wilcox Street. You won't be able to turn your back on anyone. There won't be any place you can hide that we won't hunt your ass down."

"I think she's bluffing," Chilly said, stepping towards Mary.

"Are you willing to take that chance for a measly three hundred thousand dollars?" Mary asked Scratch.

Scratch grabbed Chilly's arm. "Hold up a minute."

Chilly had had just about enough happen to him that day. Even Scratch grabbing his arm made him tense up and growl at Scratch.

"Where's Hector now? I want to see him and see what he has to say. I think Tiny might be right. Maybe it's you who is trying to steal the shit and our money," Scratch said.

"I told you Hector's not well. He's asleep in the motorhome."

"Asleep or drugged? He didn't look sick at the campground. He looked like he'd been drugged. I think you better get Hector out here right now or there's going to be trouble."

"There already is trouble and it'll be chasing your asses until it kills you and that won't take too long," Mary replied. "You don't go giving me orders. I take my orders from Wilcox Street."

Scratch had finally had enough. "Fuck Wilcox Street, she's all yours, Chilly. Tiny and I are gonna search the motorhome."

Before she could jump out of the way, Chilly had pulled his big Bowie Knife and grabbed Mary's hair. "You gonna pay now, bitch. But first I'm gonna have some fun."

Nick had been listening over the walkie-talkie which Mary had attached to the back of her shorts. Tommy, who was hiding just inside the motorhome door, had also been following the conversation, hoping things wouldn't turn out like they were about to.

"Now Tommy, move in now," Nick screamed as he listened. He had the accelerator pressed to the floor. He had never driven this fast in his life.

"*Que pasa*, what the hell are you *pendejos* doing?" Tommy said, stepping into the doorway with Mary's 50-caliber in his hand. "Let go of my *puta*."

Chilly wasn't about to let Mary go, nor was Scratch going to change his mind about stealing the rest of the cocaine.

"Hector, looks like you're feeling a little better than last time I saw you," Scratch said.

"Tell your *homie* to let go of my woman," Tommy demanded.

"He will, but just not quite yet," Scratch sensed weakness.

"I was worried she was ripping you off, that's why I stopped the motorhome," Scratch started to explain.

169

"You didn't stop it, I told her to stop it to see what you *vatos* wanted," Tommy said, doing his best to sound like Hector.

"Then why did you cause Chilly to drop his bike on the freeway and ruin his nice jacket?" Scratch was toying with Tommy.

"We didn't know who it was at first. We thought someone was trying to rip us off," Tommy replied. He knew Scratch wasn't buying it. "You need to let her go and leave or Wilcox Street will never sell to you again."

"After we take the rest of the coke you're taking to L.A., we won't need to do business with you again. So back up, we're coming in," Scratch threatened.

"You forget I have this gun," Tommy shouted.

"We didn't forget," Scratch said. "You're too much of a pussy to use it. It's written all over your face. If you don't want to die like your bitch you better get out of my way."

"Shoot him, Hector," Mary yelled.

"Shut up, bi..." but Chilly didn't finish his sentence. He had been holding tightly to Mary's hair, but Mary still had on her wig. She twisted around and kicked the knife out of Chilly's hand, then kicked him squarely, with as much force as she could muster, in the balls. She ran to the driver's side of the motorhome.

It was just enough to distract Scratch and Tiny. Tommy lifted the huge Smith and Wesson and fired it into the air, twice. The recoil from the first shot almost ripped his arm off as the gun kicked high into the air. The second shot ripped through the roof of the motorhome.

Scratch and Tiny both dove to the ground at the sound of the first shot. Scratch saw the second shot rip through the roof and he smiled. Chilly was still reeling and howling from the pain in his smashed testicles. Scratch slowly stood up.

170

"I think that's a little more gun than you can handle," Scratch said to Tommy. He signaled for Tiny to get up and move to the other side of the door.

"You better back away or else," Tommy threatened.

"Or else what," Scratch laughed. "You can't shoot us both. Hell, I don't think you're man enough to shoot either of us."

Chilly was just starting to catch his breath from the excruciating pain in his groin and began to look around for Mary.

Tommy saw he was about to go after her. He turned the gun towards the nearest cycle by Chilly and fired the gun. It sounded like a canon going off. Chilly's bike must have been leaking gas, for when the bullet hit the bike it exploded in a giant fireball throwing shrapnel everywhere. A piece from the engine flew towards Chilly hitting him in the side of the head causing a huge gash and knocking him out cold.

"I think you killed him," Scratch said. He could clearly see the fear in Tommy's face. "They're gonna put you away for a long time."

"It was an accident," Tommy yelled.

"Who's gonna believe that?" laughed Scratch.

"Hector," Mary called. "Finish it off like we planned."

Both Tiny and Scratch backed away when they heard Mary's words.

"Do it now!" she screamed.

Tommy turned and fired another shot towards where Scratch and Tiny were now standing. They both once again dove to the ground, but the shot wasn't meant for either of them. The bullet ripped into Scratch's motorcycle and the engine blew apart.

"What the hell are you doing?" Scratch yelled. "You ruined my ride."

171

Tommy fired again, this time at Tiny's cycle, but missed.

"You just made a big mistake, chump," Scratch said.

Tommy fired again and this time hit Tiny's bike blowing away most of the gas tank. Gas poured down onto the hot engine and ignited the bike.

"You are so fucking stupid," Scratch said, standing up.

Tommy turned the gun towards Scratch. "Don't make me kill you," Tommy warned.

"Kill me? Kill me with what? You're out of bullets, you stupid shit. Time for you to die." Scratch reached into his waistband for his own pistol.

"I don't think so," a voice said coming from behind the trailer.

Suddenly, the ground right behind Scratch and Tiny erupted as Nick opened fire with the AK-47. "Now drop your weapons," Nick ordered.

Both Tiny and Scratch quickly complied.

"Who the hell are you?" Scratch asked.

"You don't think we would let Hector move this much cocaine and money without backup, do you?" Nick replied.

"You ain't Wilcox Street," Scratch said. "You're Westside Capone, your tatt gives you away. I knew you guys were rippin' off Wilcox."

"Shut up, you don't know shit. Grab your friend and walk down the embankment."

Chilly had come to and was sitting dazed in front of the motorhome.

"He's not dead." Tommy said.

"Of course he's not dead," Scratch said. "His head is too hard for something like that to kill him."

"Shut up and get down that embankment," Nick ordered.

172

Slowly the three of them made their way across the shoulder and down the hill. Scratch was hoping Spike and the van would get there soon. He wasn't about to let these beaners get away with this. They'd all pay.

Nick kicked Scratch's cycle over the side and down the hill. The fire was out on both Chilly and Tiny's cycles, although Tiny's continued to give off a lot of smoke.

"You'd better kill all three of us or it'll be you who will always have to watch your back. I don't care what gang you're claiming, I'll kill all three of you." Scratch yelled. He knew they wouldn't be killed. If the Mexicans meant to kill them, they'd already be dead. "Just like the bitch said, there's no place you can hide that we won't find you."

"Except in plain sight," Nick said under his breath.

"Follow us in the car," he said to Tommy. "You better get your kit out of the motorhome and put it back in the car. I'll ride with Mary for a while. Put the money in the trunk along with your makeup kit, in case you're pulled over. I'll take the AK with me. Keep the car next to the motorhome until we are away from here. I don't want those guys knowing what we're driving. The walkie-talkie is in the car. Where's Mary?"

"I'm right here," Mary said, trying to put her wig back on straight.

Nick could see that she was shaking. "I'm sorry this has gotten so out of control. When we get back to Los Angeles, I think you should wait for us at the school."

Mary looked at Nick with fire in her eye. "How dare you treat me like I'm a helpless woman. When I joined you in this hare-brained scheme, I joined to see it through, not to be cast aside at your whim because of some chauvinistic stereotyping. Hell, you might as well paint a bull on your car when you drive to work like all the other macho Mexican *pendejos*."

173

"I don't drive a car," Nick reminded her.

"It was only a metaphor," Mary replied.

"Actually, it was an analogy," Nick corrected.

"Shut up, Nick, you're only making it worse," Tommy said, keeping an eye on the bikers down the hill. "We need to get going before the police show up. Somebody had to report the burning motorcycles."

"I only suggested that because I love you and couldn't live with myself if something were to happen to you," Nick confessed.

Mary gave Nick a hug.

"I really think we need to get going," Mary said.

"You boys just relax down there. I'm sure help is on its way. You better get that big guy to the hospital, he took quite a shot to the head it looks like," Nick said.

"The three of you will be dead before you reach L.A.," Scratch warned. "Nobody messes with the Vegas Hardass Boys."

"I'd suggest you take your hardasses back to Vegas and start packing your bags, boys. Wilcox Street will be paying you a visit soon," Mary advised.

Tommy had gotten into his car and pulled onto the opposite side of the motorhome and honked. Mary entered the motorhome and started it up. Nick stood above the bikers with the AK. "You'd be stupid to try to follow us," Nick said, and fired a clip from the AK, just above the biker's heads. Tiny dove to the ground and pulled the still groggy Chilly with him. Scratch didn't even flinch.

"Be seeing you real soon," Scratch said.

"Let's go," Mary yelled from the driver's seat.

Nick jumped into the doorway of the motorhome and stood aiming the AK at the bikers until they were out of sight.

"We've got no time to waste," Nick said to Mary. "Put her at seventy and keep her there, I know those boys will

174

come after us, so let's get a big head start. It'll be hard to hide from them now. The 15 is our only choice."

"You know there's another way," Mary said. "We could take Highway 58 from Barstow over to Mojave, and then down the 14 through Lancaster and Palmdale to the South 5 in the San Fernando Valley."

"I think that would add too much time and put us at Bolsa Chica Beach late," Nick replied.

"But aren't you afraid Scratch and his gang will follow us?" Mary asked.

"I'm sure they will, but it'll take them at least a couple of hours to arrange a way out of the predicament they're in. They won't leave their bikes no matter how shot up they are, and where are they going to find a rental car in Barstow at this time of the morning?" Nick explained. "It's impossible."

"Don't count on it," Mary replied. "We'd be foolish to count them out of the picture. Our plans should consider that they'll show up again at the most inconvenient time. We should be ready for it and, if they don't show up, then all the better."

"You're right," Nick agreed, "We need to be prepared for anything and everything. Now tell me about these two cowboys you and Tommy ran into."

"Why, are you jealous?" Mary asked.

"Who wouldn't be jealous," Nick replied.

Mary knew there was more to it than just that.

CHAPTER THIRTY-ONE

"Where in the hell are these guys headed?" Agent Jenkins said. "Do you think they're on to us and just running us in circles?"

"Nah, this is a short cut to Interstate 40. I'd bet a hundred bucks they're on the way to meet up with Scratch. He's probably spotted the motorhome and trailer. If so, we're just about in the money, partner." Agent Smith held up his hand so Jenkins could give him a high-five.

"What are you doing?" Jenkins asked.

"High five, buddy. Give me a high-five." Smith replied.

"That's so Twentieth Century. That hasn't been cool for years. Now you bang your fists together. That's the way you show how cool you are in the Twenty-First Century," Jenkins replied.

"Where did you learn that? I think you're full of shit," Smith answered.

"What, don't you ever watch MTV or the NBA?" Jenkins asked.

"Yeah, but there the guys are kissing, or hugging, or touching each other's butt and I sure as hell ain't doing any of that with you!" Smith said emphatically.

"You need to get with the program," Jenkins replied. "Who knows, it may come in handy some day when you're undercover. Hold your fist up." Jenkins held up his fist but Smith just sat there.

"Hold up your damn fist!" Jenkins yelled.

Smith reluctantly formed a fist and held it in the air.

"Now we hit them together," Jenkins said. Smith just shook his head.

Jenkins turned his head to look at Smith. "Hit my damn fist, before you piss me off."

Smith turned and smashed his fist into Jenkins.

"What the hell are you doing? You're supposed to just…. oh shit!"

Both men flew forward as Jenkins slammed on the brakes. The car skidded on some loose gravel and ran into the back of a California Highway Patrol car, just tapping the bumper hard enough to crease it and fold it under, but not hard enough to set off the airbags in their own car.

"Great," Smith said. "Show him your badge and give him one of your cards. We don't have time to sit here and exchange pleasantries. Tell him the same bullshit we told the last one about following drug dealers."

The CHP officer did not look happy as he climbed from his car. He was even less happy when he saw who had run into him.

"Do you guys have something against the CHP or against me personally?" the CHP officer said as he reached the driver's window.

"Not you again," Jenkins said when he saw the officer.

"Don't try to tell me you're following a suspect, because I've been sitting here for ten minutes and only one vehicle has gone by. You better damn well know what kind of vehicle that was if you expect to get out of here this time."

"A light blue panel van with two bikers inside. The one in the passenger seat is called Spike," Smith explained.

"Shit," the officer replied. "That's the only one that went by. I guess you can go, but be expecting another bill for the damages to this car. They aren't going to believe this back at the garage."

"Thank you, officer," Jenkins said.

"You said bikers in the van?" the officer asked.

"Yeah, but this is strictly a DEA investigation," Smith said.

"Before you jokers rear-ended me, I was responding to a call I got about two motorcycles burning on the side of Highway 40. They said a motorhome had pulled over to render assistance."

"Did you get a description of the motorhome?" Jenkins asked.

"No, just that one had stopped by the burning bikes. I'm heading there if you want to follow," the officer said.

"We will, but if the van is pulled over, just keep driving. Those bikers and that motorhome could be connected to our investigation, and we can't afford to tip them off," Smith explained.

"Will do," the officer replied. "I'll be talking to you two later. What frequency are you guys on in case I run into the van again."

"Fed 17," Smith replied.

The CHP officer got back into his car after looking at his damaged bumper. Smith and Jenkins followed him down Fort Cathy Road to the Interstate. When they reached the top of the overpass, Jenkins pulled over so Smith could use the night scope binoculars to see if he could determine which way the van had gone. The CHP car turned onto the Interstate 40 onramp heading east.

"See anything?" Jenkins asked.

"Nah, I think your little accident delayed us too long and we lost them."

"My little accident? If you weren't so behind the times this never would have happened," Jenkins began to argue.

"Whatever," Smith said, and turned the binoculars to look towards the west.

"Heh, what did that snitch Zeke say the motorhome looked like?"

178

"Just that it was brown and pulling a trailer with a picture of a lowrider painted on it," Jenkins replied. "Why? Did you see one?"

"I'm not sure," Smith replied.

"Well, we sure as hell ain't gonna follow something that you're not sure about," Jenkins replied. "We need to find that van and keep on it."

"Well, now that you've lost it, it might just prove a little difficult to find it again don't you think?" Smith replied rudely.

"Why don't you shut up trying to blame me for..." Jenkins was interrupted by a call from the CHP officer over the radio.

"Just thought you DEA clowns might like to know that I saw your blue van parked along the westbound side of the interstate about six miles east of Fort Cathy Road. That's just about where the fire was reported."

"Is the motorhome still there?" Smith asked.

"No, but I did see at least five people staring over the side of the road looking down the hill," the officer replied.

"Don't stop," Smith said, "just keep going. If there's an overpass up ahead, pull off and watch them. Just make sure they don't see you watching."

"Look boys, I'm no DEA agent. I've got my own work to take care of. You boys need to handle your own stakeouts. Call for some backup if you need help," the officer replied.

"What should we do?" Jenkins asked Smith.

"I guess we better head east," Smith replied.

"Thanks for your help, officer," Smith replied over the radio trying not to sound too sarcastic.

The two agents turned their Crown Vic onto the east onramp and floored it.

As they raced toward the van, the motorhome disappeared over the horizon to the west.

"Did you see that CHP parked back on Riverside Road?" Spike asked.

"I saw him, but I wasn't break'n any laws," the van driver responded.

"What about that other car that looked like it was following us back when we turned off the 15?" Spike said.

"Well, he ain't following us now, is he?" the driver said. "You are too fuck'n paranoid. You need to quit snort'n that shit you're sell'n."

Spike continued to watch the rearview mirror as the van entered the freeway. No cars seemed to be following them. As he watched, he missed the motorhome pulling the trailer streak by on the opposite side of the freeway.

"It should be just up ahead," Spike said.

"I don't see no god-damned motorhome," the driver replied. "Are you sure this is where you left Scratch."

"I'm positive," Spike replied. "Look, over there, ain't that Scratch stand'n by the freeway?"

"I think it is. Where the hell is his ride?" the driver asked.

"And where the hell are Chilly and Tiny? Maybe they took the motorhome somewhere already?"

The driver hit the brakes and pulled across the dirt median separating the opposing lanes. He sped up to where Scratch stood by the road.

"Look there's Chilly and Tiny. And there's the cycles at the bottom of the hill. Shit, it looks like two of the bikes burned up. Do you think they crashed?" Spike rambled.

"All I know is Scratch looks really pissed off. I'd keep my mouth shut if I was you," the driver advised.

"Get out here and help Chilly into the van," Scratch barked. "Where's your ride, Spike?"

"In the back," Spike replied, pointing to the van.

180

"Well, get it out of there, we need room for Chilly and Tiny," Scratch ordered.

"Did you see the motorhome go by?" Scratch asked.

"Didn't see nuttin'," Spike replied.

The driver looked at Spike. "I don't know where you was look'n Spike, but I saw one go by just after we hopped on the interstate."

Scratch gave Spike a nasty glare.

"Spike, I need you to wait here by our bikes until Lefty can get the tow truck here," Scratch ordered.

"What the hell happened to your bikes?" Spike asked.

Scratch didn't reply. "Give Tiny a hand with Chilly. He got a pretty good gash on his head."

"Shit, Tiny, what happened, did you guys crash or something?" Spike asked Tiny.

"Shut up and help me get him in the van," Tiny snapped back.

"If the CHP come by, you tell 'em we had an accident and someone took us to the doctor. Tell 'em you're wait'n for the tow truck. You got any shit on you?" Scratch asked.

"No, no, I got no coke on me," Spike replied.

"Bullshit," Scratch snapped. "You always got coke on you. Give it to me now. The cop will no doubt search you and I don't need nobody getting arrested right now. Gimme your gun and knife too."

Reluctantly, Spike relinquished his weapons and drugs.

"Don't say nuth'n to nobody 'bout the motorhome, you understand?" Scratch said as the van prepared to pull away.

"I understand," Spike said, even though he didn't.

The van tore down the highway, but it was old and overloaded and could barely cruise at sixty-five miles an hour, so tore might be a bit of an exaggeration.

"Pass me a cell phone," Scratch ordered. "We need to get some help."

"You ain't gonna tell them what we're after are you?" Tiny asked.

"Of course not. I'm just gonna get a few more pairs of eyes watching for that motorhome and arrange for us to borrow a couple of bikes."

"What about Chilly?" Tiny asked.

"Chilly's got a concussion. He'll be fine after a couple of day's rest. He'll stay here in the van. He won't be able to ride. We're gonna need the van to haul the coke back to Vegas. Chilly can sleep on the coke."

"What happened?" the van driver asked.

"Westside Capones are behind it," Scratch said. "At least it was a Westside Capone that got the drop on us with the AK-47. But I still don't get it. Hector is Wilcox Street and that puta seems to be Wilcox Street. They both warned me that Wilcox will be coming to Vegas to clean house. I think that's a bunch of bullshit, but now we're in too deep. We have to steal that shipment or we're out of business. If we don't, there's no way we can afford protection and we'll have to pull out."

"What's with this Westside Capone *vato*? Is he the one who torched your bikes?" the driver asked.

"No, it was Hector who did that. And something wasn't right about Hector. Maybe he was still sick, but he sure wasn't acting sick," Scratch explained.

"Maybe Wilcox has hired Westside Capones as the muscle to protect the shipment." Tiny suggested.

"I was think'n that, but why now? They ain't never worried about protection before," Scratch replied.

"Maybe they did and we just didn't know it," Tiny said.

"It makes no difference. We're gonna steal that shipment and I'll bring in some muscle to help us do it. I may have to give up a dozen kilos, but that won't mean shit once we have the rest of it safely in the van. I got to make some calls."

"You have got to be kidding me," the CHP captain said to the officer when he brought in his second damaged car that night. "You're telling me the same two DEA agents who cracked your windshield, this Smith and Jenkins, are the same ones who rear ended you out on Fort Cathy Road?"

"I know it sounds ridiculous, but these two clowns were paying no attention to anything except this van they were following," the officer replied.

"They claimed that this van is transporting drugs?"

"That's why they were in such a hurry to get away," the officer replied.

"I called the DEA and they did confirm that this Smith and Jenkins worked for them, and that they were working on an assignment in Las Vegas. However, their boss knew nothing about them tailing some van through California. According to him, they are both off duty tonight. Something you should have probably checked on," the Captain lectured.

"Give me another car and I'll go have a talk with those two agents and find out what's really going on," the officer insisted.

"Like hell you will," replied the Captain.

"That's not your job. In fact, after screwing up two cars, you aren't even going back out on patrol. We need to transport a prisoner down to Long Beach. I think that will be the perfect job for you. He needs to be there by ten in the morning, so you better get going, and don't wreck another car."

"Yes, sir," the CHP officer replied.

183

"Just be thankful I didn't stick you at a desk for the next two months," the Captain said. "Now get out of here."

CHAPTER THIRTY-TWO

"I'm going to need to stop for gas pretty soon," Tommy said over the walkie-talkie. "And I have to pee really badly."

"We are almost to the Cajon Junction," Nick said. "Why don't you pull off there. We'll keep going. I think if trouble was coming, it would have been here by now."

"I wouldn't be so sure of that," Mary said.

"I don't want to chance stopping the motorhome. That's what they'll be looking for. The sooner I can get lost in the L.A. freeway system the better. After you stop, head for school. Take our changes of clothes inside and park your car in the lot. Hold onto the walkie-talkie. When we get close to school, we'll call you and let you know to meet us out front. I don't want you standing around Cudahy at 8:00 in the morning looking like a gangster."

"No more than I want to stand out there waiting, believe me," Tommy replied. "I'll see you two in Cudahy. Be careful."

"We will, and you too," Mary answered

Nick and Mary rode in silence until they had almost reached the intersection where the 15 and 215 splits apart. A car honking jarred them both from their thoughts.

"There goes Tommy," Mary said. "Looks like he's staying to the right. He plans on taking the 15.

"It's the fastest way to Cudahy," Nick commented

"Which way will it be for us?" Mary asked.

Nick looked at his watch. It was 6:10 a.m. "Let's take the 215, the road less traveled. We still have almost two hours until we pick up Tommy."

"Let's hope you're right," Mary replied.

"What's that supposed to mean? Are you implying that I haven't been right up till now?" Nick retorted.

"Of course not," Mary replied. "It was just a figure of speech. You seem to be a little on edge."

"As if you're not?" Nick replied.

"Not quite as bad as you," Mary answered. "We're all stressed. Who wouldn't be under the circumstances?"

When the motorhome reached the turnoff for the new 210 freeway west, they passed a motorcycle traveling in the slow lane.

"Nick," Mary called. "There's a motorcycle ahead."

Nick looked out the windshield. "I don't know," Nick said. "We are bound to run into motorcycles along the way."

"Yeah, but that one is a biker, not a crotch rocket jockey. How often do bikers cruise in the slow lane?" Mary said.

"What the hell is a crotch rocket?" Nick replied.

"You know, one of those Japanese motorcycles that go over two hundred miles an hour down the freeway."

"So that's what they're called. Is that a technical term?" Nick tried to make light of the situation.

"Crotch rocket is just an analogy," Mary replied.

"No, it's a simile," Nick corrected.

"Right," Mary replied, as she signaled to pass the motorcycle.

Mary and Nick both looked at the biker as they passed and held their breath. If he was one of Scratch's gang, he did nothing to show it. His hands remained on the handlebars and his pace never faltered. They continued to watch him in the rearview mirror until traffic obscured the view.

The walkie-talkie began to chirp, startling both of them and causing Mary to jerk the wheel.

"I think we both are a little tense," Mary said, as she checked both mirrors to see how close she had come to sideswiping another car.

"Everything going alright?" Nick asked into the walkie-talkie.

"Just thought I'd let you know that a couple of bikers just roared past me on the freeway. A blue van seemed to be following them. Or at least was going the same speed," Tommy reported.

"Did it look like Scratch?" Mary asked.

"I don't know," Tommy replied. "They went by so quickly I didn't get a good look. All I know is that whoever was on those bikes was on a mission to get somewhere in a hurry."

"Thanks for the info," Nick replied. "We'll see you soon."

"Do you think it was Scratch that Tommy saw?" Mary asked.

"I think there's a very good chance it was," Nick replied.

"Where do you think they're headed?"

"Probably to Cudahy would be my guess. At least that's where I'd head if I was looking for the Wilcox Street gang," Nick replied.

"What are we going to do? We can't go back to Cudahy," Mary said.

"We have to go back to Cudahy. We have to pick up Tommy. He'll just have to meet us someplace besides right in front of school," Nick replied.

"But Scratch will be waiting for us," Mary stressed.

The walkie-talkie started chirping once again.

"What's up?" Nick asked.

"Just thought you should know that a Ford Crown Victoria with two guys, who had to be FBI, went flying past me a couple of minutes after the bikers rode past."

"Thanks Tommy. We may have to change our plans a bit," Nick explained. "When we get close to Cudahy, we'll call you, but instead of meeting us in front of school, you're going to have to walk up by the Carl's Jr. on Florence and Wilcox. We'll pick you up there. I'm afraid Scratch and his buddies will be cruising around Cudahy."

"You want me, who Scratch knows by sight, and who shot up his and his buddies' motorcycles, to walk all the way to Carl's on Florence from school? You must be nuts!" Tommy yelled into the walkie-talkie.

"That is nuts, Nick." Mary agreed. "We need to recruit some help."

"Who could we trust that would be willing to risk their life to help us out? Nobody, besides are you willing to cut someone else in our scheme and give up a third of your money?" Nick asked.

"No," Mary replied. "I'm willing to give up part of what's left of the three hundred thousand we picked up from the bikers and I know just the people to help us out."

"People? I was thinking only one other person was needed."

"I think it will take two," Mary explained. "Hear me out for a moment."

"Hold on Tommy, we'll get right back to you. We're working something out here so you won't be exposed to any danger," Nick said.

"At least any more danger than we're already in for," Mary added.

"What's your plan?" Nick asked.

For the next several minutes, Mary explained what she had in mind and Nick shared what he thought they should do. It took about ten minutes of discussion, but they soon both agreed on what they considered their best chance for success.

"I'll call my cousins and tell them what we need them to do," Mary said.

"Are you absolutely sure these two cousins of yours will do what you tell them?" Nick asked.

"They would jump in front of a moving truck on the 710 if I asked them to," Mary explained. "They are my mother's sister's only children. My mother saved their mother's life several years ago and they feel they owe my mother and her family a debt of honor. I helped arrange for them to come to California from Mexico and found jobs for them. I also paid for the truck they use on their job. They'll do whatever I ask without question."

"Just making sure," Nick said smiling.

For the next few minutes, Mary spoke in Spanish to her cousins explaining exactly what was to be done in detail.

"All taken care of," Mary announced. "One of them will park my car in front of the school and the other will follow in the truck. When Tommy sees my cousin get out of my car, have him come out the gate. The truck will be there to pick them both up. They know to drop Tommy at the Carl's Jr., then head out. Tell Tommy to wait inside until he sees the motorhome turn onto Wilcox. As soon as we make that turn, I'll make a sharp right into the Carl's Jr. parking lot. Tommy needs to run out and jump into the motorhome. Tell him I won't even stop, so be ready. We'll then turn onto Florence and head back to the freeway. Scratch and his buddies will no doubt be in the area, so tell him to stay alert."

Nick picked up the walkie-talkie, but decided it would be best if he used a cell phone. They both could be monitored, but any kid in the neighborhood with a walkie-talkie could listen in if he gave Tommy the information over

189

an easily monitored frequency. He called Tommy on the phone.

"Before I tell you the plan, I need to tell you that Mary and I realized we needed more help, so she called her two cousins who just moved here from Mexico for help, but don't worry, they don't know everything and they're not getting any of the drug money. If all goes as planned, we'll give them some of the money the bikers paid for their coke," Nick began to explain.

"If Mary says we can trust them, I believe her, and I do think we need all the help we can get," Tommy replied.

Nick was surprised at Tommy's compliance, but knew Tommy was tired and scared and the closer it came to the time of the exchange the more scared they all would become. "Watch for Mary's car. Her cousin will drop it off out front. When you see him get out of the car, you're to go out front and get into the pickup truck that'll be waiting. You'll need to bring with you the wallet from the second Capone gangster we stole back at Venice Beach and at least sixty thousand dollars of the bikers' money. Have another fifteen thousand in a separate bag. Give the fifteen thousand and the wallet to one of Mary's cousins. He'll then take you and the money to Carl's where you'll wait for us. When we turn onto Wilcox, head outside, because we'll be pulling quickly into the parking lot. If Scratch and his gang are around, they might try to stop us, so we have to keep moving. Mary will tell you the rest of the plan when you join us. Any questions?"

"Fifteen thousand is a little steep for a four-block taxi ride, but if that's what it takes, let's finish this." Tommy said.

"I'll explain it to you later. We'll see you in about an hour," Nick replied.

"Are you sure you understand exactly what you're to do?" Nick said to Mary.

"For the tenth time, yes, I know what I have to do. You worry too much," Mary said.

"You had better pull over. It's time I leave you."

Mary exited off the 60 freeway at the Nogales Street exit in Rowland Heights, and pulled to the side of the road.

"I'm going to miss you," Mary said wrapping her arms around Nick and pulling him close.

"*Pase lo que pase quiero decirte que me he enamorado de ti si tenemos éxito quiero vivir el resto de mi vida contigo en Paraguay o viajando alrededor del mundo. Me da iglual sea lo que sea con tal de que siempre estemos juntos tú eres mi matador de dragónes mi príncipe azul, mi razon de vivir,*" Mary spoke in Spanish as she had so often done before when she wanted to reveal her love to Nick, but yet could not confess her feelings.

"I've never been called a knight in shining armor before," Nick replied. "And I love you and look forward to spending the rest of my life with you as well. I know Paraguay may not be the best choice, but after we travel the world for a year or two, maybe we will find someplace where we both want to settle down. You too, are my reason for living."

Mary sat with her mouth agape. "You understood everything I just said?"

"Yeah!" Nick smiled.

"And you have understood me every time I have ranted in Spanish the past two days?"

"Yeah."

"And you understood what I said the first day I talked you and Tommy into letting me participate in your plan when I said you needed someone who could speak and understand Spanish so you wouldn't look like a couple of jerk-offs with your..."

"Yeah." Nick answered before Mary had to embarrass herself further.

191

"Are you telling me that you understand Spanish?"

"I am pretty fluent in speaking it too. So is Tommy," Nick replied.

Mary's face turned bright red. "I am so sorry I said some of those things."

"Well, I hope you meant most of what you said or I'm going to be pretty devastated. It's not often I get called a dragon slayer," Nick said smiling. "I love you more than I could ever have imagined loving someone."

"I love you more than the number of grains of sand on the Hawaiian Islands," Mary replied smiling.

"That was a simile," Tommy replied, returning Mary's smile.

"No, that was a hyperbolic conceit, and I really meant it," Mary said laughing.

"What's a 'hyperbolic conceit'?" Tommy asked.

"If you have to ask, ..."

"Here, take the walkie-talkie, and don't forget the AK," Mary reminded him, passing the pillow case holding the machine gun.

"And don't you forget that 50-caliber canon of yours," Nick replied.

Before Mary drove away, Nick removed all three locks from the trailer.

CHAPTER THIRTY-THREE

Scratch and Tiny stood alongside of their borrowed motorcycles in the parking lot of the Harley Davidson dealership in Baldwin Park along the 10 freeway. The blue van was parked next to them. Chilly was still asleep inside. "We got a call from a member of the San Bernardino Wild Ones who said he saw a motorhome pulling a trailer south on the 215 about an hour ago," Tiny said.

"Was it the one we're looking for?" Scratch asked.

"He said there was a painting of an Impala on the trailer," Tiny replied.

"That must be them," Scratch said. "Did he say which freeway they took?"

"He knows for sure it wasn't the 10, but believes it was either the 60 or 91 West," Tiny responded.

"There's a big fuck'n difference between the two," Scratch growled.

"We got men watching both freeways," Tiny said. "We'll know soon."

As they waited, three more bikers joined them.

"Wassup, Scratch? Long time no see," one of the new arrivals said in greeting.

"Horse, I didn't know you was out of jail," Scratch replied.

"Been out a couple of weeks. This here is Slim and riding the Fat Boy is Big Deuce. Boys, I'd like you to meet Scratch, one of the meanest sons-a-bitches around, next to me, that is."

Deuce and Slim both nodded their acknowledgement.

"Let's see the kilo you promised for our help," Horse said.

Scratch nodded his head and the van driver slid the door back and showed Horse the kilo of cocaine.

"It better not be bunk," Horse warned.

"Have I ever dealt in bunk?" Scratch answered, pissed off.

"Let me get this straight, if we help you take down this motorhome and steal the coke, you guarantee us ten more kilos?"

"That's right," Scratch replied.

"What kinda fight can we expect? These boys gonna have full auto?" Horse asked.

"I wouldn't think so, but you never know."

Horse didn't like the way Scratch answered the question. "How many of 'em you 'spect they'll be?"

"I know there are only two in the motorhome, but there might be another in a chase car. I would think no more than two or three with the buyer," Scratch guessed.

"Why don't we take 'hem down b'for the buy?"

"A buy means money, and if there's money, I'll cut you twenty-five percent," Scratch offered.

Horse looked at Big Deuce and Slim to see if they were agreeable to Scratch's offer. They both nodded slightly.

"I guess you gotcha self a posse," Horse said. "What's the plan?"

"The plan is we head over to Wilcox Street turf and wait to hear from our scouts," Scratch said. "Chances are the buy will go down somewhere near there."

No sooner had Scratch spoken did Tiny's cell phone began to ring.

"West on the 60 at Crossroads Parkway, got it." Tiny said. "Follow 'em, but don't let them know you're behind them."

194

"Sounds like they're heading for Cudahy, just like you thought," Horse said.

"We can be behind them in less than ten minutes if we hurry," Tiny explained to Scratch.

"We don't want to scare 'em away from the buy. You two try to beat them to Cudahy. Find a place near Wilcox to keep an eye on things. When you see them, make sure you call," Scratch said to Big Deuce and Slim.

Deuce and Slim both looked at Horse. They took orders from nobody but him. He nodded his approval and they immediately fired up their cycles and raced out of the parking lot and onto the 10 freeway.

Tiny's phone rang again. He answered and listened for less than five seconds, then closed his phone.

"The motorhome just passed the 605, they are stick'n to the 60," Tiny relayed the message.

"Call our scout at the 91 and tell him to move to the 710 and wait to hear from us," Scratch ordered

"Let's go raise some hell," Scratch said as he, Horse, and Tiny headed for the 60 freeway with the van close behind.

"It appears the motorhome has been spotted," Jenkins said to Smith. "Tiny just received a call and two of those bikers look to be leaving."

"Should we follow them?" Smith asked.

"No, we stick to Scratch. He'll lead us to the motorhome and our fortune," Jenkins replied.

"The rest of the gang looks to be getting ready to leave too," Smith said. "You know there are at least six of them now. Don't you think we may need some backup?"

"Who the hell are we going to call for backup?" Jenkins shot back. "Did you forget that we're about to steal the drugs and the money from these guys? I don't think the local DEA or Sheriff's Department would be too likely to assist us in our endeavor."

"Why can't we request a little backup without them knowing exactly what we have in mind. We can just ask the Sheriff to supply a car just as a show of force. We can tell them to stay in the car. We are bright guys, we can think of some reason to give them."

Jenkins was quiet as he thought about it. "You know, you just might be right. A sheriff's car might just be what we need. They don't necessarily need to know our names, just that we're DEA. Somebody will need to watch the prisoners while we remove the evidence," Jenkins laughed.

"Start the car, there goes Scratch," Smith said. "How are we going to get a hold of a Sheriff when we need to?"

"I haven't figured that out yet, but I will by the time we need them," Jenkins replied. "You know, it doesn't really need to be a Sheriff. A local police car will serve the same purpose."

"If it's the Wilcox Street gang behind all of this, like everyone seems to believe, then we should get the Cudahy police to help us out," Smith said.

"Where the hell is Cudahy, and do they even have a police department?" Jenkins asked.

"How the hell should I know," Smith laughed. "But I got a feeling Scratch is about to take us there."

Rudy was up early Saturday morning, pacing the bedroom floor of his mom's house on Clara Street in Cudahy.

"Chingado," Rudy exclaimed "Why in the hell hasn't Hector answered his cell phone?"

"You worry too much, *mijo*, Hector will get your car here in time for the carnival," Rudy's wife said, trying to reassure her frantic husband.

196

"It's not just the car I'm worried about, although if that *pendejo* Hector as much as rubs up against the paint job, I'll cut off his *juevos* and feed them to the dogs."

"Hector is your friend and a trusted soldier for Wilcox Street. He'll do exactly what he's expected to do," she said.

"I know, *mija*, but it's not Hector that worries me, it's those damn bikers, the Vegas Hardass Boys. Hector says they have acted like *mamons* the last two times he dropped off their supply. They haven't shown proper respect for Wilcox Street," Rudy explained.

"After the carnival, call a meeting and talk to the OGs. Let them know your concerns about these biker *putos*," his wife suggested.

"I had already planned to do that, but it still doesn't change the fact that Hector hasn't called or answered his cell phone.

"I'm going to send a couple of cars down to watch over the buy at the beach. This is one of the biggest loads Wilcox has ever moved. There's going to be a lot of money changing hands. I can't afford for anything to go wrong."

"Nothing will go wrong, but if it will make you feel better, send some of the boys down to watch. But hurry! I want you back in bed. Grandma can look after the *ninas*," Rudy's wife flashed a coy smile. Rudy got the message loud and clear.

CHAPTER THIRTY-FOUR

Tommy couldn't stop tapping his feet. He always tapped his feet when he was nervous. Actually, he tapped his feet, or his fingers, or shook his legs, pretty much constantly even when he wasn't nervous. He had done so for as long as he could remember. When he was young, he was just thought of as a very energetic young boy. Today, he would be labeled hyper-active or ADHD and placed in a special classroom, along with a dozen other kids just like him.

He had good reason for tapping his feet today. He was dressed as a Mexican gangster and about to walk outside carrying seventy-five thousand dollars and get in a car with two total strangers. Then he was to be dropped off at Carl's Jr., for god knows how long, and wait for a motorhome to pull in and slow down just enough for him to jump into it. The motorhome would probably have a half-a-dozen rabid bikers following it, trying to figure out a way to stop it and kill everyone inside. Not the way Tommy liked to start a Saturday morning.

When he had arrived at school an hour or so earlier, there were already several trucks pulled onto the school grounds setting up their carnival rides. Fortunately, the custodian on duty was over watching the activity and didn't see Tommy head into the classroom building.

Several times Tommy thought he heard someone outside in the hallway by his classroom. He was worried he would be discovered at any moment. He had brought his makeup kit back into his classroom along with changes of clothes and Nick's wig. He had plenty of cream to remove the makeup when the time came. He also had prepared two bags of money just as Nick had instructed him to do. For the fifth time in the past fifteen minutes, he checked to make sure the wallet stolen from the Westside Capone was in the bag he was to give to Mary's cousin.

Every thirty seconds Tommy would look out the classroom window to see if Mary's car had arrived. At last he finally saw it coming down the street. He watched as a young Hispanic man parked the car and got out. He never looked at the school, only down the street where a newer white Toyota Tundra pickup truck was slowly approaching.

"This is it," Tommy said, and took a deep breath. "It's show time."

Tommy listened for a moment at the door to make sure no one was in the hallway outside of his classroom. He knew it would be difficult to explain to the custodian why he was dressed that way, for he was certain the custodian would see through the costume and makeup

It took just ten seconds for Tommy to bound down the stairs and out the front door. Once out the door he slowed down and casually walked across the street where the white pickup truck was now waiting.

"Hola Señor Tommy, nosotros somos primos de Mary. ¿Tiene el parquete?"

As he was asked, Tommy passed the bag containing the wallet and fifteen thousand dollars to the cousin standing on the sidewalk.

"¿Hablas Espanol?

"Si, Yo hablo," Tommy replied.

"Por favor subase al carro. Creo que sería mejor si no los ven por aquí muy a menudo."

"Oh my goodness," Tommy said. It was one of those "dope" moments that Homer Simpson always had when he realized something that should have been completely obvious to him.

Tommy was made up to look like Hector, and Hector was from this neighborhood. Chances were someone was bound to recognize Hector and say something to Tommy or to someone about having seen Hector. How could he have forgotten something so blatantly obvious? He quickly climbed into the truck and pulled the baseball cap that he wore down around his face, hoping no one could clearly see him. He started to slide over into the middle of the front seat to allow the cousin to get in.

"*No es necessario. Mi hermano tiene un encargo.*"

Tommy watched as the cousin walked down the street. He was puzzled as to what was going on, but was too worried about being recognized to really be too concerned.

"*Yo espero en la troca contigo pero cuando mi hermano llegue te quedas solo.*"

"Thank you, I mean, *Gracias por tu ayuda.*"

The cousin drove slowly to Carl's Jr., taking a long way and avoiding Wilcox Street. He pulled into the parking lot and into the drive-through lane.

"*Necesito café, Mary nos levanté muy temprano y no tenemos tiempo para desayunar te gustaría algo.*"

"No thank you, I'm not..." Tommy was answering in English and realized Mary's cousin didn't speak English. "*Perdon por hablar en inglés,. No gracias, no tengo hambre.*"

"Ees okay, I understand a little English," the cousin replied.

Tommy smiled.

As the truck pulled up to the window, Tommy turned so as not to be seen by the cashier. The cousin paid and collected his breakfast and drove over and parked on the outskirts of the parking lot and began to eat. Tommy started shaking his legs out of nervousness, or anxiety, or both.

"Allí está mi hermano, te tienes que ir. Dios esté contigo."

"Y contigo también."

Tommy slowly opened the door. Before he got out, he checked to make sure he still had his cell phone and to see if he possibly, hopefully, had missed Mary and Nick's call to say they would be right there. He wasn't that lucky.

The cousin started the truck and Tommy knew it was the cousin's way of saying Tommy had to get out now.

Tommy exited the car and moved quickly to the restaurant. The cousin had handed him a newspaper when he got out of the car and he carried it in the same hand as the bag of money. With his other hand, he reached down to make sure he still had the 50 caliber Smith and Wesson in his waistband, although he didn't know why. He had forgotten to load it after the run in with Scratch, Chilly, and Tiny up near Barstow. The cousin backed out of the parking space and pulled up next to Tommy.

He rolled down his window and passed Tommy a cup of coffee." *Creo que vas a necesitar esto si no quieres regresar al mostrador para ordenar. Usa el periódico para cubrirle la cara."*

"Gracias," Tommy replied. Mary's cousin was wise to advise Tommy to take in the coffee so he wouldn't have to go to the counter to order. It was too risky. The paper was also a good idea to allow Tommy to keep his face concealed.

"Por nada. Buena suerte Señor Tommy," the cousin said and drove out of the parking lot and pulled in behind a large U-Haul truck.

"I'm going to need it," Tommy replied, as he opened the side door of the restaurant and sat at a booth next to the door. He immediately pulled the newspaper up in front of his face and began to pray that none of the dozen or so people inside was a friend of Hector's.

He had been sitting for less than two minutes, constantly tapping his feet, when he heard the roar of two motorcycles pull into the parking lot. He was so scared it felt as if his testicles shriveled up and disappeared. He glanced over his paper as the two bikers dismounted and removed their helmets. He let out a big sigh of relief when he realized neither of them was Scratch, Chilly, or Tiny. Still, it seemed a little too much of a coincidence. The two bikers entered, ordered coffee, and sat down at a booth right next to Tommy.

"Horse says we just gotta watch for this motorhome and call if we sees it," Slim explained.

"Fuck'n waste of time as far as I'm concerned," Big Deuce replied. "They know where the hell it is, didn't ya hear that phone call? They spotted it on the 60 freeway."

Tommy's cell phone began to vibrate. He opened it and whispered, "Hello?'

"I'm exiting the 710 onto Florence as I speak," Mary said. "Get ready."

"Just hurry," Tommy replied. "A couple of bikers are here and I overheard them say they're watching for a motorhome. I need to get out of here."

"You'll be out in just a couple of minutes. Just be ready and do exactly what we planned," Mary advised.

Mary pulled the motorhome and trailer onto Florence Avenue. There were two lights before she would reach Wilcox Street, but she hit both on green and didn't have to stop. She didn't want to have to stop anywhere in Cudahy. A car passed her going east on Florence and honked. Two people inside the car waved, but stopped in mid motion when they saw Mary was behind the wheel.

"Boy, do they look confused," Mary said to herself.

She pulled into the left-hand turn lane from Florence onto Wilcox. She would have to wait at least a minute for the light to change. She could see the two motorcycles parked in the Carl's Jr. lot, but could not see the bikers inside the restaurant. She looked in her rearview mirror, scared to reassure herself that no one was sneaking up behind her. At least she wasn't trapped in, for there were no cars in front of her waiting to turn. She watched as two cars pulled behind the trailer into the turn lane, but was unable to see who or how many were in each car.

"Look there, Big Deuce," Slim said, pointing across the street. "I bet that's the motorhome we s'posed to be watch'n for."

"Where the hell is Horse and those two Vegas bikers?" Big Deuce said.

"I don't see them nowhere," Slim replied. "Better call Horse."

The light on Wilcox changed from amber to red and the green arrow in front of her lit up. Mary hit the gas a little hard and the motorhome and trailer lurched forward.

Tommy slid out of his booth and moved towards the back door.

Slim moved to the front of the dining room to watch the motorhome drive by. "It's turning in here," Slim yelled to Big Deuce. "What should we do?"

"If they stop, maybe we should take 'um now," Deuce suggested.

As the motorhome disappeared behind the restaurant, the two bikers headed for the door where Tommy had just exited.

"Shit," Tommy said and turned around and walked back into Carl's and to the booth he had just left. The sack containing the sixty thousand dollars was lying on the bench.

He quickly grabbed it and turned to go back out the door, but the two bikers were now standing in his way.

"Excuse me," Tommy said hoping they would move out of his way, but they ignored him. Tommy took a deep breath and shoved his way in between the two bikers and out the door.

"Fuck'n beaner," Big Deuce said. "You're lucky I don't kick your ass."

"Forget about him," Slim said to Big Deuce. "What are we gonna do 'bout the motorhome?"

"Call Horse," Big Deuce replied.

The two bikers watched as the motorhome turned right in front of them and began to slow down. The door opened and Tommy jumped inside.

"That sum'bitch is with them," Big Deuce cried and ran towards the motorhome, but the door was already shut and the motorhome was turning back onto Florence Avenue.

"Thanks for the lift," Tommy said, sighing in relief. "I thought those two were going to catch me."

"I would have been more worried about some of the locals recognizing you," Mary said.

"I know, I had completely forgotten about that until your cousin picked me up," Tommy said.

"Everything should...," Mary started to speak.

"Look!" Tommy yelled, pointing up ahead. "There's Scratch and Tiny."

"With a few friends, it looks like," Mary responded. Mary accelerated, the tires screeching as she entered the south 710 onramp.

"What are we going to do? They will be right behind us."

"Not quite right behind us. Look." Mary exclaimed.

The three motorcycles had been joined by a fourth and a blue van had pulled to the side of the road behind where the bikes pulled over.

"They know we're here now," Tiny said, as the motorhome passed them with both Mary and Tommy staring their way.

"Makes no difference," Scratch said. "We'll lay back and wait for them to make their deal and then we'll move in."

"Uh-oh," Jenkins said. "Looks like we've found our motorhome."

"So has Scratch," Smith replied. "Just keep driving; we don't want them to recognize us."

Jenkins had no choice but to keep driving down Florence. He watched in his rearview mirror as the two bikers from Carl's Jr. joined the other three and the van. The bikes all made a U-turn to follow the motorhome, but were cut off by a large U-Haul truck that seemed to come out of nowhere and get in between the motorhome and the bikers.
The motorhome turned onto the onramp for the South 710. The U-Haul truck turned the same way, but suddenly stalled jerking to a stop and blocking the on ramp. Scratch and his buddies had to react quickly to keep from rear-ending the U-Haul truck.

"Get that piece of shit out of the way," Scratch yelled at the driver.

The driver only shrugged and pretended to try to start the truck. There was little room for the cycles to get around the truck. For about twenty seconds the bikes drove around in circles in the middle of Florence waiting for the truck to clear.

"This way," Scratch yelled and the six cycles and van cut across Florence to the south 710 freeway entrance from the westbound Florence lanes. No sooner had they crossed the street when the U-Haul finally started and headed down the ramp. By the time the bikers had circled around, the U-Haul was again in front of them blocking the single lane that merged onto the 710. The driver was not used to such traffic and didn't properly merge, coming to a complete stop.

"Go back to Mexico, damn wetback." Tiny said, as he jumped the median with his cycle to get around the stopped truck. The rest of the bikes followed. The van had to wait for another minute while the U-Haul truck finally was able to merge into traffic.

"Go, head back!" Smith screamed at Jenkins as he watched the cycles cut across the freeway and enter on the other south-bound ramp.

Jenkins turned sharply, making a U-turn in the middle of the intersection by the Carl's Jr. causing several cars to slam on their brakes to avoid a nasty collision. What neither Smith nor Jenkins saw was the local Cudahy police car sitting on Wilcox waiting for the light to change. As Jenkins punched the accelerator to catch up with the bikers and motorhome, the local police were right behind him with siren blaring.

"Shit, now what?" Smith yelled. "We can't afford to lose them."

Jenkins slammed on the brakes and slid to the curb. Smith was out the door by the time the car stopped. He was holding his badge in his hand as he ran to the police car.

Both the Cudahy cops had pulled their guns at the ready when they saw Smith running towards them.

"This is a god-damned emergency." Smith shouted. "We're following a major cocaine trafficker. We know the buy is about to go down. We need you to help. Follow us but stay far back, we can't let them see us until they're making the deal."

The cop looked at Smith's identification and at the Nevada plates on the car. "I don't know we'll have to check with..."

"We don't have time for you to check with anybody. They're probably monitoring the police bands and if you call in it will give us away. I'm ordering you to assist us," Smith said.

Neither of the Cudahy cops liked being ordered about, but they knew what they had to do. "Yes sir, we'll follow and do as you say."

"Good," Smith replied. "Just stay behind us, I'll let you know what to do when the time comes."

"We have to call in," one of the cops said.

"Then tell them you're going on your lunch break. I don't know, tell them whatever you need to as long as it's not the truth," Smith said.

"What kind of vehicle are we following?" one of the Cudahy officers asked.

"It's a motorhome pulling a trailer, but there are also a group of bikers and a blue van following it as well. We think they might be planning on ripping off the dealers, but you're to stay behind us until I tell you differently." Smith ran back to the car and Jenkins tore back in pursuit.

"What did you tell them?" Jenkins asked.

"I told them this was a federal emergency and I ordered them to follow us and to not to call in."

"Think they'll do as you told them?" Jenkins asked.

"They're a couple of dumb local cops. They'll do what I told them to do. Now catch up to those bikes, we don't want to lose them.

"What a *pendejo* that DEA agent was," Officer Lunas of the Cudahy Police Department said to his partner, Officer Garcia. "Are you thinking what I'm thinking?"

"I saw those Nevada plates," Garcia said. "And he did say it was a motorhome they were tailing."

"What about the bikers, do you think they could cause us trouble?" Lunas asked.

"That's probably why the DEA wants our help," Garcia replied. "What I don't understand is why there are only two DEA agents involved."

"I know, doesn't make sense. Remember Rudy told us that Wilcox is bringing in a big load this weekend. If the DEA was on to them, there'd be at least fifty agents and a couple of helicopters involved. Something just doesn't add up," Lunas remarked.

"I think those two agents are going to try to steal the cocaine and money for themselves, and they want our help in keeping the bikers from interfering or from doing the same thing."

"I think you might be right. Should we call Rudy? We might just get an extra bonus for letting him know," Lunas said.

"I don't have his number and I don't think we should call anybody else to try to get it," Garcia replied.

"You sure about that?" Lunas questioned.

"No. I do know no bonus is worth my life." Garcia replied.

"Let's just play along with those two DEA *pendejos* and make sure nothing happens to the deal, but if it does, we need to be in a position to deny we were anywhere near the place," Lunas explained.

"Better yet, this just might be that opportunity we've always talked about," Garcia said.

"You're right, this just might prove to be our ticket out of Los Angeles. If we play this right, we can't lose," Lunas replied.

"And then we'd have the Wilcox Street monkey off our backs," Garcia said. "I do like the extra money, but I hate working for a bunch of drug-dealing thugs."

"You talking about the gangsters or the police chief and his cronies?"

Lunas and Garcia both laughed.

CHAPTER THIRTY-FIVE

Paco and Chuy both awoke with a hangover.

"Chuy! Chuy! Wake up, Chuy, Hector will be here soon!" Paco yelled across the motorhome.

"*Chingado*," Chuy replied, trying to rub the pain from his eyes.

Paco knew better than to walk over and shake Chuy. He didn't want to startle him, especially since he was still clutching the shotgun he had fallen asleep with. Paco knew it hadn't been pumped, so no shell was in the chamber but, never-the-less, he wasn't about to take the chance. That was why Chuy had been selected to help guard the money and collect the drugs. He wasn't afraid to kill if the situation required him to do so.

It was already a little past nine in the morning and Hector was due at ten. Hector was never late. At least he had never been late the past three times Paco had made the buys. Paco also knew Hector would be in a hurry today. Paco had heard about the carnival and car show in Cudahy and knew Hector was bringing Rudy's new Impala out for the show. He knew the deal wouldn't take long. Just long enough for Chuy to move the cocaine from Hector's motorhome to his own. Paco would handle the exchange of the money, all ten million dollars. It was more money than he had ever seen in his life. It had been neatly boxed in four used Corona cases. Just like the cocaine would be neatly boxed in twenty-five Budweiser boxes. Oddly enough, no one seemed to pay any attention to campers on the beach exchanging cases of beer.

"You want a breakfast burrito," Paco asked Chuy. "I'll throw one in the microwave if you do."

"*Dos burritos, por favor,*" Chuy replied. "So this Hector, he come by himself?"

"Always," Paco replied, "But I know he's got backup cruising out on PCH if he needs it. I seen 'em!"

"Why don't he bring a homie along?"

"Don't need to when he got you to do all the work," Paco laughed.

"*Chingado!*"

"Where did that truck come from?" Tommy gasped as he watched in the mirror as a U-Haul truck stalled at the start of the onramp.

"The truck was part of the plan that Nick and I worked out. He knew they'd be behind us. We just don't want them crashing the party until the correct time. That's one of my cousins back in the U-Haul truck," Mary explained.

"I hope there's more to Nick's plan than that," Tommy said.

"Oh, there'll be much more, just wait," Mary said. "Did you remember to bring my Smith and Wesson?"

"Got it right here, but it's out of ammunition," Tommy said.

"Look in my bag. I brought extra, just in case," Mary smiled.

Tommy pulled the bullets from Mary's purse and tried to figure out how to put in the new bullets.

"You have to take the old cartridges out before you load the new ones," Mary said.

"I thought they flew out when you pulled the trigger," Tommy said.

"You're thinking of a semi-automatic. These you pull out. Here, give it to me and I'll do it," Mary said.

"You're driving," Tommy said.

"Like I don't multi-task when I drive to work in the morning? Give me the damn gun and bullets," Mary insisted.

Tommy did as he was told.

"You know I don't see those motorcycles anywhere back there," Tommy said.

"Oh, I'm sure they're there," Mary said. "They aren't about to let us get out of their sights now that they're so close."

As Mary took the connecting road to the 105 east off the 710, her cell phone started to ring. Mary looked at the incoming number before she answered.

"*Hola*," Mary answered. She listened for about twenty seconds, "*Gracias primo*."

"What did your cousin want?" Tommy asked.

"He just wanted to warn us that an unmarked car with two white men and a Cudahy police car are both following behind the bikers," Mary said.

"We should let Nick know," Tommy said.

"It really won't make any difference and Nick warned me not to use the walkie-talkie. There's too great a chance someone would be listening," Mary said.

"Ri-vet!" They both looked at each other when the heard the frogs croak.

"Ri-vet!"

"Please tell me that's not a frog in your pants," Mary said to Tommy.

Tommy reached down into his waistband and pulled out the walkie-talkie.

"Riv-et!" it croaked again.

"What happened to the cricket chirp," Tommy asked.

"Something in your pants must have pushed a button to change it. Well, aren't you going to answer it?" Mary said.

Tommy pushed the talk button. "Hello?"

"What took you so long?" Nick asked.

"The damn radio croaked instead of chirping like a cricket. We weren't sure what it was at first," Tommy replied.

"I know I said not to use these, but is everything going all right?" Nick asked.

"A couple of law enforcement friends seem to have joined the parade," Mary said. "They seem to be more interested in the bikers than in us. I really don't see it as being an issue."

"Let's hope not. Is everything ready to go?"

"Locked and loaded," Tommy replied. Mary looked quizzically at Tommy, who explained to her: "What? I heard it on Law and Order one day."

"I'll be in touch," Nick said, and ended the transmission.

Mary and Tommy rode in silence for the next five minutes, both thinking about what was about to go down. Thoughts about the money had long disappeared, now focus had shifted to survival. As the 105 came to an end, Mary took the south 605. Tommy was constantly watching in the rearview mirror, keeping track of the bikers and trying to see if he could spot the police cars tailing them.

"Do you think the bikers know they're being followed?" he asked Mary.

"I don't know. I keep looking for helicopters and there are none. You would think that if the police were on to us there would be at least one if not two or three helicopters in the sky. I haven't seen one all morning."

"Wouldn't there be more than two police cars?" Tommy asked.

"I would think so. My *primo* said the unmarked car had Nevada plates on it and the other was a local Cudahy police car," Mary explained.

"That doesn't make any sense," Tommy replied.

213

"You know all those Cudahy cops are on the Wilcox Street gang payroll," Mary said.

"I know, I read that article in the *L.A. Weekly*. Supposedly, they're the most corrupt police department in California. Do you think it's true?"

"I know it's true." Mary replied.

"Then why do you think they're following us?" Tommy asked.

"I think it was happenstance that they got involved. My cousin said he saw the police car pull over the unmarked car for making a U-turn in the middle of Florence."

"Just who is in that unmarked car?"

"It can't be any local Nevada police agency, at least not acting in an official capacity. It would have to be the FBI or the DEA to cross state lines tailing somebody and if that were the case where is all of their backup? Something is not right."

"Why are the Cudahy police now involved? Tommy asked.

"Sheer happenstance I would surmise. I bet they pulled the unmarked car over and then either volunteered or got drafted into helping out. Regardless, you can bet they're there to help make sure Wilcox completes the deal."

"You think the two men in the unmarked car are corrupt?" Tommy asked.

"It's beginning to look like everybody involved in this is corrupt," Mary said, as she eased the motorhome onto the transition road and onto the 405 South. As soon as we get off on Seal Beach Boulevard, you're going to have to take over driving. Hector will be expecting to see you and, now that the Cudahy police are involved, I'd bet Wilcox will have a few of their gangsters keeping an eye on things."

"What if some of the Wilcox gangsters try to join us? They'll know I'm not Hector," Tommy said, concerned.

"Remember what the real Hector told us. Paco only dealt with him and too many people around wasn't conducive to a calm, smooth transaction. We won't be bothered by any gangsters. It'll be tough enough trying to explain my presence."

"Once he sees those, he'll understand why you're with me," Tommy said, pointing to Mary's breasts.

"Don't embarrass me," Mary replied. "Hold on, I'm going to be taking this exit rather quick."

The tires squealed as Mary turned onto the Seal Beach exit. Right behind the trailer, the U-Haul truck that Tommy had seen in Cudahy turned sharply causing it to flip on its side and block the off-ramp. As Tommy watched, he saw one of Mary's cousins climb out of the cab. He was wearing a crash helmet. As soon as he was out, he ran into the bushes and up the embankment. Traffic was already beginning to snarl and stop on the 405 freeway.

"What the hell," Scratch said to himself as he watched the U-Haul flip on its side. There were several cars in front of the bikers that had all stopped to either assist the crash victims, who were nowhere to be found, or because they had no choice in the matter.

"That's the same fuck'n truck that blocked us in Cudahy," Tiny shouted to Scratch.

Scratch signaled for the bikers to follow as he headed to the shoulder. Nick had chosen well, for it was impossible for even the cycles to squeeze by.

"Cut through the grass," Scratch told the other bikers. "Tiny, go back and tell the van to pull up to where the cars merge onto the freeway and use it to get back to the street."

Tiny looked at Scratch in disbelief, but knew better than to question his judgment and turned around, driving

215

against the direction of traffic along the shoulder of the 405 looking for the van.

Horse was the first to try to get around the truck on the grass. The sprinklers were on and seemed to have been on for quite some time. It was like a marsh next to the exit ramp. Almost immediately, Horse's heavy Harley was stuck in the thick mud.

Big Deuce and Slim parked and went to help pull Horse's cycle out.

"Follow me," Scratch yelled at the two other bikers, who had been the scouts. He gunned his engine and roared under the overpass to where traffic was merging onto the 405 and turned against it, sticking as close to the shoulder as possible. Cars slowed and several stopped to avoid a possible head-on collision. Thirty seconds later the rest of the bikers and the blue van were attempting the same maneuver.

"Okay, you better drive from here," Mary said, as she waited for the light to change. "Any sign of them?"

"None at all. I think it must have worked," Tommy replied, sliding into the driver's seat.

Mary saw her cousin jump into the white Toyota Tundra waiting atop the overpass, and watched as it sped down the boulevard.

"You know the route," Mary said. "Take a deep breath and let's get this over with."

"My thoughts exactly," Tommy replied. "I only wish Nick were here."

"*Te amo con toda mi alma,*" Mary confessed.

"*No puedo vivir sin ti,*" Tommy replied, as he hit the accelerator as the light turned green.

"What the hell is going on?" Jenkins said to Smith.

216

"Looks like some kind of accident up ahead," Smith replied.

"Either that or it's some kind of diversion," Jenkins replied. "Look, one of the bikers is heading this way."

They watched as Tiny pulled up next to the blue van.

"Heh, look!" Jenkins yelled. "Scratch and his buddies are taking off."

"And the van looks to be following them," Smith said. "Get around these cars, don't lose them."

"What the hell are they doing?" Jenkins asked.

"They're turning back onto the onramp. That's idiotic." Smith said.

"It's what has to be done," Jenkins said, and braked sharply, turned a hard right on the gore point and headed down the shoulder, honking his horn and praying traffic would get out of his way.

"I ain't gonna do that," Garcia said to Lunas. "Those guys are fucking nuts."

Lunas and Garcia pulled along the shoulder and watched as the DEA agents drove against the merging traffic.

"Head on down the 405 and take the Warner exit. I heard Rudy talking about Bolsa Chica State Beach as one of the spots he used to make the exchanges. I'd bet that's where the motorhome is headed," Garcia said.

"Better than trying to commit suicide like those chumps," Lunas replied.

Garcia turned on the siren and lights as Lunas merged into the traffic.

217

CHAPTER THIRTY-SIX

"Somebody's waving at me," Tommy called to Mary.

"Wave back," Mary said.

Tommy, disguised as Hector, smiled at the car full of gangster soldiers and waved back to them.

"Did you recognize any of them?" Mary asked

"No, but they sure seemed to know the motorhome and me. They must be Wilcox soldiers.

"Probably sent as your protection," Mary suggested. "Nick said we would probably see some backup."

Tommy turned right into the Bolsa State Beach parking lot and pulled up next to the kiosk.

"Mr. Contreras, nice to see you again," the man said, smiling. "Just stopping by for the day, I see. I reserved your usual space." He handed Hector a pass to place in the window.

"Thanks," Hector replied.

The attendant smiled, looked around to make sure no one was watching, and then flashed the Wilcox Street gang sign. Tommy had seen his students do the same almost daily and he himself had even practiced it at one time. He quickly flashed the sign back to the attendant and he was waved on through.

The access road inside the beach parallels PCH. Just before the motorhome reached its assigned site, Scratch and his gang were driving down PCH and saw the motorhome. They continued on for a couple of hundred yards past where the motorhome was pulling in. He made a U-turn and the rest of the bikes and the van followed.

"Three of you wait here. The rest of you go back past the motorhome a couple of hundred yards and wait there. Horse, Tiny, and I will head inside the beach with the van. The four of us should be enough to take care of business," Scratch explained. "But keep a sharp eye out. If there's trouble, come in fast."

Big Deuce and Slim looked to Horse for permission to do as Scratch said. Horse nodded his head and they both headed up past where the motorhome was parking.

"There it is," Jenkins said to Smith. "Looks like Scratch and his boys are already getting into position."

"We could sure use those damn cops now. Those chicken-shits wouldn't go up the onramp. I don't know where the hell they went," Smith said.

"Well, I know where we need to go," Jenkins said and pulled quickly into the park.

Rudy's cell phone began to ring.

"This better be good news," Rudy said.

"We saw Hector pulling into the campground," Nacho said.

"Everything look alright?"

"Everything looked fine. He smiled and waved to us," Nacho said.

"The *pendejos* cell phone must be busted," Rudy exclaimed, feeling much better now that he knew all was going according to plan.

"Let's head to the carnival," Rudy said, turning to his wife.

"I'm tired of you always talking on that damn phone. Why don't you leave it at home so we can enjoy the carnival as a family without worrying about business?" She explained.

It was a tough thing for Rudy to do, but he tossed his phone on the bed and they headed out the door.

"*¿Que pasa*, Hector?" Paco said, as Hector pulled the motorhome to a stop.

219

"I been sick," Tommy replied, trying his best to sound like Hector. "Let's get this done so I can drop off Rudy's car and get in bed. I feel like shit."

"You look like shit too, amigo," Paco laughed. Then he noticed Mary.

"What's this shit, what's the *puta* doing here?" Paco said.

"Rudy sent her along 'cause I was so sick. She helped drive."

"I hope she helped with something else too, amigo," Paco smiled

Mary paid no attention to Paco and closed the bedroom door.

Tommy led Paco outside and to the side door of the trailer. Chuy was already there waiting. When Hector saw him, he stopped.

"This is Chuy. The OGs sent him along to help protect the money," Paco explained. Tommy nodded at Chuy, who nodded in return.

"What about the code?" Hector asked.

"*Chinga* that stupid code. I know it's you," Paco said.

"Shit's inside the trailer. Twenty-five boxes," Tommy said.

"Chuy, get the money and bring it in here. I want to take a look at Rudy's Impala. He's been talking about it for weeks. Before Tommy could stop him, Paco entered the side door of the trailer.

"Is there a light in here, I can't see shit?" Paco said.

No light," Tommy answered. Paco opened the door on the other side to let in more light.

"That's more like it," Paco said. The rear end of the car could now be seen and Paco whistled at the incredible paint job. "That paint job must have cost thirty thou alone."

"At least," Tommy replied. "We need to handle business," Tommy said, trying to speed things up.

Chuy brought the third Corona case over and dropped it behind the Impala and picked up two more Budweiser cases and carried them to their motorhome.

"Ten million is a lot of money," Paco said. "I hope you got some backup to keep it safe."

"Lots of backup," Tommy replied.

"Yeah, Chuy and I saw a car full of your homies cruising back and forth out there."

Tommy opened the trunk of the Impala and removed the two canvas bags Nick had placed in there earlier. He pulled the money out of the Corona cases and spread it evenly between the two bags, then tossed them in the trunk of the Impala, but didn't close the trunk.

Chuy was just about through moving the Budweiser cases from the trailer to the motorhome when Mary came strutting up next to the trailer. Tommy and Paco came out of the trailer and Chuy stopped what he was doing and watched as Mary bent over to pick something up off the ground.

"Mama, you really turn me on," Paco said, as Mary looked up and smiled.

"Looks like I turn your homie on too," Mary said, making fun nodding towards Chuy.

Paco and Tommy looked over and laughed at Chuy's embarrassment.

All four of them turned when a trash truck pulled up and one of the trashmen walked over and grabbed the trash bag out of the can near Paco's motorhome. He quickly fit a new trash bag into the can and threw the full one into the back of the truck. His partner had done the same on the opposite side of the street. They both got back in and drove to the other side of Hector's trailer where they repeated the process.

Jenkins and Smith had entered the beach campground and pulled their car into the far end of the road that led to Hector's motorhome and trailer. The road was blocked by the trash truck forcing them to turn into an empty space and head on foot to Hector's trailer.

Garcia and Lunas had reached the campground and arrived at the opposite end of the road nearer the trailer just as Jenkins and Smith exited the car.

"Looks like the deal is still in progress," Garcia said. "Those two *pendejos* are moving in on foot."

"Here come the bikers," Lunas said, as Scratch, Horse, and Tiny approached with the van right behind them.

"Decision time," Garcia said. "We gonna help out Wilcox Street or are we gonna try to get a piece of the action for ourselves?" Just as he spoke, the car of Wilcox gangsters pulled onto the side of the road and they all piled out having seen the bikers and knowing something was going down.

"It's about to get too out of hand," Garcia said, as he reached up and turned on the police car's siren.

CHAPTER THIRTY-SEVEN

The wailing of the siren froze everyone in their tracks. The police car shot forward and blocked the bikers and the van from continuing down the road. The Wilcox gangsters all stopped next to their car to try to figure out what to do now that the bikers were blocked.

"What the hell are those asshole cops doing?" Jenkins said. "I thought you told them to make no move until we gave them the signal?"

"I did, god-dammit, now we have to hurry," Smith replied.

"It's the cops, we got to get out of here," Paco yelled, as he and Chuy grabbed the last four Budweiser cases from the trailer. In his haste, Chuy tripped and the four bundles inside one of the cases came flying out. One of the bundles hit the open door of Paco's motorhome and split open. The towel inside the fake bundles of cocaine caught on the corner of the door and hung there while the two bricks, the packages of sheets, and the socks all tumbled to the ground.

"What the fuck," Paco yelled.

"*Chigada*," Chuy yelled, grabbing his shotgun.

"Everybody, freeze!" Jenkins yelled, as he raced around the front of Hector's motorhome with his gun drawn.

Paco dropped the two cases in his hand and Chuy lowered his shotgun, but didn't drop it.

"Where are the other two?" Smith asked.

Paco turned around, but Hector and his *puta* were nowhere to be seen.

The trailer shook as the engine of the Impala roared to life. The rear door had been opened during all the commotion. The Impala tore from the trailer, shooting into the air, making a loud scraping noise as it landed on the asphalt road.

"That *mamón* Hector stole our money." Paco yelled. "He stole our ten million dollars."

"What about the cocaine?" Smith asked.

"Ain't no cocaine, nothing but this shit," Paco said, pointing to the sheets, bricks, and socks on the ground.

Scratch had just rounded the back of the trailer and heard what Paco had said. He was holding a 9MM Glock.

Jenkins, Smith, Scratch, Chuy, and Paco all looked at each other as if it were a scene from *The Good, the Bad, and the Ugly*. They all knew what was at stake and they all intended to be the one to get their hands on the ten million dollars. Instantly, they all took off running in different directions to give chase to Rudy's Impala.

Paco was the first to get moving since he and Chuy were right next to his motorhome. He didn't even bother to disconnect any of the power or water lines he had connected when they arrived the previous evening and ripped them from the trailer space in their haste.

Jenkins and Smith headed for their car, but it was now blocked in by the trash collectors. They quickly returned to Hector's motorhome. The keys were still in the ignition and Smith jumped into the driver's seat. He shifted into reverse. forgetting that the trailer was hooked to the motorhome. It jackknifed on him and plowed into the motorhome parked across the road.

"Damn!" he shouted.

"Cut it hard right," Jenkins shouted.

Smith did and circled through the empty space Paco's trailer had just vacated. The trailer had hooked the bumper of the motorhome across the street and now, as Smith turned and accelerated, he dragged the neighbor's motorhome with

224

him, at least for about twenty feet until the bumper and much of the front panel ripped away.

Across the street, the bikers that had been told to watch started their cycles and moved to intercept the Impala and the motorhomes as they headed to the beach exit. The Wilcox gangsters saw this and made an effort to get in the way. Threats were made by showing the firepower each other possessed but, as yet, no one was ready to shoot until they knew for sure what was going on and exactly who to shoot at.

"There goes Hector," Garcia said, as he watched the Impala race towards the exit.

"What's he doing?" Lunas asked.

"I have no idea, but if he expects to get away he better stop it," Garcia replied.

Nick had been waiting inside the trailer the entire time, ready to come out blasting if necessary. He had the AK, but was praying he wouldn't need to use it. The siren sounding was the perfect distraction to allow Tommy and Mary to get into the trailer and then the Impala. Tommy slammed the trunk closed after making sure the two bags were still inside.

"Paco knows the bundles are fake." Mary yelled, as she jumped into the car.

"It doesn't matter now," Nick said and hit the gas.

The Impala flew out of the trailer hitting hard. The impact caused the Impala's hydraulics to malfunction and the car began to raise and lower at random at all four lift areas.

"What's going on with the car?" Tommy shouted.

"I think the drop screwed up the hydraulics," Nick said.

As the car slowed at the exit, the front end began to hop up and down.

225

"Can't you make it stop doing that?" Tommy asked.

"I would if I knew what was making it do that," Nick replied.

Mary hit a switch and the entire car seemed to lift two feet into the air.

"At least it stopped bouncing," Tommy said.

The car dropped down like a rock bottoming out on the pavement.

"Green light, go, go, go!" Mary shouted.

As Nick hit the accelerator, all three of the passengers were jarred when Paco's motorhome rammed into the back of the Impala. Nick floored it and headed up PCH, pulling away from Paco.

"That's going to leave a mark," Tommy said.

"Yeah, Rudy isn't going to be very happy," Nick replied.

"Get next to him and shove him out of the way," Jenkins yelled at Smith.

Paco's motorhome had stalled when he ran into the back of the Impala.

Smith pulled next to Paco and swung over when the trailer was next to him. The trailer smashed into Paco's motorhome, but did little more than scrape and dent the aluminum side panels on each. By the time Smith stopped fishtailing, Paco was right behind him.

Big Deuce, Slim, and the two scouts had pulled their Harleys up next to both motorhomes waiting for Scratch and Horse to catch up and tell them what to do. They were not the kind of men to make decisions or even think on their own. They took orders, and until they had orders, they would do nothing.

"*Chingado*," Paco cried out when he saw the bikers on either side of him

"I'll get rid of them," Chuy said, as he pulled up his shotgun.

"Hold on, I'll take care of these *pendejos*," Paco said, as he swerved sharply to the right and then to the left.

Big Deuce and Slim were alert and ready for Paco's attempt to run them off the road and slowed to avoid contact. The two scouts on the right of Paco's motorhome were not as lucky and went sailing into the marshy wetlands next to the PCH. One was fortunate in that he skidded on the gravel over the bank and just fell into the swampy muck; the other, not so lucky, hit a raised embankment and he and his cycle parted ways as they both flew through the air and into the marsh.

"Tommy, pass me some of that sixty thousand you brought," Nick said as they approached the PCH and Seal Beach Blvd. intersection. "Let's test my plan."

The Impala pulled to a stop at the corner and continued its up and down random motion. Even though they had a green arrow allowing them to turn right, Nick hesitated. He took a handful of hundred-dollar bills and tossed them out the window as he turned the corner. Cross traffic had just started to pull across PCH when cars suddenly stopped, as their drivers and passengers leapt out and began grabbing the bills fluttering in the wind and falling to the ground. Within seconds, most of the occupants of the cars waiting at the stoplight to continue up PCH were also out trying to collect the money. Nick's plan worked and his entourage tailing behind were all delayed as the traffic snarled.

"Watch him, watch him," Smith yelled to Jenkins as he swerved to the shoulder trying to pass the cars and people filling the intersection.

"He must be headed back for the freeway," Jenkins said. "Probably back to Cudahy."

Jenkins and Smith both were jarred as they spun sideways as Paco rammed his motorhome into the back of the trailer. Several of the people trying to collect the money on the ground barely managed to get out of the way, although several of their cars were smashed by the fishtailing trailer.

"Take him now," Chuy yelled, as Paco's motorhome pulled alongside of Jenkins and Smith. Both motorhomes accelerated up Seal Beach Blvd ramming their sides together as they went.

Scratch, Tiny, and Horse, followed by the blue van, pulled into the southbound lanes of PCH to get around the chaos, but were quickly stopped by the congestion that now clogged the intersection. The bikes were able to quickly weave their way through the scattered cars, but the van was caught up in the melee, until it was able to ram into two smaller cars opening a path.

Behind them Garcia and Lunas had their siren screaming and their lights ablaze, but those collecting the bills failed to heed the warning. The two drivers whose cars had just been smashed by the van tried to flag down Lunas and Garcia's approaching police car. The drivers were standing in the path the van had just taken and Lunas had to swerve to avoid them, smashing one of the driver's cars and pushing it into two others, before rushing on.

The car of Wilcox gangsters had caught up to Big Deuce and Slim, and tried, as had Paco, to run the two bikers off the road. They were more concerned with stopping the bikers than with the stopped traffic in front of them and, at the last minute, the driver had to swerve sharply to the right to avoid smashing into several of the cars stopped at the intersection. The gangster's car flew into some bushes and through a chain link fence surrounding the Seal Beach Naval Weapons Storage installation.

The base had gone on alert when the U-Haul truck had overturned on the Seal Beach offramp less than an hour ago. There were fears of a terrorist attack. Now, with the breaching of the outer fence, they thought their fears had been realized and all the fury and might of the personnel assigned to guard the facility came down on the gangster's car like swarming hornets.

The Wilcox Street gangsters were no longer participants in the chase. The scene around the intersection was one of complete chaos as cars were strewn everywhere and people walked everywhere talking on their cell phones and looking for more of the hundred-dollar bills.

CHAPTER THIRTY-EIGHT

"I don't see any of them yet," Tommy said, as he stared out the rear window of the Impala.

"Try another of those switches," Nick said to Mary. "All this jumping up and down is making me seasick."

"We're not in the water," Mary corrected, "It is making you motion sick."

"Yes 'ma'am," Nick replied, smiling.

"Here they come," Tommy said.

"Here who comes?" Nick asked, trying to see in his rearview mirror.

"The two motorhomes are in the lanes behind us and three of the bikers and a blue van are coming on the wrong side of the street."

Several other cars had also turned or continued on Seal Beach Blvd., hoping the occupants of the Impala would throw more money from the car. The Impala was approaching Westminster Avenue, and Nick had a decision to make. Would he stop at the red signal ahead, or run it? If he stopped, he knew the bikers would surely catch up to him, and chances were, they all had weapons and were inclined to use them after the incident in Barstow. If he ran the light, he was confident he could avoid the cross traffic and it really made no difference if he attracted the attention of a police car, for that was inevitable.

"Hold on," Nick said, "We're blowing through this intersection." He turned onto the right shoulder barely slowing down.

"Mary, you look right, Tommy, you look left," Nick instructed.

"Okay on the left," Tommy shouted.

"Just go quickly!" Mary pleaded.

Nick floored the gas and the Impala shot through the intersection, just missing the rear of an SUV and causing two others to slam on their brakes and turn to avoid a collision. Tommy and Mary had both screamed and ducked down to brace for impact.

"Well, that went well, considering," Nick said, as the sound of screeching brakes could still be heard. Nick had bought himself enough time to make it safely to the freeway.

"Pass me a few thousand more dollars," Nick asked.

"Let us do it this time, Mary insisted. "You need to concentrate on driving."

"Are you inferring that my driving is less than adequate?" Nick replied.

"On the contrary, I think you're doing an exceptional job of driving. It's all the other cars on the road I'm concerned about," Mary said smiling.

Nick turned onto the north 405 onramp. "Wait till the other lane merges with this one," Nick advised.

Tommy and Mary did as they were told and as soon as the two lanes merged tossed another six thousand dollars out the car windows. Immediately, the offramp was blocked by cars.

"That should tie them up for a while," Nick said.

"Hector sure knows what he's doing," Garcia said to Lunas. "What a smart idea tossing out a little money to slow everybody down."

"Smarter than you and me. How we gonna explain plowing through those parked cars like that?" Lunas asked.

"We'll just tell them we were in pursuit of several armed gangsters shooting at each other from their vehicles," Garcia replied.

"If that's the case, we better call it in to the CHP for backup to cover our asses."

"Good idea, but don't mention the Impala. Only the cycles, van, and motorhomes," Garcia said.

"What about Hector's motorhome? The one that belongs to Wilcox Street?" Garcia asked.

"We have to report it. It might be the only way to keep the heat off the Impala," Lunas said.

"I'll call it in," Garcia replied.

Big Deuce and Slim had finally caught up to Paco's motorhome. Big Deuce pulled up along the passenger's side signaling them to pull over and showing them the pistol, he had pulled from his belt, to get the point across. Chuy smiled, lifted his shotgun, and pumped it. Big Deuce got the message just in time ducking, as a basketball size hole blew out the side of the motorhome, right where his head had been five seconds earlier.

"*Changada*," Paco yelled. "Don't fuck'n kill anybody. At least not yet. Wait till we get the money back. Then we'll kill all those *pendejos*."

"Watch out," Chuy yelled, just as Smith and Jenkins slammed their motorhome into the side of Paco's. Parts were falling off everywhere as the two continued their demolition battle as they headed up the boulevard.

"Hard right, hard right," Chuy yelled. Paco had been too worried about Hector's motorhome to see the stopped traffic at Westminster. He turned sharply onto the right shoulder and plowed through the intersection without slowing. Fortunately, cross traffic had stopped after the Impala had barreled through moments before and the pedestrians standing around got safely out of the way as they heard the dueling motorhomes approach. Paco was now out in front of the chase pack.

"Ram that SOB." Jenkins yelled to Smith.

"I am god-dammit." Smith replied.

"Blam!"

"That sounded like a shotgun," Jenkins said.

"Well, it wasn't at us if it was. Where are the bikers and that cop car?" Smith asked.

"The bikes are about to pass us on the left, along with that blue van. The cops are way back there," Jenkins replied.

"I'll put a stop to that," Smith said and pulled sharply to the left to both avoid the stopped traffic and slow the cycles down.

"The Impala is turning onto the 405 north," Jenkins said.

"Good, at least we won't have any cross traffic to contend with. Hold on." Smith said, as he hit the accelerator and the trailer fishtailed to the left smashing into the blue van, but only managing to slow it down.

"Where am I?" Chilly said, as he sat up in the back of the blue van. He had been sleeping since he'd been hit on the head along the Interstate 40 in Barstow.

"Just stay down," the van driver advised. "Things could get a little hairy."

"What ya talk'n 'bout," Chilly said, and began to stand.

At that very moment, Hector's motorhome sideswiped the van. Chilly lost his balance and went headfirst into the side door, knocking him out.

"I told you to stay down, you dumb ass," the driver said, and continued the chase.

It was difficult for Scratch and Horse to communicate with their gang members and coordinate any real plan to stop the Impala. Horse and Slim had seen what happened when

233

Big Deuce pulled up next to Paco's motorhome, and weren't about to repeat that mistake. Scratch knew his best chance at getting the money was to stick close to the Impala and either pin it in when it stopped or run it off the road. The chances of the bikes running it off the road weren't good, but the motorhomes would have no problem doing so with their bulkier weight and size. He and his boys just needed to be there when it happened. He knew he had numbers on his side and probably had them outgunned. At least he knew he had the two DEA agents outgunned. He had heard the shotgun blast, and if that was the biggest and baldest weapon they had, then he knew he had them outgunned as well. His only concern was that cop car that was chasing them. He figured it was there to help out Hector. He would have to do something about them.

CHAPTER THIRTY-NINE

"KFWB news 98! This is traffic on the 'ones'," the announcer said. "Let's go to Jeff in jet-copter 98."

"Thanks Bob, here's one you don't hear every day. According to the CHP, someone is driving north on the 405 throwing handfuls of hundred-dollar bills out the window. You can be sure this is causing quite dangerous conditions as people stop to pick up the money. I would recommend that you avoid the Long Beach section of the 405 if possible. Also, in Seal Beach we have reports of some kind of chase going on that involves several vehicles and motorcycles. There have been several accidents reported because of this and CHP is on the way to investigate."

"Do you think these two reports are related somehow, Jeff?"

"They are near each other, but I have no information that indicates they are," Jeff said.

"Well, I think it's good advice telling people to stay out of the area, but think about it, if you knew someone was driving down the freeway throwing out handfuls of hundred-dollar bills, would you avoid the area?"

"Let's hope they do, Bob. I'm headed that way now to check it out. This is Jeff in jet-copter 98. I'll report back in ten minutes."

Nick, Tommy, and Mary were almost to the 710 interchange when the motorcycles came into view.

"If that damn thing would stop going up and down, we could go a lot faster," Nick complained.

"I've hit just about every switch there is to hit," Mary said. "There isn't much else I can do."

"I know, and thanks for trying. I just hate being dizzy. Yikes, looks like traffic is backing up."

"I can see both the motorhomes coming," Tommy said

"Throw out some more money," Nick ordered, as he pulled onto the 710-north transition.

Tommy and Mary did as instructed, but the wind blew all the bills off the transition and into the Los Angeles River channel below.

"That didn't work," Tommy said.

"I guess we're just going to have to outrun them," Nick said.

"That might be a problem," Mary replied. Two of the bikers were now on either side of the Impala and two were in front trying to slow them down.

"Just stay on the accelerator," Tommy advised, "they'll get out of the way."

"Here come the motorhomes," Mary announced.

Jenkins and Smith had managed to pass Paco on the 405. Paco had convinced Chuy it would not be wise to shoot at DEA agents, so Smith and Jenkins were able to move ahead with only minor sideswiping occurring.

"Watch out for that blue van," Mary said. "I think it's going to try to get in front of us and stop.

Nick could see the van three lanes over starting to pass the truck in the lane next to the bikers.

"Hold on," Nick yelled, and suddenly swerved in front of the two bikers on the left, forcing them into the path of the large truck.

The semitruck was a large open truck carrying a carnival ride. At the front of the truck was some type of large supporting base for holding the big Viking ship that was attached to the center of the truck. It looked like the kind of carnival ride that would swing you back and forth high into the air. At the very end of the trailer was a large dragon's head with two long, white fangs. This head would be attached to the front of the Viking ship to complete the effect.

As the two bikes swerved to avoid Nick, so did the semi, locking its brakes and jackknifing in the middle of the freeway. Most cars were able to avoid it, although there were several minor fender benders. The straps holding the ship and dragon's head broke free and the ship tumbled off the trailer onto the freeway, the head flying into the air and smashing into the passenger windshield of Hector's motorhome where it lodged in tightly as if it were hooked to the front of the boat.

"Look out," Smith yelled, as the huge heavy plastic dragon's head broke free and flew into the windshield.

Jenkins dove towards the back, avoiding the head, but was covered in the shattered safety glass of the windshield.

"Get rid of that thing," Smith shouted.

Jenkins tried several times, but the head was tightly lodged in place, making a comical picture as the motorhome continued in the chase. The first lights of the approaching CHP cars were now appearing in everyone's rear view mirrors.

Without asking, Tommy grabbed another handful of hundreds and tossed them out the window. It did nothing to slow the bikes, van, or motorhomes, but it did bring the freeway to a halt, stopping the CHP from catching up.

"That's pretty spooky-looking," Mary said, pointing to Hector's motorhome. "It looks like a dragon is chasing us."

"This is Jeff in KFWB jet-copter 98 over the 710 freeway and Del Amo Blvd. We have quite a mess down here. It looks like a carnival truck has jack-knifed in lanes spilling its ride onto the freeway. Dozens of cars have come to a stop, even though there's room on the right for traffic to get by.

Apparently, the report about someone throwing money out of their car is true. I can see bills all over the freeway and people running everywhere trying to pick them up. Now the southbound side is stopping as several of the bills have flown over there as well."

"Jeff, this is Bob, is the CHP on the scene?"

"I see three CHP cars, but they're trapped inside this mess of stopped cars. They won't be going anywhere until this mess is sorted out."

"Do they know who is throwing out the money?" Bob asked. "Is it some kind of publicity stunt?"

"From the CHP scanners I just heard that they were chasing two motorhomes, a blue van, and several motorcycles that all might be involved with the money. If it's a publicity stunt, it's gotten completely out of hand and is putting the lives of a lot of people in jeopardy. I'm going to head north and see if I can spot anything up ahead."

"Thank you, Jeff."

"This if Jeff, in jet-copter 98, for KFWB, news 98."

As the news report ended, hundreds of drivers all converged on the 710 freeway for their chance to score the hundred-dollar bills.

Suddenly, the Impala started bucking up-and-down like a wild bronco.

"Yikes!" Nick yelped. "There's no way we can get away with the car doing this."

Mary started hitting switches again and smoke poured from the control box. "Now we have some issues," Mary said. The car finally stopped bucking and went back to its random corner lifting.

"Everybody's about to catch us again." Tommy shouted, "and it looks like a CHP unit up ahead on the side of the freeway."

"Time for plan B," Nick said.

"You have a plan B?" Mary asked.

"Actually, plan A was really plan B, and plan C won't work now, so this is really plan D or E, I get them confused," Nick replied. "Hold on," Nick cut sharply to the right crossing two lanes of traffic and headed down the Artesia Blvd. exit ramp. Behind him cars, motorhomes, motorcycles, trucks and vans all slammed on their brakes and followed.

"What the hell is going on?" Smith shouted. "Who are all these people?"

"I think they're after the money Hector is tossing out," Jenkins said.

Suddenly, Paco came roaring past in his motorhome knocking several of the cars out of the way that had gotten in-between the Impala and the motorhomes.

"Tommy, more money," Mary said.

Tommy grabbed several thousand dollars and passed half of it to Mary.

"Wait till I turn onto Artesia," Nick said. As he skidded around the corner to the right, Mary and Tommy threw the money out the window. Several of the cars that had been following screeched to a stop and the occupants ran out and began grabbing the money. It gave Nick, Mary, and Tommy just the break they needed to put some distance between them and their pursuers.

CHAPTER FORTY

"This is Jeff in jet-copter 98. The mess on the north 710 only seems to get more bizarre as time goes by. I'm looking at a motorhome pulling a trailer that has a giant dragon's head attached to the front of the motorhome. It appears to be chasing, or is being chased, it's hard to tell, by a second motorhome. There also seems to be six motorcycles and a blue van involved somehow. I'm not sure, but there could be six or seven other cars also participating in this chase."

"Jeff, this is Ruth, is it one of the motorhomes that's tossing the money?"

"Hello Ruth, I'm not really sure. They all have exited onto Artesia Blvd east-bound right now and it looks like there are several cars stopped and people picking up money at the end of the offramp. Wait a minute, both the motorhomes have turned onto the bike path on the west side of the Los Angeles River. I see two motorhomes and now the cycles and blue van are following. There're also several cars behind them now. Looks like a couple of the television news copters have joined me here. This is the first chase I've ever covered that so far doesn't involve any police or the CHP. Rather strange."

"Well Jeff, get back to us as things continue to develop."

"Will do, Bob, this is Jeff in jet-copter 98."

"Are you sure about this?" Mary asked.

"Yeah, is there enough room under all of these bridges for us to get through?" Tommy asked.

"It's a bike path. A person sitting on a bike is taller than this car," Nick explained.

"Maybe not when it's raised way up in the air," Tommy replied.

"We have no worry about the overpasses. We only need to worry about everybody behind us," Nick said. "And if you haven't noticed, this path is so narrow that no one can pass us."

"I think you spoke too soon," Mary said, as a parallel road suddenly appeared right next to the path they were on. Paco's motorhome started gaining on the Impala and Chuy readied to fire at the Impala just as a news copter swooped down into the river channel. Chuy pulled the shotgun back, backed off the accelerator, and pulled in behind the Impala. It was the kind of break Smith and Jenkins had been waiting for.

"Pull up next to him and hurry before we run out of road," Jenkins said, looking up ahead.

Smith pulled Hector's motorhome up next to Paco's. Paco looked over to flip Smith off just as Smith rammed into the side of Paco. The bike path was too narrow and there was no shoulder to forgive the swerve of Paco's motorhome. It wasn't a sheer drop, nor was it a gradual incline, but the cement embankment into the river bed was steep enough that had Paco not turned into it, he would have rolled the motorhome down the hill, toppling several times. As it turned out, it was a sharp and sudden drop, then a bang as he reached the bottom, but still in one piece.

"That takes care of those chumps," Smith said to Jenkins. "Now let's concentrate on getting rid of those cycles."

"That could have been us," Tommy said, as he watched the motorhome come to a rest in the river bottom.

"I won't allow that to happen," Nick said assuredly.

"Look up ahead," Mary said. "It looks like we're going to have to go over instead of under."

"Looks like you're right," Nick replied.

The CHP car had pulled onto Somerset Blvd. At least it was Somerset once you reached the river. Before that it was called East Compton Blvd, but the City of Paramount didn't care for the name Compton for one of their main thoroughfares. As he approached the river, the Impala shot across the street in front of him. Right behind it were two motorcycles, and behind the motorcycles was the motorhome with the dragon head. Following the motorhome were three other motorcycles, then a blue van. As the officer looked down the bike path, he saw a few other cars coming but much more slowly. He decided now was the time to join the chase. When the other cars following the path saw the CHP car pull on ahead of them, they all decided their excitement was over for the day and they headed their separate ways hoping to avoid arrest.

There was no room for anyone to pass, so the chase continued in order, up the bike path next to the river. At several of the overpasses, cars had stopped and people had gathered to cheer on the chase, which was now being broadcast live on several local television channels.

"Watch out for the bikes." Mary screamed.

"I hope they move," Nick said. "Those titanium racers are no match for Detroit steel."

A group of bicyclists had come racing south down the bike path. They had seen the cars ahead, but knew they had the right away and weren't about to break their pacing. That is, until they had no choice. Just yards before what would have been a horrific collision, the pack split apart with some of the bicycles sliding down the cement embankment to the river below, as others took to the brush to the left of the approaching caravan.

As if in slow motion, one of the bicycles smashed into the front of the Impala and flipped over the hood, cracking the windshield before disappearing over the roof of the car.

"Where was the rider? Did anyone see the rider?" Nick was frantic.

"He's safe," Tommy said, looking out the back. "I saw him bail off into the weeds before the collision

"Are you sure he wasn't hurt?" Nick asked.

"No, but he's throwing rocks at the motorhome behind us," Tommy replied.

"Thank God we didn't kill anyone," Mary said.

"At least we haven't yet," Tommy replied.

"Let's make this interesting, shall we?" Nick said.

"Like it hasn't been up to this point!" Mary quipped.

The parade of vehicles was approaching Imperial Highway. At this point in the cement river, the Rio Hondo Channel connects to the L.A. River Channel. There are several access roads at this junction. Just before the Impala reached the Imperial Highway overpass, Nick took the right fork in the path that led down onto the concrete river bed. Everyone followed. The moss was slimy and thick in areas along the river bottom. Big Deuce's cycle hit a slick spot and slid into the center channel of fast-moving water. Big Deuce was out of the chase. When Smith and Jenkins reached the riverbed, they were suddenly jarred as someone slammed into the trailer from the right.

"What the hell was that?" Smith asked. Jenkins had to lean out the window to see, since the mirrors had long been gone from an earlier collision.

"It's that other damn motorhome. He must have been driving along the river bed trying to keep up," Jenkins said.

"Well, he did a damn good job, I thought we'd knocked him out for good."

The rest of the chase pack had now reached the river bed, including the CHP car. As soon as the 710-freeway cut across the river above his head, Nick pulled the Impala sharply to the left and went back up the embankment to the bike path. Jenkins and Smith were right behind. As they slowed going up the hill, Paco rammed the trailer and knocked it off the road, causing it to dangle over the steep embankment. The weight of the trailer started to pull Hector's motorhome along, with Jenkins and Smith, after it back towards the river bottom, but the hitch snapped and the trailer tumbled to the river bed below, allowing the motorhome to shoot ahead relieved of its heavy ballast.

The CHP unit was driving south on the 710 freeway, headed for Long Beach, when he heard the call for any available unit. The officer driving responded and was told to exit on Florence Avenue east, turn south on Eastern, then west on Clara Street. There on the north side of the street he would find an entrance to the bike path along the west side of the Los Angeles River. He was told to take that entrance and then turn back south when he reached the path, intercepting the chase, blocking its progress. The officer did as the dispatcher instructed.

"We must be getting close," Mary said.

"There, right there, that's the elementary school," Tommy shouted.

Nick heard them but was looking straight ahead. A CHP car was turning onto the bike path in front of him.

"This is going to be close," Nick said. "Brace yourself!"

244

"I never liked the game of chicken," Mary said.

"Me neither." Tommy cried, and closed his eyes and ducked behind the seat.

"Nor me," Nick said, and cut the wheel sharply to the left and onto the exit and through the gate, bouncing hard against the retaining wall, then onto the Clara Street South Road. The trunk of the Impala popped open and one of the bags flew out from the impact.

"Nick, we lost one of the bags, you've got to stop." Tommy shouted.

"There's no time. If we stop, the bikers will kill us." Nick shouted back.

Mary and Tommy looked at the three bikers who were now right behind them and knew Nick was right. They would have to leave the bag. Half of what they had worked so hard to get this far was now lost.

The CHP officer slammed on his brakes, expecting to impact the Impala and skidded past the spot where, at the last possible second, the Impala had turned. However, the motorhome behind was unable to follow, now that the CHP cruiser blocked the path, and the dragon's head came crashing into the officer's windshield, just missing the ducking officer. Paco's motorhome crashed into the back of Smith and Jenkins' and the blue van crashed into the back of Paco's motorhome. The CHP car that was following the chase had been joined by three others and they all managed to stop before adding to the pileup. Scratch, Horse, and Tiny all managed to avoid the pileup and squeeze by to continue to follow the Impala. Slim was not as fortunate and went down the embankment towards the river bed. His misfortune turned into good fortune, at least for a while, as he was able to get away continuing along the river bottom until police, guided by the helicopters that had been following the chase, moved in and arrested him.

The CHP surrounded the blue van. The driver gave himself up, just as Chilly was gaining consciousness.

"Come out with your hands up," one of the officers yelled.

Chilly, still dazed, opened the van door and stepped out. What he didn't know was that the van was right on the edge of the embankment. When he stepped out, he went tumbling down the cement embankment to the river bottom below. He would not wake up for several more days.

Chuy and Paco both took off running after the crash. Chuy headed down into the river. He jumped into the swiftly flowing channel that ran down the middle of the giant cement ditch they called the Los Angeles River. He thought he was going to get away, until he realized he couldn't get out of the fast-moving current. It took the fire department's swift water rescue unit to save him. Paco made it into the local neighborhood where he was able to hide out for several hours, avoiding the police. That would turn out to be his misfortune.
.

"Come out of the motorhome with your hands up," said the officer who just missed being impaled by the giant teeth of the dragon head.

"Shit, now what are we going to do?" Jenkins asked.

"Just give him your card and tell them we were chasing a drug suspect," Smith said. "We can work out our story later."

"Just hold your badge above your head when you climb out," Jenkins reminded Smith.

"Officer, we are DEA agents in pursuit of..." Jenkins stopped in mid-sentence.

"You guys again? Not this time. This is the third car you've wrecked of mine in the past twelve hours. My Captain is finally going to believe me, because you guys aren't going anywhere until my Captain talks to your boss, so don't give me no story about 'being in pursuit of a suspect', crap."

Smith and Jenkins looked at each other. They knew they had a lot of explaining to do over the next couple of weeks. And when it was all said and done, being fired would turn out to be the least of their worries.

CHAPTER FORTY-ONE

"This is Jeff with jet-copter 98 with an update on the wild scene here next to the 710 freeway. It's happening along the L.A. River Channel here in Bell Gardens. It looks like the chase has finally come to somewhat of an end. The motorhome with the dragon head has run into a CHP unit coming south on the bike path near Florence Avenue. A second motorhome and a van seem to have piled into the first motorhome in a chain reaction collision. There appears to be two, no make that three, individuals running from the vehicles. Let me make a correction, one of the individuals appears to have only fallen and rolled down the embankment into the river channel. I see one of the motorcycles heading north inside the channel, and three other motorcycles headed west on a side street. They might still be pursuing another vehicle, but at this point I can't be sure. The CHP have guns drawn and one person from the van is in custody. Two men from the dragonhead motorhome at first had their arms up, but now seem to be standing and talking to the CHP officers."

"Jeff, we're watching the broadcast on one of the local stations, and Ruth and I were wondering if those two men from what you call the dragonhead motorhome are in custody?"

"No Bob, they seem to just be standing there next to the motorhome. I can't really tell what's happening."

"Jeff, you stay on it and let us know what transpires with this strange and bizarre chase that seems to have started in Seal Beach and has now ended at Florence Avenue and the Los Angeles River."

"Will do, Bob!"

248

"There's a helicopter overhead," Tommy said, as the Impala pulled onto Clara Street and headed for the high school.

"Make that two helicopters," Mary added.

Scratch, and Horse were right behind the Impala as it raced towards the school parking lot entrance. Tiny had stopped and grabbed the bag of money that had flown out of the trunk.

"Slow down, there's a cop right by the gate. At least the car quit rocking after hitting the wall," Mary said.

"You are such an optimist," Nick replied, and turned on the right turn signal, then realized it had been broken away much earlier in the chase.

The bikers had also seen the police standing in the street and backed off from the Impala.

"Wonder what all the helicopters are doing?" the officer directing traffic by the gate said to his partner. Neither was really a policeman, but were police cadets in uniform to help with traffic control for the carnival. Most of the local Cudahy police were involved in a softball game against the Wilcox Street gang.

"This entrance is for the car show only," the cadet said to Nick.

"That's what I'm here for," Nick replied.

"Are you entering that in the car show?" the cadet asked, puzzled.

"Of course, it's a classic 64 Impala," Nick replied.

"If you say so," he replied and waved the car through.

Scratch, Horse, and Tiny tried to follow, but were turned away.

"This entrance is for the car show only," the cadet said, trying to act tough.

Scratch was about to force his way inside when the sound of sirens coming from down the street changed his mind. The three bikers roared away, knowing they had lost the chase.

One of the helicopters overhead took off after the cycles, while the second continued to hover over the parking lot Nick had just entered. Inside the parking lot was another police cadet who waved the Impala through into the school area where the other lowriders were parked.

"How much of that money is left?" Nick asked.

"At least ten thousand," Tommy replied.

"Give some to Mary and some to me," Nick ordered. "In about one minute, if not sooner, police will be all over this car. As soon as I stop, jump out, throw the money into the air, disappear into the chaos and hightail it back to Tommy's classroom. Remember to stay under the walkways so the helicopter can't see you," Nick said.

"What about the bag in the trunk? Who's going to grab it?" Tommy asked.

"I'll take care of that," Nick said, looking at Mary. "You two just get safely to your classroom."

Before Tommy or Mary could reply, Nick stopped the Impala. "Go fast!" Nick yelled and they all opened their doors. All but Mary, whose door had been so badly damaged in the crash it wouldn't budge.

"My doors stuck." Mary screamed to Nick as he tossed the wad of hundred-dollar bills into the air.

Tommy turned to help, but saw two CHP officers heading his way. He took a handful of the money and tossed it towards the crowd standing between him and the CHP. "Free money!" he yelled. Dozens of people rushed towards him blocking the officers.

Nick ran back to his door and grabbed Mary around the waist and pulled her out of the car. The Cudahy police officers were almost on them when Mary remembered the money in her hand and tossed it into the air. She didn't need to say anything, for the crowd swarmed the area for a chance at getting at hundred-dollar bills. Word of the money traveled quickly through the crowd at the carnival and several of the more prominent Wilcox Street gang members headed over to see what the commotion was.

"Maybe my sweet Impala has finally arrived," Rudy said proudly. "It'll be the star of this show."

There was no time nor was there the opportunity for Nick to grab the bag out of the trunk that was still ajar. The two CHP officers were standing right behind it. Nick and Mary turned into the frenzied crowd, blending in, and disappeared, just as Tommy had already done.

Rudy had gathered several of the Wilcox gangsters and several friends together to parade them over and show off his ride.

"*¿Que pasa?*" Rudy asked as he came upon the wild melee of people scrambling to pick up the hundred-dollar bills.

"Hector and two homies tossed all this money into the air when they pulled in. There's money everywhere."

Rudy couldn't understand why Hector would do such a crazy thing or who the two homies were who arrived with Hector. He was, however, pleased to hear that Hector had arrived. That meant his Impala was ready for the show.

"That *pendejo* Hector better not have put any fingerprints on the paint job," Rudy said to no one in particular.

A collective gasp went up from the group surrounding Rudy.

"*Chingado, miá dió Purisimo*," Rudy yelled. "*Mi carro*! I'm going to kill Hector!"

As if on cue, the spent hydraulic system finally succumbed to all the abuse and the Impala dropped to the ground, emitting what sounded like a sustained fart.

Several other CHP officers had now arrived and the search was on for Hector and his two companions.

"Hector better pray the police find him before I do." Rudy yelled.

Tommy, Mary, and Nick had all made it to Tommy's classroom safely. Mary changed quickly into her usual frumpy style and removed her wig. She brushed out her hair and in less than two minutes no one would ever have known that she and the buxomly tart that arrived with Hector were one and the same.

Tommy had prepared large towels with special crème spread on them to remove the makeup on him and Nick. Upon entering the room, Nick ripped off his gangster clothes and with Mary's help began to wipe the dark makeup and fake tattoos off of his skin.

Tommy just sat at his desk and began to cry. "It was all for nothing, a complete waste, we lost all the money." Tommy was beside himself with grief.

Nick and Mary looked at each other. "We still have over two hundred thousand left of the biker's money we can split," Nick said, trying to hide a smile.

"No," Mary corrected, "I promised that to my cousins if everything went as planned. That money belongs to them."

Tommy looked up, shocked. "But nothing went as planned. We lost both bags of money. The bikers got one and the other we left in the car."

"Are sure about that?" Nick asked.

Tommy looked up, puzzled. "What are you taking about, of course I'm sure."

"Have you ever been to Las Vegas and watched one of those really good magic shows?" Mary asked Tommy.

Tommy looked really confused. "You guys are crazy. What are you talking about?"

"I'm serious, have you seen a good magician work?" Mary repeated.

"I...I guess so," Tommy replied.

"Well, if you have, what makes a magician so good is his ability to misdirect everyone's attention."

"Usually he does the switch or the trick in the first couple of seconds and the rest is just show and misdirection."

"Stop, stop, stop!" Tommy yelled. "What are you two trying to tell me?"

"We're trying to tell you that the money was never in the Impala," Nick said.

"What! Where is it then?" Tommy responded, getting mad now.

"Shhh, not so loud," Mary warned. She looked up at the classroom clock. "I would say it's sitting in the living room of my house at this very moment."

"How..., why..., who...?" Tommy tried to speak but couldn't.

"If you're as anxious to go see the money as we are, you had better quit sulking and get that makeup off before someone sees you and the whole plan is blown," Nick advised.

In less than five minutes, the three conspirators looked like their old boring conservative selves, at least Nick and Mary. Tommy never looked boring.

"You can bet they'll be searching the rooms, so Mary will take the two hundred thousand and her gun and head out the front before they secure this place," Nick said. "I'll follow her with the costumes."

"What about the towels with the makeup all over them? That's a dead giveaway," Mary said.

"I'll handle that," Tommy replied. "There's a washer in the home economics room next store. I use it all the time for washing the makeup out of these towels. Nobody will know the difference," Tommy said.

"Don't hang out long," Nick said.

"No, I'll just start the wash and leave. Don't worry, Ms. Flowers is always on me about forgetting to put the towels in the dryer."

"Then we will meet you at Mary's house in about a half-hour," Nick said.

"You can count on it. Then you can explain to me how you pulled off this slight-of-hand, misdirection, crap you're talking about. Is the money really there?" Tommy asked.

"It's really there!" Mary confirmed. "I'll see you within the hour."

CHAPTER FORTY-TWO

"What took you so long?" Nick asked Tommy.

"My car was in the teacher's parking lot and a couple of CHP cars had me blocked in. It was still total chaos when we left."

"Did you see Rudy?" Mary asked.

"Boy, did I. He had gone completely nuts. When he tried to take the duffle bag out of the trunk, the CHP threatened to arrest him. He would have been arrested, had the Cudahy police not intervened. All he could do was watch as they opened the bag and poured the trash out. I couldn't tell if he was happy or just relieved to see that it wasn't the money."

"I'm sure Wilcox Street has most of its members out searching for that money right now," Mary said.

"Look!" Nick shouted, and pointed to the television. The news was showing a rerun of the end of the chase at the L.A. River.

"Tommy watch this. Nick and I have already seen it four times," Mary said.

Tommy watched as the van door opened and Chilly stepped out and tumbled down the cement embankment.

"That had to hurt," Tommy said. "I actually feel sorry for the guy."

"Not me," Mary said, sounding cold and serious.

The news then cut to a newscaster interviewing several people who had collected some of the hundred-dollar bills that were tossed out of the Impala and wanted to turn them in.

"You got to be kidding me," Tommy said. "There's no way I would do that."

The next news switched to the CHP finally catching Scratch, Horse, and Tiny. It showed them opening the duffle bag and pouring out the trash. Finally, it showed the Impala and Cudahy High School. The newscaster talked a little about the community carnival and then showed the Impala arriving and the three of them exiting and throwing the money into the air. It was impossible to tell where Nick, Mary, and Tommy disappeared to in the free-for-all. The last clip they showed was of Rudy going berserk and pounding on his battered Impala.

"He'd better be careful or he might scratch the paint," Nick said, laughing.

"Is this really the money?" Tommy asked, looking at the two bags in the middle of the floor.

"It most certainly is," Mary replied.

"Can I see it?" Tommy asked.

"Of course you can. You can even touch it if you want. One third of it belongs to you," Nick replied.

Tommy started to open one of the bags, but changed his mind. "Tell me, just how did the money end up in your living room?"

"I know it was pretty crazy at that moment, but do you remember when you were out by the trailer with Paco and his partner and then I walked out?" Mary said to Tommy.

"Sure I do," Tommy said.

"And as we were talking, the trash truck pulled up and that guy in the white outfit pulled the trash bags out of the can and fitted a new bag?"

"Yeah, so?" Tommy replied.

"You had already switched the money from the Corona boxes into the two bags and packed them in the trunk, right?"

"Yeah," Tommy said.

"And if you remember the other side door had been opened so Paco could see the Impala."

"Yeah, that's right. I was worried that Paco might see Nick waiting in the car," Tommy replied.

"When those two trash collectors picked up the trash in the can on the other side of the motorhome, they pulled out the two bags of money and dropped them in trash bags and replaced them with two other duffle bags filled with trash. Those were my two cousins. The same ones who picked you up and kept getting in the bikers' way with the U-Haul they rented with the money you gave them," Mary explained.

Tommy smiled and thought for a second. "Won't the police trace the U-Haul truck back to your cousin?"

"Oh I'm sure they'll trace it back alright," Nick said, "but it won't be to Mary's cousins. It'll be to that Westside Capone gangster whose wallet you also turned over to Mary's cousin."

Tommy lay back in the chair and put his feet up on one of the duffle bags, full of money. "So where are your cousins now?"

"When I arrived, I gave them the two-hundred thousand that was left from the biker's money. I told them it would be a good idea if they went back to the ranch in Mexico for a while, until things calmed down here. I also told them not to buy anything extravagant with the money for a few months. They assured me they wouldn't. They plan to use the money to attend the University in Mexico and study agriculture. They also eventually want to buy the land next to their mother's ranch and farm it. I hated to see them leave, but they guaranteed me they would finish their education," Mary said.

"So now what?" Tommy asked. They all remained quiet and looked back and forth at each other until smiles grew on each of their faces. Nick and Tommy each grabbed a bag and poured the contents onto the floor.

"Ten million dollars, ten million dollars, ten million dollars," Tommy began to chant and Mary and Nick joined in, grabbing armfuls of the bundled hundred-dollar bills and caressing them.

After about five minutes of fantasies racing through his head, Tommy spoke up. "What do we do with the money till the end of the school year?"

"I'm leaving mine with Mary's in her gun safe. There's no place in my apartment where I feel it would be safe," Nick explained. "Besides, I'm planning on being around to keep an eye on it."

"I was hoping you would say that," Mary said, giving Nick a passionate kiss.

"Maybe I should buy a safe too," Tommy said.

"That would be a good idea, but make sure you go to one of those home remodeling warehouses and pay cash. I'll help you move it into your house. We don't want any written records of a safe being bought with your name attached to it or delivered to your address," Nick said. "We can do it tomorrow if you like."

"That'd be great," Tommy said.

"Remember, no big, extravagant, or out-of-character purchases until after the school year ends and we have all quit and moved away," Mary reminded everyone.

"I swear," Tommy said.

"Scouts honor," Nick replied.

"If you want to, and I think you should, you can leave your share of the money here until you get your safe tomorrow," Mary offered.

"I believe I will," Tommy replied.

The three friends counted, divided, and then loaded the money into the safe.

"Nick are you ready to head home?" Tommy asked.

Nick looked at Mary. "I think I'll be staying here tonight.

Tommy smiled widely. That's nice to hear. Then I'll call tomorrow about getting the safe." Tommy paused. "I can't believe we pulled it off."

"I never had a doubt," Nick replied.

"Right," Mary and Tommy replied.

CHAPTER FORTY-THREE

The train was running late again, something not too
uncommon for a Monday. Nick stood back away from the
crowd that had been gathering by the spot, his spot, on the
platform, where the door of the car would open. That is, if
the train ever showed up.

"Here it comes," the stranger said to Nick. "I can hear
it."

Nick didn't even bother to look down the track. The
man said the same thing every time the train was late.

"Haven't seen you much lately," the man said. "Been
driving in?"

"Yeah, driving in," Nick replied, trying to ignore the
man.

"Sure was something those folks throwing out all that
money on the freeway a couple weeks ago. I heard they
threw out almost twenty thousand dollars," the stranger said.

Nick just nodded, hoping the man would move on and
annoy someone else. This was only the second time since the
carnival that Nick had spent the night at his apartment and he
didn't like it one bit. He managed to avoid further
conversation until the train arrived. As usual, seats were few
and far between, but today it didn't seem to matter quite so
much to Nick.

No seats were available on the main floor, so Nick
headed up the stairs. Here he found one inside seat opposite
an obese man whose snores rumbled throughout the car.
Next to him was a lady painting her fingernails. Why they
allowed women to do that on the train Nick couldn't
understand. The smell always gave him a migraine and he
was sure others were affected similarly.

Nick headed up the steps to the top set of seats. There was one near the front, but the acrid odor of the fingernail polish still hung heavy in the air. There was only one seat available at the far end of the car. It was one of the seating areas with a table. Sitting there was a mother with her two children and she was feeding them some sort of porridge that the sight alone was enough to make you want to hurl.

"It's a good day to stand," Nick said to himself and headed back downstairs.

When he arrived at Union Station, Nick was accosted by the usual number of beggars and panhandlers, and he gave his favorite the change from his pocket. When he walked outside, Tommy was already waiting.

"Hey Nick, I've missed you. It's just not the same driving to school without you."

"I miss your company too, Tommy, though I hope this will be the last time I will need a ride in the morning."

"Did you get your apartment cleaned out this weekend, like you had hoped?" Tommy asked.

"Pretty much so. I gave almost everything away to the Goodwill. They came by yesterday and picked most of it up. Today they're coming by for the big furniture. I won't need any of it after the end of the year."

"I know what you mean. I've already listed my condo for sale, furniture and all" Tommy said. "But I don't plan on moving to Paris until the end of the summer. There are still a couple of things I have to handle before I make the move."

"Mary has already received an offer on her house. We've set up escrow to end the week school lets out," Nick said. "We already have an agent looking for a place in Paraguay for us, but we intend to travel for at least two months before we head there. We both always wanted to see

Prague. They say it's the most romantic city in the world. We intend to find out."

"Well, if it's romance you're after, make sure you take a drive down the Romantic Road in Germany. You stay in these thousand-year-old castles all the way to Munich," Tommy said. "I saw it on the Travel Channel."

Nick and Tommy both sat silently the rest of the commute, thinking about the end of the school year.

Mary was waiting in the parking lot when the two pulled up.

"I decided I don't like sleeping alone anymore," Mary said kissing Nick.

"Me neither," Nick replied.

"Guys, somebody is going to see you," Tommy said looking around.

"Let them look," Nick replied, and kissed Mary again.

"Did you notice there haven't been so many students parking here lately?" Tommy commented.

"I've noticed that several students in my classes are no longer around," Nick replied.

"I heard Rudy's entire family had to move to keep from being killed," Mary said.

"Not only Rudy's, but Hector's, and about a dozen other families with members in Wilcox Street," Nick said.

"Did anyone ever hear what happened to Hector?" Tommy asked.

"I heard a lot of things that first week after the carnival," Mary said, "but most of it was exaggeration and the rest speculation."

"Same here, but I sure as hell wasn't going to question any of the students about it," Nick said. "But I did read in the paper that they found Paco beat up pretty bad over by the river Sunday morning."

"You know all the classrooms were searched again this weekend," Mary said.

"Sounds like Wilcox Street is desperate," Tommy said.

"They still have no idea who is responsible for what happened," Nick surmised. "Nor will they ever know for sure."

'Two more months," Tommy said, and they all headed to class with smiles on their faces.

The students were just as rude, defiant, and apathetic as they always had been. The administration was just as ineffective and annoying as ever and the teachers just as disgruntled and negative, but not for Mary, Nick, and Tommy. If there were such a thing as rose colored glasses, all three could be accused of wearing them. A future as bright as the dawning of a new day grew nearer with each passing hour. And that was a metaphor they all understood. Or was that an analogy?

EPILOGUE

Mary and Nick had settled into their new hillside estate in Paraguay. It was a huge open house with a pool and a guest house. The best part about it was that they were able to purchase it with the money they made from the sale of Mary's house. They had hired a full-time cook, groundskeeper, and housekeeper. They had deposited five of the almost seven million of their shares of the gang's money in a Swiss bank account. The rest they spread across several banks in Paraguay, California, Mexico, and the Bahamas. They had taken Tommy's advice and traveled the Romantic Road through southern Germany and had fallen in love with the walled city of Rothenberg. They made plans to return there during the Christmas holidays.

They had not heard from Tommy for over two months. They knew he was planning on moving to Paris, but said he had some business to finish before he moved. They were very surprised when a package arrived for them from Paris.

"It's from Tommy," Nick said excitedly, as he tore it open. Inside were two envelopes, one with Mary's name and one with Nick's name on it. There was also a letter written to the two of them.

Bon Jour Nick and Mary,
I have arrived in Paris and already have a position as a make-up artist for Jer duBley, one of Paris' most exclusive fashion designers. I have purchased the loveliest apartment in the sixteenth district, I am told it is the most exclusive district in all of Paris. It is very near the Eiffel Tower and I have a

spare room whenever you want to come and visit. And that had better be soon. My French allows me to get by better than expected. What you hear about the Parisians being very rude is true, but the rude sassiness makes me feel right at home.

I want to apologize to both of you. Mary, if Nick didn't tell you, I took a bundle of cocaine from the motorhome, but I want to assure you I didn't use any of that ghastly stuff nor did I sell it. I hope you don't think poorly of me for what I did with it, but after hearing what that assistant principal did to you, Mary, I felt he had to pay for his immoral behavior. I also want to assure you again, Nick, that I had never used the Ketamine on anyone before we gave it to Hector. However, I was forced to use it once again and I hope you'll forgive me for what I've done. As you can see, I've included an envelope addressed to each of you within this package. If you decide to share the contents with each other, that's your decision. I hope to see you soon.

Love, Tommy

"I'm almost afraid to open the envelope," Nick said.

Mary had no such reservations and ripped open the smaller envelope and poured out the contents. Several newspaper clippings fell out and she picked one up and began to read. Tears started to run down her cheeks as she read.

"What is it?" Nick asked.

Mary grabbed another and began to read it.

"Is everything all right? Duh, of course it's not or you wouldn't be crying," Nick said.

"He's in jail," Mary said.

"Who's in jail?

"The assistant principal, the one who raped me and all those other teachers," Mary replied.

"They arrested him for raping a teacher?" Nick asked.

"No, according to the article, they arrested him for possessing and using cocaine on a school campus, for posting gay pornography of himself on the web, and for having gay and child porn on his school computer," Mary said.

"How did they catch him?" Nick asked.

"The article says that the school custodian found him and an underage boy naked in his office at school with lines of cocaine on the desk. He claims it was all a setup; however, they found traces of cocaine in his system along with Ketamine. It says over a kilo of coke was found in his office desk and in his car."

Neither spoke for a moment. "Tommy did this for me," Mary said.

Nick opened his envelope. Inside were the photos the assistant principal was accused of placing on the web. Tommy had scribbled a note on one of the photos.

I'm sorry I did this, but the man deserved it. Just so you know, everyone in these photos is over eighteen, although, they sure don't look like it. A dear friend owed me a favor and helped arrange this for me. You decide if Mary should see these.

"What's in your envelope?" Mary asked.

"Some pictures I really don't think you need to see," Nick explained. "Tommy included them just in case you needed them for closure."

"I think that part of our lives is already closed," Mary said, and kissed Nick.

"I think you're right," Nick replied, as he threw the photos into the fireplace. "How about a margarita?" Nick said, stroking his beard.

"Make mine a double," Mary replied, with a wicked smile.